Paris Noir: The Suburbs

EDITED BY
HERVÉ DELOUCHE

Translation by Katie Shireen Assef, David Ball,
Nicole Ball, and Paul Curtis Daw

AKASHIC
BOOKS

BROOKLYN, NEW YORK

Published by Akashic Books
©2022 Akashic Books

Paperback ISBN: 978-1-61775-755-6
Library of Congress Control Number: 2021935244

Series concept by Tim McLoughlin and Johnny Temple
Paris map by Sohrab Habibion

This work received the French Voices Award for excellence in publication and translation. French Voices is a program created and funded by the French Embassy in the United States and the FACE Foundation.

FRENCH
VOICES
FRENCH
VOICES

French Voices logo designed by Serge Bloch.

The front cover image is adapted from a photograph by Paul Fleury. The original can by viewed on Wikimedia Commons here:
https://commons.wikimedia.org/wiki/
File:Les_Choux_de_Créteil_-_panoramio_(8).jpg

Akashic Books
Brooklyn, New York
Instagram: AkashicBooks
Twitter: AkashicBooks
Facebook: AkashicBooks
E-mail: info@akashicbooks.com
Website: www.akashicbooks.com

ALSO IN THE AKASHIC NOIR SERIES

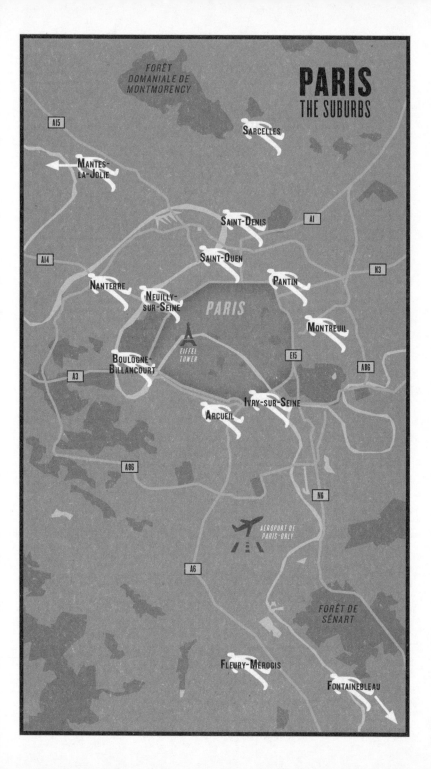

TABLE OF CONTENTS

PART III: SCARFACES OF THE SUBURBS

PART IV: GHOSTS FROM THE PAST

INTRODUCTION
EXPLORERS OF THE SUBURBS

To Claude Mesplède
Translated by Paul Curtis Daw

C hoosing a title for this collection hasn't been easy . . . Unlike other works in the Akashic Noir Series, this one doesn't pertain to just one municipality or to a defined playing field for writers who like to write about city neighborhoods, be they in London or Delhi, Beirut or Barcelona, Washington or . . . Paris (which entered the series in 2008). So, we mulled this over quite a bit.

The term Greater Paris is in vogue today, for it has an administrative cachet and seems to denote a simple extension of the capital—as if a ravenous Paris need only extend her web. However, it was not our goal to embrace the tenets of the metro area's comprehensive plan, aka the *Grand Projet*, envisioned as a future El Dorado by the planners and developers. Rather, our aim was to depict the Parisian suburbs in all their plurality and diversity. Without pretending to encompass every spot on the map, we instead opted to give voice and exposure to the localities chosen by the writers who have been part of this adventure. Thus, we decided to adopt the word "suburbs"—in the plural, obviously, for the periphery of the capital is not a homogeneous bloc, nor is it reducible to a cliché like "the suburban ring."

Over the course of the nineteenth century, and even well into the twentieth, the word *banlieue* ("suburb") still had overtones of pastoral poetry; of Verlaine writing, "We go to the suburb by train / which carts us several leagues / to the true land of cheap and decent wine"; of Reda Caire singing in 1934, "The lovely Sundays of springtime, when we would go to Robinson . . ."; of the era of the festive, open-air *guinguettes*; of the dream of rural fulfillment portrayed in Duvivier's classic film *La belle équipe* (*They Were Five*); of the Marne riverside, to which many flocked on the weekend, and where for a while they could elude the workaday world—the other face of Paris's outskirts, dominated by assembly plants and manufacturing complexes.

For a long time, the suburban fringe comprised the Communist-led Red Belt. The word "suburb" was synonymous with "factories" and with the departments directly bordering Paris: the Petite Couronne, populated by "the working class, the dangerous class," in an epoch when there was work to be done. From Ivry to Boulogne-Billancourt, la Courneuve to Gentilly, Clichy to Montrouge, the flagship industrial firms were riding high, mass-producing cars, turbines, matches, batteries, cookies, ball bearings . . . They were printing, they were bleaching paper and textiles . . . and workers, in their rebellious moments, would gather on cobblestone streets to pry and fling those very stones. Nowhere has that history been better recounted than by Alain Rustenholz in *De la banlieue rouge au Grand Paris* (La Fabrique, 2015).

And then came the first public housing projects. No doubt to correct the perception of Le Corbusier, who regarded the suburbs as "the degenerate offspring of the *faubourgs* [districts beyond the city walls, later absorbed into the city]." The urban planners imagined spacious living units, cultural activities, greenery . . . The futurist Léon Bonneff declared in 1922 in *Aubervilliers* that "the factories, which today risk destruction only in periodic conflagrations, will disappear, and on their ruins will rise buildings erected with consideration of workers' health." As adroitly described by Marc Bernard in *Sarcellopolis*, the utopian vision of the new-towns movement was symbolized by the construction of the emblematic housing development of Sarcelles, begun in the late 1950s with no public input. In numerous instances, such communities turned dystopian by reason of the social crisis, a policy vacuum, and their relegation, at best, to secondary priority . . . It took the 2005 riots, around Paris and in other French cities, to expose the extent of their deprivation.

However, the late Thierry Jonquet, who observed the aberrations, including criminal ones, of certain housing projects (see his novel *Ils sont votre épouvante et vous êtes leur crainte*), went far beyond a simplistic, reductive vision. Thus, in the exhibition *Banlieues buissonnières*, he wrote ironically: "*Banlieue*. On the cathode-ray screens, this mysteriously named character—could it be a pseudonym?—occupied a choice position, outfitted with death-dealing gear worthy of the worst creatures of blood-and-gore films." And in his narrative of a walking tour in the Seine-Saint-Denis department, he noted, near the town of Stains, that plots of land dotted with shacks and enclosed vegetable gardens were scattered in the midst of dilapidated tower blocks, exclaiming to himself, "So, at the very base of one of the most sinister monuments of the architecture of destruction, the fearless countryside reclaims its rights . . . A pointless defiance! An affront to concrete! Stains! Crisscrossed, who would have believed it, by shining paths!"

So, let's not get it wrong: the Parisian suburbs cannot be summed up as a triptych of detached homes, large-scale public housing, and shopping centers. Rather, they form a kaleidoscope of contrasting landscapes and architectural forms. Of inhabitants who are very much alive and not just itinerant ghosts. It was in quest of those people and places that François Maspero decided to set out in 1990, accompanied by the photographer Anaïk Frantz. They began with the sadly plausible observation that "many Parisians view the suburbs as a formless lava flow, a desert of ten million souls, a succession of undifferentiated gray structures, a circular purgatory centered by a Paris-Paradise." Those two inquisitive Parisians undertook a station-by-station exploration via the train from Roissy to Saint-Rémy-lès-Chevreuse to absorb both history and the present. That resulted in a stunning book, *Les passagers du Roissy-Express*, an encounter with the "real world" and "real life," when the whole of Paris had become one big shopping center and a cultural Disneyland.

That real world, that real life, pulses and throbs in this collection too. The authors of these thirteen stories are neither sociologists, ethnologists, nor journalists. They aren't impelled by a yen for the exotic. Residing in the departments that buttress the capital, or fond of roaming through them, they know their territories. Some are active in local life, and all are "explorers of the suburbs" in the image of those inveterate walkers of Paris, Léon-Paul Fargue and Henri Calet. And they've chosen noir, the literary genre that witnesses its era, illuminates the shadowy areas, and captures life's quicksilver moments. Using the whole gamut of colors that compose the lively and the ephemeral, from the tragic to the amusing, without omitting a possible touch of the lyrical or the fantastic, they offer us candid snapshots of those places. Foregrounded by characters of flesh and emotions, frequently misfits, or at least men and women whose existences have been upended.

* * *

Some ghosts from the past are in store for you. In "The Shadows of the Trapèze," Anne Secret evokes the memory of the defunct Renault factory through a young woman's inquiry into the murder of her blue-collar father. Quite a slice of social lore that history writ large has neglected. The narrator of Anne-Sylvie Salzman's "Strange Martyrs" recreates the neighborhood of her youth at the foot of the Arcueil aqueduct, with its Villa Byzantine, marked for demolition, its dark places, its mysteries . . . and a singular character with ghastly collections. It was a news item that brought the writer Patrick Pécherot back to Nanterre in "The Day Johnny Died": an overly boisterous youth from the projects murdered by a longtime fan of Johnny Hallyday, who was mourning the singer . . . An occasion to recall a bygone Nanterre that "feels like a village," not yet effaced, only a stone's throw from the gargantuan office complex of la Défense.

Familiar figures, scarfaces of the suburbs, also appear. The northern tier of suburbs has changed, Rachid Santaki tells us right off in "To My Last Breath": "Saint-Denis is blighted by the refuse of Paris . . . And yet, it used to be a fine kingdom." Descending directly south, to Ivry, a trio of drug dealers imagined by Guillaume Balsamo, closer to the Three Stooges than to Tony Montana. His "Men at Work: Date of Completion, February 2027" leads us to the criminal underside of a pleasant housing complex, with the Chinagora hotel and restaurant as a piece of the exotic, the dream. Don't be misled: as for drugs, the more upscale localities of the suburbs are not slumbering. Hauts-de-Seine and Neuilly are fertile ground for the narcotics traffic, and it's there that "The Baroness" by Marc Fernandez takes place.

Those who are misfortunate in life are not necessarily reconciled to their fate. They sometimes risk attempts at escape.

One such, conjured by Marc Villard, is Lucienne Berthier, who at age fifteen hangs out "Beneath the Périphérique," near Saint-Ouen. In the midst of the destitute *biffins*—Roma, Africans, a whole population shoved beyond the boundaries of Paris and struggling to survive. A getaway; that's the treat the young couple want to give themselves in Jean-Pierre Rumeau's "The Donkey Cemetery." A nocturnal expedition to the forest of Fontainebleau, an adventure sixty kilometers from Paris. A setting serene in appearance, but capable of reserving some surprises, in the manner of James Dickey's *Deliverance*! The narrator of "Pantin, Really" by Timothée Demeillers has to flee from Albania and then finds himself sequestered at Pantin, nursing frustrated dreams of the Eiffel Tower and the Arc de Triomphe. And it's through his new perspective that we discover derelict warehouses, aging cafés, and modest workingman's cottages . . . not so different from Kukës or Tiranë.

When the suburbs are dumping grounds for the excluded, they breed insulted and rebellious individuals. Merely for a brash wisecrack, Sofiane is arrested in the midst of Islamophobic hysteria—providing an occasion for Cloé Mehdi to depict the Fleury-Mérogis Prison and to brandish her title like a cry of rebellion: "I Am Not Paris." With "The Morillon Houses," Karim Madani shows us another face of Montreuil, far from the ideal suburb touted by the media: Montreuil's public housing, cut off from everything and occupied by the "little soldiers" of Bilal, the local drug kingpin . . . For her part, the female narrator of Christian Roux's "The Metamorphosis of Emma F.," a housekeeper at the Hilton and a resident of the grim Val Fourré housing project, is about to undergo a veritable metamorphosis in order to restore "a little order to this rotten world." At Sarcelles, twenty-two-year-old Mani wants to create a place where kids can find educational support and self-esteem. But the authorities put up roadblocks and even resort to arson. In "Seeing Is Believing," Insa Sané sums up one of the objectives of this collection: to "cry out to the world that the inhabitants of the deprived suburbs truly exist."

In 1992—in the review *Gulliver*, created by Michel Le Bris in the spirit of the Étonnants Voyageurs literary festival—longtime Ivry resident Jean-Bernard Pouy offered up a story, "Transports en particuliers," in which he writes, "And perhaps the love of the suburbs persists, thanks to those who knew them *before*, that is to say, before they became bedroom communities, when the smallish cities all around Paris still operated as a red belt, preventing the huge, blubbery stomach of Paris from spilling over into the countryside. But it's surely true that everyone now living there is in search of new myths and that the housing projects will inspire as many colorful tales as the detached homes or vacant tracts of yesteryear." Here are thirteen such stories, decidedly noir, to be savored without sugar or sweetener.

Hervé Delouche
Paris, France
November 2021

PART I

THE INSULTED AND THE REBELLIOUS

I AM NOT PARIS

BY CLOÉ MEHDI

Fleury-Mérogis

Translated by Paul Curtis Daw

They'll say it's an attack, and maybe they'll be right. I'm slumped in front of the BFM news channel, which is showing balaclava-clad cops fanning out in a Toulouse neighborhood for a raid on suspected terrorists. As I watch, I'm wondering how the authorities who prosecute me will present their case. If the fact that I have a Muslim name will suffice to tip me over into the category of Islamic terrorism, or if they'll take the trouble to look in front, behind, and on the sides.

I glance guiltily at my smartphone, abandoned on the coffee table. I've spent the day trying to make an explanatory video, without knowing if it's meant for those closest to me or for the whole of France. I haven't managed to produce anything, knowing that the media will pounce on everything they can fit within their own logic, which is already fully developed. I don't want to confide in the social networks either. In fact, I would have preferred to carry out my plan without justification, with a mere snap of the fingers, and let my action be explained by all that had preceded it. But it only takes turning on the television or looking at online commentary to know that no one grants anyone the slightest leeway these days. And that people have no interest in understanding those who are different.

They'll say I'm confused, and they'll be right.

Podcast / January 11, 2015, on France Info radio:
A sidewalk interview, on the edge of a demonstration honor-
    ing the victims of terrorist acts on the seventh, eighth, and
    ninth of January.
REPORTER: Are you familiar with Charlie Hebdo?
SOFIANE: No, no, it isn't relevant to my generation.
REPORTER: What is it that motivated you to attend this
    march?
SOFIANE: Me? But I'm not in the march. I'm walking my
    cousin to the gym. (Laughs.) Sarah, he thinks I'm part of
    the march.
SARAH: (Laughs.)
REPORTER: You think the march is funny? May I ask why?

Why did we stop to answer the reporter's question? I was already late for my boxing class, and I was throwing exasperated glances at my cousin to make him get in gear. Since then, I've replayed a thousand times in my head those fifteen seconds when everything became inevitable. I've had plenty of time for regret. Maybe if I'd kept my mouth shut the interview would have ended with no consequences.

SOFIANE: Charlie Hebdo, I mean, who's that? Those
    guys who draw ugly cartoons of naked politicians? Yes,
    the same ones who drew the Prophet Muhammad because
    they asked each other, "Hold on, which group hasn't taken
    enough shit this year? Oh, yeah, the Muslims! The me-
    dia never fuck with the Muslims, that needs to change!"
    Charlie Hebdo! And we're supposed to shed tears for
    those guys who never felt sorry for anyone?

REPORTER: *They ridicule everyone, not just Muslims . . .*

SOFIANE: *I'm not even a believer. But faith should be respected! That's what France doesn't understand! She respects nothing, not even her own recognition of the rights of man. France no longer believes in anything, and she's suddenly going to give us lessons in tolerance?*

SARAH: *France believes in the freedom of expression! (Laughs.) That's become the French religion.*

SOFIANE: *Exactly! That's what the marchers in the street are calling for! But hey, is that all you've found sacred in your lives? That's all you care to defend? Freedom of expression? (Laughs.) That's rich!*

REPORTER: *And you, what do you believe in?*

SOFIANE: *The Kouachi brothers!* (Laughs.)

At that moment, no one—neither Sofiane, nor I, nor even the reporter—suspected the turn this was going to take. It was a bad joke that spiraled into a nightmare.

The reporter was about twenty, a little younger than my cousin. He looked at his mic with bemusement, as if he felt guilty for holding the device that had registered Sofiane's wisecrack. To my eyes, he resembled a cross between a philosophy major and a business student. His hair was carefully disheveled, his threads expensive yet casual, and he had the little mug of someone who was first in his class. I found out later that he was an intern on his first sidewalk interview.

His dazed expression told me this was going to turn to shit. I let out an embarrassed giggle and grabbed Sofiane's sleeve: "Let's get moving, I'm running behind." He had the same feeling I did—a bit late, yes, always too late. That was a quality

---

* The Kouachi brothers were the perpetrators of the attack on the *Charlie Hedbo* headquarters in 2015, killing twelve people and injuring eleven others.

that defined us and a host of others; in a world going so fast, you have to strain to follow the rhythm. At times I tell myself that therein lies the root of the problem: that tricky rhythm.

On the screen, the cops are entering the buildings. Since when do reporters trail them closely in real time? Since when do we find it normal to observe a police operation from A to Z, or to encounter the faces of attack victims before their own families do? To absorb such a tragedy on a live telecast, while sitting at home on our sofas, snacks on our laps? And in the long run, how does that transform our perception of a grim event?

I stare at the TV, unable to switch it off, with wide-open eyes made dry by lack of blinking. I avidly partake of something that disgusts me. That's typical of this society, isn't it? On an individual level, you become part of the problem. And I wonder if they've orchestrated that or if it just happens. I believe in humanity's infinite capacity to sabotage itself, and I'm not convinced it takes bad leadership to make that happen. It's on that point that my view differs from Sofiane's. But, as my mother says, "No one asked for your opinion, sweetie."

At the time, no one had understood the magnitude the *Charlie Hebdo* attacks were about to assume. There had long been terrorist incidents on what seemed almost a daily basis, but not at home, not here, not in France, not in Paris, not at *Charlie*. The republic rose up as one, and when the republic rises up (I understood this only later), you'd better brace yourself, because she'll be looking to whip someone's ass.

I was nineteen years old, and I experienced the events as a witch hunt. Robust in its vaunted enlightenment and disavowing a preference for any sect or creed, the "great secular republic" nevertheless began to hunt down the heretics, just as in bygone days she used to indoctrinate the natives of her colonies. She drew the very distinctions she was pretending to deplore: friend or enemy, Charlie or not Charlie, assimilated Muslim or Muslim fundamentalist. One by one, the imams were backed up against the wall, forced to pledge allegiance to the great republic or be dragged through the mud by the media and public opinion. The whole strategy was nurtured by catchphrases that pretended to bring everyone together: "tolerance," "freedom of expression," "national unity." If you listened to them, you were convinced that the entire population was pulsing with a common sentiment of belonging. Suddenly, France was once again patriotic, united, and indivisible.

The whole nation was Charlie.

They found Sofiane via the surveillance cameras and the details provided by the young reporter. Because, obviously, Sofiane's remarks had gone out live over the radio. Three days after the sacrilege, they arrested him at my aunt's house and dragged him into custody. Forty-eight hours later, he was taken to an expedited court hearing.

With such a brief interval, it was difficult to prepare or even think of a coherent defense. Sofiane and his court-appointed lawyer didn't get smart with the judge; there's nothing amusing about a defendant on trial for the offense of glorifying terrorism. My cousin didn't defend his joke. He apologized about forty times, and the judge said straight to his face that people like him were nauseating. The judge sentenced him to five months in prison, beginning immediately. The hearing had lasted twenty-five minutes. Like a little girl, I burst into tears in the arms of my mother and aunt. Sofiane looked at us, his eyes opened wide, barely registering what had just happened. I believe he was still trying desperately, and once again belatedly, to sync up his rhythm with that of the tribunal. With that of France. And failing at it.

The machinery of justice had made an example of my cousin. With one voice, social media celebrated his conviction, though some complained about the lightness of the sentence. Sofiane's sister, Hayet, was spat upon at her lycée. The French Republic had swung her arm and brought down the broadsword. Her blows struck several people in succession, doling out prison sentences to each. Without apparent difficulty, the state passed from the cult of free expression to the imprisonment of all those who had exercised that freedom to say, more or less forcefully, that they were not Charlie. I imagine this was considered the price to be paid for preserving national unity.

The republic tightened its ranks. My country had never seemed so suffocating to me. I began to spend my time watching BFM, training my gaze on France and trying doggedly to understand her, she who ascribed importance only to her own values. I wanted to know who she really was, myth or reality. And what image she had of herself. My efforts were futile; I didn't understand.

Sofiane, in the visiting room of Fleury-Mérogis, didn't even try to understand. Each visit, he would spout an interminable monologue. He didn't ask for news of his friends and relatives. He only thought about the injustice of his situation and how to make "them" pay. My mother and aunt begged him to watch what he was saying in such proximity to the guards: "Don't spoil your chances for a reduced sentence." Beyond the subject of his release, there was, as always, the question of money. Sofiane's family had to send him some every month so he could live in tolerable conditions. Everything at Fleury was expensive, from a Twix bar to the cost of renting a radio, not to mention cigarettes. Sometimes, my aunt would erupt when he complained, and she'd scream that he was there by his own fault; that he could've kept his mouth shut for once in his life; that he shouldn't have counted on France being indulgent; and that, had he any sense, he would've known this. Sofiane would clam up then and hang his head for the rest of the visit.

I used to tell myself that if I'd just grit my teeth and wait, the five months would pass quickly. I was puzzled by the anxieties of my aunt and mother, who seemed to fear that Sofiane would never get out of prison. It turned out that they understood the system better than I did. After six weeks' confinement, Sofiane slapped a guard who'd refused to let him out his cell for the regular exercise period. As a result, his sentence was extended by three months. Several weeks later, during an inspection, a guard found the cell phone Sofiane used to call us after lights-out: two more months tacked on.

From one extension to the next, his release date stretched out to a distant horizon. My aunt was tearing her hair out. I could hardly eat. The whole family closed in on itself, living in a fixed routine of visiting Sofiane, doing his laundry, and sending the regular remittances.

Meanwhile, the media frenzy was gradually abating. We could breathe a little easier but were careful not to huff and puff. We tiptoed to avoid troubling the republic's light slumber.

And then, on November 13, 2015, came the coordinated terrorist attacks on Paris. I was at the laundromat with a tote bag full of Sofiane's laundry. There was no TV, but the attendant turned up the volume of her smartphone, and the customers gathered around her and the little screen as we all listened to the words: a hail of bullets, grievous attack, Stade de France. I thought: *God, let this be a fascist plot or fake news.*

After several hours of mourning, the republic drew a breath, opened her mouth wide, and spewed the contents of her lungs onto the Muslim community. Secure in the knowledge of what is sacred and what is profane, what plainly provokes indignation and what can be laughed off, the "great secularism" deployed her theoretical and practical weapons. On the talk shows and newscasts, her emissaries proclaimed to all who would listen, and even to those who covered their ears, that everyone could be free in their beliefs so long as they were aligned with the republic's values. That she didn't want to stigmatize anyone, but . . . well, Islam. But . . . well, Muslims. She said, "Spare us the sight of those archaic practices we don't want to see anymore." She seemed unwilling to tolerate, in her streets, the beliefs she didn't understand.

I believed in a perplexing god, a god of fog and smoke screens, who could not be encompassed by any word or book but only by my own intuition. Even so, I wanted to envelop myself defiantly in a hijab to announce to the republic that I hadn't bowed to its codes of thought. My mother, although a Muslim and herself veiled, barred me from doing so, saying it would be sacrilegious to wear it for such a reason.

And then the impossible happened.

The whole citizenry rose up in support of the republic, waving tricolor flags and small models of the Eiffel Tower. Wherever the camera lens had the misfortune of focusing, people were professing their solidarity. Apparently, attacks reported elsewhere had never occurred. This was the first time people had been murdered randomly, without "deserving it." Take my aunt, who closely followed the news of constant bloodshed in Palestine and elsewhere: she was disgusted by the notion that only terror in Paris is worthy of our attention. Because people had been gunned down not in Nablus, or Damascus, or Tunis, but in Paris, in a country that was wealthy and officially at peace. They'd entered the ranks of global martyrs to "blind and barbaric hatred" not while on their way to a bazaar or holed up for safety, but instead while merely enjoying a concert or having a drink on a terrace. Still, what about all the others? What about those before and after, killed by similar terrorist gangs, or by non-Islamic governments, including France? Hadn't they also lost their lives? Who decides *which* procession of the dead is most tragic?

And who was manufacturing the weaponry that was blowing holes in all those bodies?

In the visiting room, Sofiane could hardly have been more enraged and frustrated by these developments. I was too sad to find the words that might have calmed him. Which words even needed saying? The money for his remittances was getting harder to come by. Intent on mending his finances independently, he'd started dealing weed, and had gotten caught and sentenced to yet another eight months. My aunt was conflicted about continuing to visit him.

She phoned my mother on March 28, 2016—crying. She'd just received a call from the prison warden. Sofiane had died the night before of unexplained causes. An autopsy later linked it to an asthma attack. We wanted to know how such a common and treatable condition could have killed him, but no one responded to our questions.

The truth, or part of it, came that summer. A certain Arthur Vianney, Sofiane's ex-cellmate, contacted my cousin Hayet on Facebook and told her about the night of his death. According to Arthur, the warden hadn't lied, but the guard who had responded to Arthur's appeal had not taken the situation seriously. Despite the cellmate's pleas and Sofiane's convulsive wheezing, the guard simply continued on his rounds. My cousin expired during the night.

At the same moment, the summer's great controversy, the prohibition of the wearing of the burkini, broke out in the media. One after another, politicians, sociologists, philosophers, and even some imams spoke out to denounce the ultramodest burkini as an incalculable transgression and to prescribe how a respectable woman must dress within France—ostensibly a tolerant, equitable, and nonsexist society.

They'll say it's an attack, and maybe they'll be right.

On BFM, tired of waiting for the results of the umpteenth raid, the presenters pass to another news topic: the nationwide strike by prison guards. It began at Fleury-Mérogis after five prisoners "assaulted" two guards who tried to force them into a four-person cell, which was also beset by standing water. The striking guards refused to take any prisoners from their cells to the visiting room, to their activities, or to the exercise yard. Transfers within and between prisons were suspended. Meals were reduced to one per day, the food served cold. The guards have demanded increased staffing and higher pay. The camera is filming the entrance to Fleury, where the guards have set up a picket line. A union representative is explaining that hoodlums run rampant inside and that the state practices a pro-prisoner policy to the detriment of the guards.

With determined effort, I tear myself from my lethargy. I turn off the TV and survey with a critical eye the disorderly state of my studio. I lack the heart to straighten it up before leaving. My eyes fall one more time on my smartphone, and I think of the video I haven't managed to make. So, I tear a sticky note from its pad, scribble the first words that come to mind, and set it conspicuously on the coffee table.

It reads, in part, "It's September 1, 2016. My name is Sarah and I'm 21."

Clutching the steering wheel of my car—actually, it was Sofiane's—I drive to the immense prison complex at Fleu-ry-Mérogis. The guards are there, as well as several cops on foot and a small contingent of reporters. I don't know if the scene is on live TV. I don't know if I want it to be. I try not to think of my mother as I press down hard on the accelerator and head straight toward the picket line, my mind resolutely fixed on the last line of my note, which they'll find as my sole explanation and which in any case they won't understand: "I am not Paris."

THE MORILLON HOUSES
BY KARIM MADANI
Montreuil

Translated by Katie Shireen Assef

ilal's goat makes its way across the place du Morillon, shits on a Nike shoebox, and returns to its favorite spot by the door of the Esperanto community center. It's a chilly October day, one of those when you can feel that summer has truly packed up and gone. Steven peeks in through the window: ten a.m. and the first watchmen are already at their posts. Their hot spot is the lobby of the building wedged between the neighborhood library and a Pakistani bazaar. Bilal's little soldiers are already here, wearing the uniform of the Dionysian dealer: black North Face parkas with hoods lowered over their faces, black jogging pants and running shoes. Beneath the hoods, Steven can make out their dulled eyes, their brown skin turned the color of ash from so much stress, monotony, routine.

Denise, his aging mother, never takes off her wool bathrobe anymore. She constantly complains that it's too cold in the apartment and that the management company still hasn't turned the heat on. The place smells of cat litter and chronic depression. Denise was born in Morillon and will most likely die there. Steven gets a chill just thinking about it. He wants to get the hell out of Montreuil, leave Seine-Saint-Denis for good. When he hears journalists refer to "the ninety-three," thinking that they're *with it*, he wants to puke. He's had it with the fucking ninety-three. It's not some Parisian news team's fantasy. It's his reality.

The goddamn goat is munching on the rotten grass that grows between the cracks in the sidewalk. The place du Morillon is circular; when you step out of a car, they can spot you within seconds. The watchmen have sharp eyes, but they also have lookouts standing guard in dozens of apartments.

The people who live here are bored out of their minds. When they're not sitting in front of the TV, they're looking out the window. They're intrigued by new faces. No one pays much attention to the customers; they know that business is business. They keep an eye out for cops, though, and for anyone who looks a little different, or has an odd way of walking. Everyone is watched and everyone keeps tabs on everyone else. If Steven had read Foucault, he might have been shocked that the writer's panopticon so closely resembles his own neighborhood. It's the most isolated part of Montreuil, at the edge of Fontenay-sous-Bois in Val-de-Marne. No metro, no RER. Only one bus you can take to go up the hill—the 122.

Outside, the goat is chomping on wilted daisies. Steven isn't in the mood to listen to Denise's bitching and moaning. Or her criticisms, either. The rent, the bills, the fridge that he should be doing his part to help fill. He slides a CD into the old stereo that belonged to his dad. Charles Aznavour. At twenty-five, Steven still lives with his mom and is a bit of a romantic. The song opens up a recent wound: his girlfriend, Sarah, wants to break up. He can't believe it. He's madly in love with her, but you can't say these things openly in the neighborhood.

"When are you going to find a job?" Denise mutters as she sips her coffee and pets Guillotine, their fat old cat. Steven's dad, Philippe, was the one who chose this name. They never knew why. On the morning when Steven was getting ready to celebrate his twentieth birthday, the phone rang and the cops told Denise that her husband had thrown himself in front of a metro car. At the RATP, they call it "a serious accident involving a passenger." Very discreet. Denise identified Philippe's body and then fainted at the morgue. Since then, she's been on a diet of coffee, Prozac, and buttered bread.

Steven had never been close to his old man. When Philippe met Denise, he was a working-class kid who lived in a miserable furnished studio by Croix de Chavaux. She was living with her parents in a dilapidated apartment on Robespierre. Then he'd landed an interview and was hired by the SNCF, first as a simple maintenance worker and then as a ticket inspector. And the city had found him a three-bedroom apartment in a rent-controlled building in Morillon. It had changed their life, a little—except Philippe was still chronically depressed and always moping. A bit of an alcoholic too.

When Steven's friends found out that his dad was a ticket inspector—a job that was as reviled in Morillon as cops and bailiffs were—he'd taken a lot of flak for it. Bullying. His dad was constantly telling Denise that they should move. "We're the last white people here. It's no place for us anymore."

The lyrics of the song "Mourir d'aimer" fall onto the gray carpet, like the crumbs from a piece of stale and bitter bread.

> I reach to touch the walls around me.
> The shadows of the night surround me.
> Alone I face my destiny: to die of love.
>
> They say our love has been forbidden,
> but what we feel cannot be hidden.
> It's very possible, you see, to die of love.

The little dealers all work for Bilal, and they all still live with their parents. Some pray five times a day to the east, while the customers keep coming from the western side of the projects. Customers "score" and dealers "serve up" or "sling." Quite a few sedentary Roma make their home in Montreuil, and their slang blends perfectly into the language of the neighborhood; they speak all in *verlan* and snatches of Arabic. A broken tongue. Anyone who's a little different is considered a moron. A freak. A pussy.

Steven had had it with this word. A word that ostracizes you. Excommunicates you. And then, little by little, he'd made something of a name for himself. Mainly on the soccer field. The older kids said he had a good left foot, but his mom never signed him up for a team. The practice fields were too far from the neighborhood.

Steven met Sarah about a year ago. Well, "met" isn't the right word, since you don't really meet people in Morillon. You know them from when they were little, and maybe one day they show themselves to you in a new way. Sarah had been a chubby girl, always in jogging pants. Then, a few years ago, she lost some weight and started wearing skirts. Now she's beautiful and independent. She works down at the city hall, near the areas in Montreuil with metro access and a decent bus network.

He never would've thought that Sarah would give him the time of day. Him, the little white kid who hung around the main square all day with a lost look on his face? And he didn't even deal—a freak indeed. But Sarah isn't attracted to dealers. She even wishes they would leave the neighborhood, but no one says these things out loud. When she runs into

Bilal, she greets him with the same timid deference usually reserved for local bigwigs, like the mayor or his secretary. Letting Bilal see how much she hates him would have serious consequences: he could make her parents' and younger siblings' lives hell.

When she gave him her number, Steven couldn't believe it. Something about him had gotten under her skin, she said; she couldn't express it in words. They started seeing each other in secret. It was hard to carry on this kind of relationship out in the open in the neighborhood, because of how people gossiped. And Steven is white, Sarah Arab. Sarah's parents are the traditional type; they see their daughter going down the path of endogamy, like they did. Only, Sarah thinks for herself. At least he thought so until yesterday, when she told him to meet her at a bar by Croix de Chavaux.

She wanted to break up. Too much pressure. At twenty, she doesn't see herself settling down anytime soon. Steven had brought her a present, a ring that cost him two hundred euros, all his savings blown on this tiny royal-blue box. She refused it. He'd wanted to tell her about his plans for them: he'd find a job and they could leave the neighborhood, go live somewhere away from the city, put at least six hundred kilometers between themselves and Morillon.

"And you'd abandon your mother?" Sarah asked. She didn't want to leave her parents, they were annoying as hell but you don't choose your family, blah, blah, blah, she adored her sisters and her little brother, and had lots of girlfriends she hung out with at the community center in Morillon. Steven took it all in, stunned. He told her he was in love with her. How important all of this was to him.

"We're not on the same page anymore," Sarah cut him off, right before leaving the café with a determined stride. He can still hear the sound of her little heels clicking on the tiled floor. He called her all that night, but she'd turned off her phone.

From his window, he can see the building where the Belkadis live. Sarah's building. He taps the name *Sarah Love* on his smartphone and starts the call, gets her voice mail again and again. He'd like to tear out its automated vocal cords. A dull pain and an even colder anger strain his muscles and bones. A nasty migraine pounds his skull.

"You'd better go get some groceries, we're out of everything," his mom calls from the living room, where she's watching TF1. He puts on a pair of gray jogging pants and a denim jacket. His mom's left a twenty on the table, along with a big plastic bag. The elevator takes forever to arrive, and when it does, it stinks of piss and defeat. On one of the cabin walls, someone's written, *Drink up bitches my sperm is free—come and get your STDs.*

The neon lights in the Leader Price store are pallid. He peers at his reflection in a mirror; he looks like a junkie. Totally pale even though he spent the summer under the sweltering sun in Morillon. He drags his feet in the aisles where severe-looking mothers fill their shopping carts with enough soda and snacks to kill an army of diabetic kids. He throws a tub of margarine and a loaf of sandwich bread into the cart. A pack of sliced ham. A bottle of Coke. A carton of milk and some Ricoré instant coffee. On his way out, he runs into Bilal's goat. The soldiers are still stationed in the recess of the hallway. A watchman known as the Smurf looks Steven up and down, barely hiding his contempt.

Once, Bilal offered to hire Steven. He was short-staffed and had started recruiting. Bilal speaks like a manager, like he's fresh out of some slick business school. He talked about his "business plan," his "teams," "productivity," "flexible hours," "maximizing profits," "cost killing." Yes, Bilal would have been a huge success in business school. Except in a real company, you can't bring your pet to the office, especially if it happens to be a goat. Bilal always wears jeans and a button-down shirt; he could almost pass for a Celio or a C&A model.

Steven managed to decline the offer without injuring the dealer's pride. Bilal had just wanted to do a good deed. "Listen, man, you can't spend all your time hanging out on the street, kicking a soccer ball around. There's no point anyway, since they've blocked off the old playing field." The politics of urbanism move in mysterious ways, like God. At least the soccer field gave the kids something to do in the afternoons. Steven never understood why the city decided to block it off.

A cold wind starts to blow. The neighborhood is practically deserted. All the kids are at school, and the few people with jobs have left early. The unemployed families go straight from Leader Price to the couch to switch on TF1. It's the truth, even if it's hard to hear. The neighborhood is heading south. The only people who have any real work here are dealers, plenty of them doing night shifts to keep business going around the clock, and often for pitiful salaries, considering the risks involved. It's always the boss who rakes in the jackpot, the same shark who controls the entire turf. The shop never closes. Steven didn't really understand when Bilal talked about "savage neoliberalism," but he senses that the guy manages his little enterprise as if it were a Burger King. With efficiency, discernment, and, above all, rationality.

The typical bullshit that goes on in the projects isn't tolerated. A working business means a calm and quiet neighborhood— no drama, no police raids. When the cops come to Morillon, it's because a resident's reported a car fire or a trash bin in flames, a watchdog's bitten a kid, or some teenagers have picked a fight with the manager at Leader Price or tried to steal some halal meat from the butcher shop. No one would ever put it this way, but Bilal has his own community center without walls, a kind of shadow organization: he helps people, invests a little money in a project, pays someone's overdue rent here, a car-loan payment there, buys presents for the kids on Christmas or during Ramadan. It's more complicated than what you see on TV. Steven knows there's more to it than the bad guys on one side and the good guys on the other. Morillon is a huge gray area where people try to give some meaning to their lives and spend most of their time just keeping their heads above water.

Steven shakes a few hands and makes his way toward the halal butcher; his mom asked for a pork chop and Leader doesn't sell them anymore. A cut of halal veal should do the trick. He gives a little nod to the dealers, some barely fifteen. He's seen them grow up, knew them when they were munch-kins who'd get homework help at the community center. He'd spent quite a lot of time there himself, after school, working on his math and French. One day the ladies at the center had invited a historian, a guy who specialized in Montreuil, and he'd told them that the neighborhood was named after a pair of Resistance members imprisoned by the Nazis during the Second World War.

After leaving the butcher's, Steven stops briefly near the square, right where there used to be a kind of pond. Older residents talk of a swimming area where they'd hang out on holidays and in the summer. Denise says there were fish, and claims that Steven, barely four years old, would amuse himself by trying to catch them. Anyway, the pond and the fish have disappeared, buried beneath a ton of cement and memories clouded by nostalgia.

He turns his head, already knowing what he's about to see: a bunch of dealers killing time, talking shit. Some of the soldiers are depressive. They know that life will offer them few possibilities, that dealing is only one shitty option among others, like working your ass off in the pit of a garage for six hundred euros a month—and that's if you can pass the mechanic's exam. Flip burgers chez Ronald the clown to make peanuts, and that's if you can give a halfway decent interview. All their years on the street have deprived these boys of a whole battery of communication skills.

It's all the same, though, to those who've fallen into an almost nihilistic despair. The projects or the hole, what fucking difference does it make? There's the exact same feeling of being trapped. And it takes careful planning just to get out of Morillon, if you don't have wheels. Steven would know. He's decided he won't spend his life suffocating in a packed 122 bus, or worse, at a bus stop waiting for the next one to pass. He never leaves the projects, except to file the occasional paperwork at the town hall annex on Blancs-Vilains. You were born in Morillon, and sometimes you died there, like Saïd, shot to death by the owner of a corner grocery whose nerves had been worn thin by customers' late payments. Saïd had nothing to do with any of that. It was just the wrong place, wrong time. The grocer who killed Saïd often lent money to kids. That was how it worked around here. Try finding a grocer anywhere else who'd lend money to his own mother! Around the neighborhood, they called him "the bean counter."

Steven sees Sarah. It's her day off. She's walking into the Leader Price. He rushes toward her, his heart beating fast.

"Hey, Sarah, what's going on? You won't even answer my calls."

She doesn't stop. She just gives him an icy glance and says, "Don't come near me."

It takes his breath away. She's never talked to him like this before. One of the watchmen throws him a contemptuous look.

Okay, he needs to calm down. He'll go home and have lunch with his mom and pass by the community center to see Sarah in the afternoon. Good with numbers, she has a diploma in accounting and tutors middle schoolers in math. She'll be more comfortable talking there; it's too stressful on the street, everyone's always watching everyone else—they're all hungry for gossip, for a break in the routine, anything that will allow them a momentary escape from the crushing lethargy of their lives.

"Lethargy." Steven learned the word one afternoon at the local library. He'd dropped out after ninth grade, just before high school, but he likes going to the library to leaf through books or comics, especially in winter when it's freezing and there's nothing else to do. Samia, the librarian, is a cool lady; she always finds him a book to read, something interesting and not too difficult. He's never asked for a library card. He prefers to hang out there. It's better than rotting away in the apartment, where Denise watches TV with the sound blaring because she's going deaf. Reruns of *Confessions intimes* at full volume; it drives him insane.

Denise makes ham-and-margarine sandwiches, and they eat in silence. The afternoon goes by in slow motion. Steven has a violent pain in his stomach that has nothing to do with the sandwich. This situation with Sarah is killing him. How could

she do this to him? Stomp all over his heart. Refuse the ring.
He tries to take a nap, but it's impossible to fall asleep. The
anger and frustration are razor blades that cut right into his
guts and ravage his nervous system.

He paces around the apartment, checking his phone: not
a single message from Sarah. Still two hours to kill before she's
at the community center. He looks out the window. The soldiers haven't moved. Bilal's goat trots back and forth across
the square. No one says a word. No one has a thing to say
about the presence of this goat. Not the residents, not the
assholes from the town hall; they all just pretend it's not there.
It's a nice goat, sure, but it shits everywhere. The dealers with
guard dogs take long detours to avoid the animal. You get the
feeling Bilal has the whole neighborhood under his thumb.

It's four fifteen. Thank God. Steven puts on his nicest
jogging pants, sprays himself with cologne, checks his hair in
the mirror, and leaves the apartment. When he gets to the
center, Sarah's already there. She's talking with Sophie, one
of the employees. He also sees Adama, the manager of the
after-school program, and Betty, in charge of the arts and language classes.

"Can we talk for a minute, Sarah?" Steven asks. He's nervous because he's just interrupted her conversation.

She barely glances at him. "I can't now, I'm busy."

"Come on, don't be like that. I just want to talk."

"Leave me alone, Steven. I don't have time to talk to you.
I don't *want* to talk to you."

He grabs her by the arm. "Why are you acting like this?
I'm your man, aren't I?"

"Don't touch me!" Sarah shakes herself free. "No, you're
not my man. I don't want to see you anymore, Steven. It's
over."

He has tears in his eyes. Her words hit him like a punch in the gut. He grabs her again and squeezes her arm hard. "Why are you doing this to me?!"

He feels someone pushing him up against the wall: Adama and his six-foot-three, 220-pound frame.

"You get out, now. Out. The kids will be here soon. We don't want any of that here."

Sophie, Betty, Adama, and Sarah are all looking at him with disgust, as if Steven were a turd on the brand-new linoleum.

"The kids? You let the kids take presents from Bilal, but you lose your shit when I raise my voice in front of them? Is that what you call morals, you piece of shit?"

Adama grabs him by the collar and drags him toward the exit. He opens the door with one hand and pushes Steven out into the cold with the other, as if he were an old plastic mannequin.

Steven slips and falls on his tailbone. The pain is immediate, excruciating. The dealers are laughing, calling him a loser. A woman leans out her window, seeming to enjoy the show. Shame floods Steven's foggy brain, then hardens into hate. He runs home. Goes up to the apartment and asks Denise where she put the keys to the cellar.

"Hurry up!" he yells at her.

He goes down to the cellar and finds what he's looking for: his dad's old rifle. He'd showed Steven how to use it in his grandmother's garden, out in the country, on his thirteenth birthday. It's loaded. Cold and heavy in his hands trembling with rage.

He rushes back to the community center, the rifle hidden beneath his denim jacket. He opens the door. Adama quickly approaches.

"Didn't we tell you to stay away from here?"

Adama freezes when Steven opens his jacket to show him the gun. The hallway is crammed with kids waiting for their afternoon snack. Sophie lets out a gasp.

"Shut up, bitch! I just want to talk to Sarah."

A few of the kids start to cry. A sixth grader asks Steven if the gun is real.

"Get them out of here!" he orders.

Adama obeys and leads the children outside. Steven walks up to Betty and points the rifle at her head.

"I want to talk to my girlfriend. I won't hurt anyone. I'm taking Sarah with me and we're getting out of here."

Sarah stands there, her teeth chattering. "Steven, I can't leave with you. Put down the gun."

He motions to Adama to not let anyone in, and for everyone to throw their cell phones in the trash can. There are at most a dozen people in the center, all adults. He leads them into the homework-help room. They're all pale with fear. A tall Senegalese man who's looking for work has even opened his Koran. As if a book could protect him.

"Get your jacket, Sarah. We're leaving. You have your car keys on you?"

She shakes her head.

"We're leaving the neighborhood, baby. We're getting married."

Steven stands in the doorway to keep an eye on both the hallway and Adama.

"Steven, you know the cops will be here any minute. You've already done a very good, a very fair thing—you let the kids go. The judge will take that into consideration."

He's about to run off with his woman to get married and she wants to talk to him about a judge? He points the rifle down.

"Do you love me, Sarah?"

She looks at the floor, then at Betty and Sophie. She says yes; it rings false, of course, but he smiles.

"I love you too, baby."

The hallway door opens. Adama steps aside. Bilal's goat trots onto the linoleum, followed by his master.

"Hey, man, what are you doing? The gendarmes won't waste any time getting over here . . . You know what that means? With the new security protocol and everything, after the terrorist attacks? It means they're gonna beat your ass."

Bilal is wearing a peacoat over a sky-blue chambray shirt and tight jeans. A real business-student look.

"I'm leaving," says Steven. "I'm taking Sarah with me. I'm not gonna make any trouble."

Bilal rubs his jaw. "I know, I know. But the cops will come anyway. And it's a good day for me. Paris is playing Manchester. It'll be crazy busy in a few hours."

He's talking about his customers, the ones who'll buy hash and weed to smoke while they watch the match. And what Steven's doing isn't good for business.

"Drop the gun and I promise I'll pay for you to get a good lawyer. They'll help you plead temporary insanity. A crime of passion—even if there hasn't been any crime, that's how they talk. Trust me, kid, the neighborhood doesn't need this. They'll make us look even worse. You know that. Morillon just needs a working economy, that way everybody wins. No drama, no cops. We turn a profit. That's how things are, and we've got to keep it that way."

The goat's rubbing right up against Steven's crotch.

"Let me leave here with my girl, Bilal."

"Come on, man, she's not your girl anymore. You know it. Be reasonable. You're making me lose time and money here." Bilal glances at his watch.

Then comes the sound of a helicopter circling above, over Morillon.

"Come on, drop the gun. You're fucking up my business. It's not cool." Bilal sniffs. "Jesus, man, you reek! You fall into a vat of perfume or something?"

Steven's finger tightens over the trigger.

The gun fires. Accidentally. The goat takes a round in the gut. Blood flows out of her. Steven throws the rifle down and holds his head in his hands. The hostages take advantage of the moment to run toward the exit, screaming.

Bilal kneels over the animal's body. "Marilyn, you shot my Marilyn," he sobs.

This goat's been frolicking around the neighborhood for years and no one knew its name. Bilal throws a last look at Marilyn and runs off, the goat's blood all over his nice shirt.

Sarah has left. Steven picks up the rifle. It seems so heavy in his hands. The sound of helicopter blades is growing louder and louder. He can hear the sirens of the cop cars too, and a megaphone spitting out instructions.

He picks up his phone and calls Sarah. A cop answers.

"Are there still people inside?"

"No, just me."

"A hostage just came out, covered in blood. We weren't able to identify him. Did you shoot him?"

"No, no, it's . . . that's his goat's blood."

"His goat?"

"Tell Sarah I love her."

It occurs to Steven then that he's talking to a negotiator, like in a bad American TV movie. He hangs up.

A few seconds later, the phone rings. Steven stares at the little goat's lifeless body. He picks up.

"Is it true what they're saying on BFM?!" his mother yells.

"You've done something horrible, haven't you?" Her voice is shaking. "The gendarmes are saying you have to let the kid go."

Steven checks all the rooms and offices in the center. He looks underneath all the tables. No one's hiding anywhere. (They'd learn later that a sixth kid had skipped his tutoring session to go play video games at a friend's house without telling anyone.) Denise is surrounded by more cops than Morillon has ever seen—Steven knows it.

"Mom, there's no kid here with me. I killed Bilal's goat." His voice is choked by sobs. His mom is crying too.

He hangs up.

He heads toward the main entrance and looks through the window.

He's put all the dealers out of work.

Not a soul in the hallways.

Dozens of cops from the special forces have surrounded the building.

He can make out the barrels of the sharpshooters' weapons pointing down from the roofs of the surrounding buildings.

He smiles and returns to the director's office.

To live in Morillon. To die in Morillon.

At least his dad had the courage to go and die outside the neighborhood.

The phone rings. It's Sarah. He answers.

"I'll leave with you if you let the kid go."

She really is a terrible actress. She takes him—they all take him—for an idiot. Sarah, everyone at the community center, Bilal and his soldiers, the cops. All of them. Even his poor mother, who must be sitting there shaking her head, cursing God for giving her a fuckup husband and a son just like him.

He throws the phone in the trash and sits down on the

desk chair. He pushes the barrel up under his chin, holding the rifle vertically, wedged between his thighs.

Shit, he forgot to lock the door to the basement.

All their stuff will be stolen.

It's the last thought that runs through his mind before the buckshot pulverizes his brain.

SEEING IS BELIEVING

BY INSA SANÉ

Sarcelles

Translated by Paul Curtis Daw

Our eyes are for seeing, and that's often what blinds us. Where the firefighters and onlookers saw only a burning building, Mani was seeing the destruction of his sacrifices, his history, and his Library of Alexandria. Likewise, no one understood what was driving the young man to want to brave the flames. To Mani's eyes, there was still something to save: a book, a page, a sentence, a word, a memory . . . Shedding any semblance of rationality, he sprinted toward the building entrance. He was almost there . . . when, at the last moment, a fireman tackled him to the ground, soon to be assisted by Daniel Aimand of the crime-fighting brigade.

"Fuck! I beg you, let go of me!!! Please . . . please."

Our eyes are for seeing, but unfortunately, they can also make us blind. The cops had handcuffed Mani—for his own good. Most of them didn't know him except through his brushes with the law.

"Mani! I repeat: Mani! Mike, Alpha, November, India. Gender: male. Race: Black. Height: five foot eight."

His police file depicted him as an impulsive and rebellious individual. Daniel still remembered their first run-in.

Daniel, the Cop

Go back four years. Daniel Aimand had just joined the Anti-

Crime Brigade. In a heartbeat, he'd been compelled to give up the tranquility of his provincial city and go on patrol in the midst of Sarcelles's public housing tower blocks. It was hard at first. You know in your mind that you're still in France, but even so, you feel homesick. Those vast blocks of concrete and glass that stretch as far as the eye can see and commune up close with the clouds. It all made him dizzy. Worst of all, there were legions of individuals who came from all four corners of the world. Danger lurking everywhere. Daniel had never learned the languages of Babel, still less those of the savages. Like everyone, he had thumbed through the history books affirming that his ancestors were Gauls. It was unquestioned lore that Charles Martel, in his crusade against the Saracens, had needed only one battle to crush them. There was something suspicious in the faces of those foreigners.

One evening, Daniel and his team had received orders to support their colleagues from the municipal police, who were inspecting identity papers in front of a building—the same one that would collapse in flames four years later. Agent Aimand confronted Mani at the checkpoint. Barely an adult at the time, Mani refused to produce his papers, pleading police harassment. He showed so much defiance and disrespect toward the uniform that Daniel and his colleagues were obliged to use force. Mani spent twenty-six hours in custody, refusing to eat any food or submit to administrative procedures. At an expedited hearing, he was ultimately ordered to pay a fine, on the basis of the affront suffered by one of Daniel's colleagues, and given a suspended sentence of three months' confinement.

The young man was not one to express remorse, and information passed on by the mayor's office was unequivocal: Mani, under the cover of a nonprofit association pretending to have educational and cultural objectives, was a Black activist who was advocating a dangerous form of racial separatism. The intelligence service had its eye on him. Daniel had even been instructed to investigate the association's sources of financing. Still, he never managed to establish any kind of link between the group's treasury and the narcotics traffic. His report earned him the ire of his superiors, who had conveyed by hints that it was easy to manufacture evidence, given that Mani's circle of friends included unsavory fanatics who had already been put away several times for their illicit activities. Daniel pretended not to understand.

Today, with four years of service under his belt, Sarcelles seemed less forbidding to him. You can get used to anything, maybe. Even the worst. He ended up accepting that it wasn't those poor saps who had created the architecture of their city. And that no one had consulted them on the day when the authorities decided to stack up squalor behind a fanciful stage setting, far from the "free world" that prefers to forget their plight. To ignore it so obstinately that Daniel Aimand was overcome with compassion for the inhabitants of those towers of Babel, those "little children of the century," who, according to the well-known novel of that name, were pawns of a dehumanizing system.

Mani finally looked away from the burning building, and turned to glare at Daniel.

"So, Monsieur l'Agent, do you feel at all guilty? This time, once again, the authorities will see no reason to investigate? I suppose our classroom fell victim to spontaneous combustion? And you're only doing your job, of course . . . What are you paid for, after all? To protect the population, is that it? Well, it's been said that a good many residents of Sarcelles were skipped over in the last census. Let me go or take me away, but I don't want to stay here!"

Some of the cops sneered malevolently. Not Daniel. He knew what Mani was talking about. When the agent approached his prisoner to remove the handcuffs, his colleagues voiced their disapproval.

"He hasn't done anything wrong!" said Daniel, defending his action.

"Yes he has!" rejoined one of the officers. "He violated a public order by crossing the security cordon. I'm sure there's enough to charge him with an offense . . ."

Daniel shook his head. This time, he was refusing to be party to injustice. And what the hell, he was the highest-ranking agent on the scene. In a kindly tone, he said to Mani, "Go home and move on to something else. And whatever you do, don't make any waves. I'm sure there'll be an investigation."

We have eyes to see, and yet we prefer to conjure up mirages. Both men sensed at some level that nothing would be done to determine the cause of the fire.

Mani was angry. No, he was enraged. He was no longer willing to be preached at. While still a child, he'd been trained by his respectable immigrant family: "First and foremost, don't let yourself stand out." But how can you go unnoticed when you're Black in a very white world? Mani had learned early on that turning his other cheek would allow an aggressor to deck him without breaking a sweat.

He turned his back on the building that had been almost completely consumed, and while moving away he encountered Malika, a reporter for a local daily. Now was the time for him to be completely up-front.

Although Malika sensed Mani's distress, she nonetheless hurried toward him to capture his reaction in the heat of the moment. She wanted to ignore the fact that he had called her number twice, and she hadn't answered.

Malika, the Reporter

Malika felt great tenderness toward Mani. She must have been thirteen when he, as a six-year-old, had arrived from his native country. The others in the housing project used to make fun of him because of his plastic shoes and his rustic, African-style clothing. She had immediately taken him under her wing. The boy was rather like her, in a frizzier-haired and darker-pigmented version. Malika was born in Sarcelles, the youngest of seven children. She was in some sense a daughter of *Le gone du Chaâba*: like the title character of that book, her parents had settled in a shantytown within a France that was enjoying the vaunted decades of prosperity following World War II. Malika herself had not experienced the shacks made of sheet metal and scrap wood, hidden away in a wasteland beyond reach of the city lights, but she was to some extent an inheritor of the chaotic divorce between France and its colonial history.

Her parents were quick to remind her that she was French-born, having drawn her first breath in a clinic wedged amid the tower blocks. But the xenophobic attacks to which people like her were subjected, beginning at the end of the 1960s, indicated that France didn't want them. So, hard as iron, the family matriarch proclaimed that home was . . . elsewhere. Her homeland was a mountain enclave perched on the heights of Kabylia, somewhere in northern Algeria. At their Sarcelles dwelling—an apartment set on the seventh floor of an eleven-story building—they spoke Berber and convinced themselves that any day they would return to their real home. But visits to the Kabylian backcountry happened only once every two years, and only for the two months of summer vacation. In the village, her cousins mocked her French-accented Berber; in the recreation area of her school in Sarcelles, her peers scoffed at her mop of hair that got kinkier whenever a cloudy sky brought humidity. Quickly, Malika felt torn between the two lands. In the school run by the French Republic, the teachers exhorted her to be a model student, but she never, ever behaved "like the French." And yet, she was fond of her blacktopped schoolyard oasis and her own accent of the working-class suburbs, spoken in tempo with the laughter of carefree kids thrilled to be living in the moment, far from the mad scramble of the adults.

With the other kids from the housing project—boys and girls whose parents came from Portugal, Spain, Italy, Poland, Morocco, Mali, Senegal, Cameroon, and Cambodia, and who were Christians, Jews, Muslims, Buddhists, and African animists—she built tree houses in the orchard; swam in the outdoor pools dotted among the towers; played hide-and-seek in the basements; and spouted curse words in all the languages. Her generation nurtured the hope that, in the year 2000, humanity would blast off aboard a spacecraft piloted by Captain Kirk and Mr. Spock . . . Shit, why not? Didn't mankind walk on the moon?

The problem was that, well before the millennium and its bug, Malika's world was upended. She had come home from school, her panties soiled by her first period. She had wanted her mother to explain the cause of the bleeding, but the timing was terrible . . . Malika became a woman at the same time that her oldest brother died of an overdose. It appeared that he was the first addict in the project to die from drug abuse. Plenty of others would follow. And just two years later, Malika lost another brother. He had caught the "homo disease," as it was cruelly called back then. Ancient Egypt had undergone its plagues; Sarcelles endured its own. The ravages of drugs and AIDS deprived numerous households of their firstborns. The third blow was the general rush to the exit. To protect the children, you had to move out. The ensuing exodus deprived Sarcelles of its white middle class. Then the municipal administration, which for years had sailed under the Communist ensign, pitched abruptly to the right. It was vital to shift expectations downward. The era of "austerity" had arrived.

For Malika, the Indian summer pointed her in another direction. Her enjoyment of life in the outside world was no longer limited to gazing at it through her bedroom window. Her parents were afraid for her. They didn't want her, at the outset of womanhood, to be smitten by the first seducer to come along, especially if he was not of the Muslim faith. But Malika was hungry for freedom, and it's impossible to stop Icarus from flying toward the sun, even at the cost of igniting his wings. At eighteen, Malika had run away from home and into the arms of a Romeo who knew how to say "I love you" like in the Hollywood films.

The word *nif*, Algerian Arabic for "nose," also means "pride," "honor." On the southern shores of the Mediterranean, a person's nif is sacred. By rejecting her parents' authority and protection, Malika had gravely offended them. From then on, they never spoke to her, and the door of their apartment was closed. Malika would have liked to tell her story in a novel blending fiction and reality—a kind of testament to her "sacrificed generation"—that would cry out to the world that the inhabitants of the deprived suburbs truly exist. But her narrative didn't interest the Parisian publishing houses, who gave no credence to authors with minority backgrounds except when they produced sensational documentaries. Fiction existed to portray heroes, and until proven otherwise, the Berbers and Saracens were on the enemy side. Unable to become an author, Malika pursued a career in journalism. She envisioned it as a way of being useful to her own kind. Our eyes are made for seeing. Malika had chosen to write what she saw.

But mastering the language of Molière wasn't sufficient to break the mold. Besides, the only assignment given to her by the editor in chief was compiling news-in-brief items. The more lurid the story, the happier he was. Nevertheless, when Mani had come to Malika, confiding to her the tactics used by the new mayor, a former government minister, to harm his association, Malika was convinced that she could help him. She wrote a piece detailing the pressures to which Mani had been subjected: the unexplained shutoffs of water and electricity, the vexatious changes of locks, the identity checks, the systematic body searches carried out on members of the public who frequented the association's premises . . . A scandal! Malika had investigated, observed with her own eyes the excesses of the new city administration. However, her editor tore her article into confetti, claiming that Malika lacked objectivity. He threatened to fire the reporter if she persisted in compromising herself in the partisan struggles or if she divulged her findings to any third party. She'd been forced to swallow her nif before announcing to Mani that her article would ultimately not be published.

His immediate reaction was to absolve her. He understood that she had tried, but that was just how things were . . . "Maybe the old people are right: this place is not our home."

"Okay," Malika said. "But if it's not here, where exactly is our home?"

She sincerely wanted to help him reach his promised land. And yet, when he once again called on her for support, she was less able than ever to help. Someone had vandalized the classroom used by Mani's association. They had spray-painted on the walls: *Filthy apes. Go back to your jungle and gobble bananas.* Hate is blind. Often it compromises itself. In a letter intended to be anonymous, those cowards came out with death threats, referring to lynchings inflicted on "the darkies in Mississippi." Nevertheless, at the police station, not one officer was willing to investigate the lead. Mani had no one to turn to. No one to defend him in the country of the Declaration of the Rights of Man and of the Citizen. Because he was not regarded as a man, and still less as a citizen. Malika knew she was powerless, but she told him that she'd do her best. She lacked the courage to write an article on the subject, nor could she bring herself to confront Mani's disappointment when his calls reached her cell phone. She preferred to bury her head in the sand and hope that things would settle down.

And now, did she really want to support him, or was she solely motivated by the scoop?

"What do you want?" snapped Mani. "As if there haven't already been enough vultures circling my carcass . . ."

"Mani, people need to know—"

"Wrong! Everyone knows already. But no one cares. It's not your fault. No one can do anything. I know what I have to do."

At that moment, Malika saw something alarming in the black of his pupils. Something like this: *I have nothing more to lose, you didn't need to come looking for me. I'll hurt you just as intensely as I once hoped for your love.*

That frightened Malika. Our eyes are for seeing, and sometimes we choose to lower them. She put away her notebook and pen and moved out of Mani's way.

Monsieur Benisti had just arrived on the scene. From his living room window, he'd noticed the unnerving column of smoke. He'd feared the worst, but as the blaze died down before his eyes, the worst had already happened. He could tell from Mani's expression that the bitter harvest had ripened. Monsieur Benisti had gotten to know Mani when he was the young man's high school history teacher.

Monsieur Benisti, the Teacher

Monsieur Benisti, first name Joseph, had entered the world in the city of Sétif, Algeria, of Jewish parents holding French citizenship. Before the Algerian War of Independence— euphemistically called "the events"—he was just a kid in the streets like so many others, singing the hits of the pop singer Cheikha Rimitti without really grasping the meaning of the words: "*Dour biha ya chibani, dour biha . . .*" His parents were no better off than the native Arabs and Berbers, who were collectively called "the Muslims" to distinguish them from French citizens. Joseph, the family's youngest child, had enjoyed the privilege of being schooled. His family had bled itself dry to pay the tuition. But he had asked for nothing, and hadn't been consulted when it came time to decide his future.

His dream was to become a soccer player. He wanted to be the people's gladiator, following the example of Eusébio or Algeria's own Rachid Mekhloufi. Our eyes are for seeing, and Joseph burned with the desire to be cheered in the center of the arena. After school, awaiting his hour of triumph, he would take off his shoes to kick the ball around with the neighborhood kids. On the vacant lot, there were no distinctions between Muslims and colonists, big kids and little ones. There was only sweat, scoring goals, and strong or weak players.

But then that bitch of a conflict, the War of Independence,

broke out. When you haven't even lost all your baby teeth and a war breaks out, you really don't know who's right and who's wrong. Joseph knew only that from then on, he was forbidden to play with his neighborhood pals, because "that's how it is. Don't ask questions!" In any case, between those whose families were interned, those who'd suddenly disappeared, and those no longer allowed to speak to him, there was no one left to play with. It didn't help to close your eyes; you still heard the rumors. Along the route from school to his home, people were talking about attacks, reprisals, torture, massacres, minefields, and checkpoints. Just like Cheikha Rimitti's songs, he wasn't sure he understood what he was hearing. Sharing his daily life with the indigenous Algerians, he saw point-blank the destitution that surrounded him. It was unjust to die at nine years of age, unjust not to have employment, unjust not to be respected in your country of birth.

His childhood had been stripped forever of its light-hearted innocence when, in the depths of night, he'd been awakened by his oldest brother. Rubbing his eyes, Joseph saw the suitcases: the family had to flee. To go where? No one had told him. His mother was sobbing as she finished putting her affairs in order. Your eyes are there to shed your body's tears. When he saw his mother whimpering, the youngest Benisti was truly afraid for the first time. He remembered a quotation from an author whose books he'd studied at school: "If that's what justice is, I prefer my mother." So Joseph made no fuss at all. He didn't insist on taking his leather soccer ball with him to their mysterious destination.

It was upon his arrival in France that Joseph knew he would be unalterably "a Jew." Like thousands of others, his family was allocated a residence in a new development north of Paris: Sarcelles. They could have been housed in less desirable quarters. After all, those grand housing complexes plunked on top of marshlands and fields were very strong evidence that mankind had set down its toe at the edge of the twenty-first century. The concrete masses felt like the future. Our eyes are for seeing. At Sarcelles, the concrete extended to the horizon. The project architects had calculated that each resident would walk the same number of steps to the bakery, the school, and the hairdresser. The irony was that none of those great experts would ever live in the low-to-moderate-income habitat they'd designed. From the pleasant dream to the harrowing nightmare is just a short step—as you make your bed, so shall you sleep in it, and sometimes you wake up in a lather.

It had taken time for Joseph to make a new life for himself in a new country. First, the voices and faces of his former chums faded out. Then his old playing field began receding from memory. The Arabic words for describing the world disappeared one after another, until the smells of Sétif Province drifted away, leaving only a dream . . . a memory in ruins: the ancient Septimian temple rising from the high plains.

We have eyes for seeing, and if we have two legs, they're certainly not for standing in one place all our lives . . . We're constantly advancing toward the infinite. His mother would often speak wistfully of the time when they were "back home" in the imaginary country that had been theirs. But Joseph knew that it now consisted only of yellowing black-and-white photos in an album that would permit future generations to muse about a bygone era. So, he decided to plant his flag in Sarcelles. He wouldn't be a demigod of the stadium. He had read Albert Camus's *The Stranger* and been contaminated by the plague: the stubborn refusal to remain a foreigner.

Joseph became a history teacher because instructing those

who were younger was a legitimate means of making them feel at home in their new surroundings. He'd see them pass through with hair that was black, brown, red, sometimes kinky . . . the adopted children of Marianne, whose image personifies the French Republic. Their parents had arrived from other parts of Europe or from the rest of a planet that had been ravaged by the stinging victory of global finance over societal needs.

Joseph taught them that a nation is a collection of individuals who join together because they've decided to adopt ideals, symbols, myths, and common values: those beliefs put them all on the same footing. A nation has its dogmas: "Remember the mud of the Soissons battlefield." Clovis could never have uttered these words: "Soldiers, consider that from the top of those pyramids forty centuries of history are gazing at you!" But what if it was a simple foot soldier who pronounced them, and not the future emperor Napoleon? And what if, when it came down to it, Joan of Arc had never heard voices? And if Charles de Gaulle had never really understood the French people? And if Vercingetorix had been a cannibal? And if Cleopatra's nose was nothing but a simple nif? And if you could look forever for the promised land, without necessarily finding it? . . . For a long time, his welcoming speech was enough to establish a rapport with the students. For a long time, Joseph was in the right . . . until the machinery broke down . . . until the shadow of a doubt began to loom over his certainties.

In 1989, Mani was fifteen. He entered high school and Joseph became his homeroom teacher. That year, France was shaken by two events: the fall of the Berlin Wall, and the polemic surrounding two female students who attended their public school while wearing the veil. One alternative to the capitalist system was collapsing just as another was coming to light. Mani belonged to that first generation of "French insubordinates." Cold stares. Scorn. Anger. Fear, as well. And only limited comprehension. Lacking the words to express it . . . his voice stifled by a gag fashioned from a material not of his making. The media picked up the controversy over fundamentalism and ran with it. They called it a one-way form of integration. It was inevitably deemed the stranger's fault if his existence was folded in on itself. It was considered rich to disdain pork in the country of wine, bread, and packets of little dried sausages. And definitely over the top to call yourself Muhammad when you supposedly wanted to become French!

Never had a student posed such a challenge for Joseph. Mani seemed motivated only by an eagerness to debate. Where most of his colleagues saw only an insolent kid, Joseph detected a real pearl. It was true that Mani sometimes kept bad company. Certainly, once distanced from the benches of the Lycée Jules-Ferry and delivered to the school of life, he had contracted an acute form of Sarcellitis—the malaise affecting persons living in public housing towers. But Joseph knew that under Mani's jeans-clad external shell, a gem was lurking. Sometimes eyes are for perceiving the indiscernible. Thus, the teacher set about burnishing the jewel. One day, when Mani complained about the scarcity of suitable study space for the city's three thousand high school students, Joseph had taken up the challenge of finding a solution on his own, without waiting for the institutions.

Mani never lost his enthusiasm, and he founded his association as one step in the process. To bring his plan to fruition, he needed a facility of some kind. Thus, letter after letter, meeting after meeting, he obtained from the then mayor a classroom in a disused junior high school. The building, located in a remote corner of the city, was seriously run-down. No matter! The space was the only help that Mani had requested from the mayor's office. He wanted to provide a learning center where the local kids could do their homework, take remedial classes, discuss the world that surrounded them, and, above all, reclaim their own image while cultivating self-esteem. Naturally, the key to his project was preserving its independent management.

He'd therefore found it necessary to raise money to pay the teachers who would assist the students. The postsecondary students would be obligated to support the high schoolers. The latter would impart their learning to the junior high kids, and so on. The association was called l'Arbre à palabre, its name alluding to the baobab tree, beneath which African elders would sit to work out their differences. Membership was open to all young people, without regard to gender or religion. Mani worked hard to cobble together the funds needed to operate the center. On weekends, he sold knickknacks and clothing at the flea market, and at the end of the year he went door-to-door selling calendars. He had hit the bull's-eye. Every night of the week and Saturday afternoons, the center was filled with young people who had nowhere else to work undisturbed. Joseph was so proud of his ex-student that he taught his class there three times a week at no charge.

Mani was wearing the sullen face of his bad days . . . the days when he'd been taken over by his evil genie. His jaw clamped, his brow furrowed, he wormed his way through the small knot of bystanders who stood gawking. Joseph hurried toward him. Mani raised his fist before realizing that it was his former teacher and present friend who was coming to place an affectionate hand on his shoulder.

They took several steps to separate themselves from the crowd that was continuing to grow. Mani remained silent, his gaze seemingly riveted on something no one else could make out. Joseph managed to plant himself in front of the young man.

"Mani . . . look at me."

He finally looked at Joseph. "Fuck it all! The bastards! They've burned the classroom . . ."

Joseph pulled Mani toward him and held him tightly in his arms, trying to soak up his overflowing rage. And Mani began to cry. Crying the way a man must never do, especially if he comes from the projects and he's grown up being one of the guys in a fairly rough bunch. Mani opened his fists and embraced the elderly Joseph.

"Monsieur Benisti, I know what I have to do . . ."

"Mani! The only thing lost is physical property . . . They want you to crack. Don't give them the pleasure. They didn't kill you, so you'll come back that much stronger. For the moment, go get some rest. You can be sure that all the people who helped you get started will help you rebuild. Believe me. And I'll be there too. So promise me you won't do anything irresponsible. Look at me, Mani."

Mani wiped his tears. He gripped the hand of his mentor. It was a pact. Joseph watched him leave in the direction of his apartment, his head hanging.

Mani, the Young Man

We have eyes to help us choose our path. Mani could have turned out very badly. He'd seen others take that route, childhood friends loitering against walls, ending up in prison, going insane, or getting themselves killed on the streets. He wasn't better than the others, but he was undoubtedly better supported. By his parents, whom he had long resented because they'd decided to leave their homeland. By teachers like Monsieur Benisti, who was urging him to aim always for excellence. By friends who would be there if he stumbled.

Mani dedicated his association to the young people who hadn't had such good fortune. He'd quickly understood that equality was an illusion. Was it fair to judge the students without taking into account their social affiliations, family situations, and backgrounds? Through l'Arbre à palabre, he wanted to correct that injustice. And he was delighted to see that even the parents encouraged their children to frequent the learning center. Yes! He'd finally found a reason to live. The struggle was noble, even though the battleground was a mucky pit.

Mani's decision not to accept subsidies from the city at once freed and endangered him. Apart from the classroom space, the mayor's office had no leverage over the association. And each adult within Mani's wide following represented a potential vote that the various political parties eyed avidly. That's where the whole business got complicated.

In 1995, when a long-fanged politician had coveted the mayor's office in Sarcelles, he made quite an effort to woo Mani's support. As a former government minister overseeing industry and foreign trade, the candidate pledged that his reputation would induce companies to relocate to Sarcelles, thereby reducing unemployment and the dizzying local tax rates. But Mani had no desire to endorse a campaign that would forget its promises as soon as the election was over. He therefore opted to stay uncommitted. But this wasn't happening in neutral Switzerland; once the Socialist Party heavyweight was elected mayor, any prospect of further support for Mani and his association was off the table.

Mani witnessed the successive disappearance of all the amenities that had enabled the youth of Sarcelles to keep their dreams alive, like the municipal theater and the recording studio that had launched artists from the city onto the national scene. Even though he had observed the ravages caused by the new administration, he maintained his distance from the political realm. No one found it strange that in order to stay in power, the team leading the city was buying social harmony with big dollops of phantom jobs, arrangements bordering on mob tactics, and handouts to the various religious communities.

It was all far removed from the era when Mani played at trading punches with his friends, far from the days when he thought the year 2000 was bound to be an adventure . . . far from when he believed neutrality would be the best strategy for rebuilding the future. Since the mayor wanted to play at "who's got the biggest one," Mani had to respond with the equivalent of fire and brimstone. But no! He wasn't going to behave like the punk that the mayor surely imagined he was. Monsieur Benisti was right: Mani had to act subtly and efficiently.

It was decided, then: that afternoon, he would convene his allies. Among them, he could count on his childhood friends. He would likewise assemble the individuals who were considered the dregs of the city's various housing projects: they all owed him a favor. The students who frequented the learning center would represent far from the least of his reinforcements. The strength of their numbers would make the mayor give way. Mani was sure of that.

We have eyes for seeing, but Mani hadn't noticed . . . His hands in his pockets, alone on the sidewalk, he was in the midst of plotting his counterattack when a car screeched to a halt not far from him. Three men got out. In the most electrifying fiction, Mani would have defended himself like a lion. Wielding fists and feet, he would have taken out his assailants. But in life, real life, being in the right doesn't ensure that you come out on top . . . In the ordinary world, you have no chance against three big goons who are seasoned brawlers. Taken by surprise, Mani quickly found himself pinned to the sidewalk, wrists bound. He struggled with all his might.

It was only when he was shoved into the backseat, sandwiched between two of the bruisers, that he understood. This was chess. He was two moves behind his opponent. Thus, he'd have no opportunity to recoup.

The car pulled off again. A deathly silence reigned. The driver and his three confederates were hooded, proof that they were not there to talk things over. But Mani wanted to understand. To understand how they were going to justify his death.

"You think you can get away with this? There'll be an investigation for sure."

The four men started laughing.

"For a stiff, you talk a lot."

"Especially for a guy who's about to top himself."

We have eyes for seeing . . . but we never envision the worst.

THE METAMORPHOSIS OF EMMA F.

BY CHRISTIAN ROUX

Mantes-la-Jolie

Translated by David and Nicole Ball

> *But I have sometimes thought that a woman's nature is like a great house full of rooms: there is the hall, through which everyone passes in going in and out; the drawing-room, where one receives formal visits; the sitting-room, where the members of the family come and go as they list; but beyond that, far beyond, are other rooms, the handles of whose doors perhaps are never turned; no one knows the way to them, no one knows whither they lead; and in the innermost room, the holy of holies, the soul sits alone and waits for a footstep that never comes.*
> —Edith Wharton, "The Fullness of Life"

I read in an article that *someone* spotted her when she was fifteen, in an H&M store. *Someone* spotted her. That means she was there, doing fuck all, looking at clothes or God knows what, trying them on maybe, and *someone* went into the store and *someone* saw her and *someone* said to herself, *She's marvelous, I must have her in my stable . . . Someone:* let's imagine a woman of fifty-three, slender, perfumed, nicely made up, who's trying not to admit that her youth is just a memory and death's already torching her face. She's the director of a modeling agency, a "connection girl," or whatever they say in English, my English is pathetic. So anyway, Mylène walks in—Mylène's the name I'm giving this poor middle-aged woman who doesn't know she's screwed—bumps into the girl, finds her impeccable, incredibly well proportioned, and proposes a photo session. And then, the article says, "one thing led to another." And seven years later, after she's displayed her beautiful flesh in fashion shows, the girl's on the poster for a film in competition at Cannes. *Such a Pretty Girl*, the movie's called. And the whole Croisette is crazy about her. "Already her name is on everyone's lips," says the article. "She has 'star quality,' as the Americans say: she's fascinating." All she needs now is to be rich and idolized. Just because she's built like a prick's wet dream.

Me, I've never seen a real prick, I mean with my own eyes. Guys fuck me in the basement and in the dark when they have nothing better to do. Some are generous. "That fat cow has to have some fun too! And her cunt's the only nice thing about her." I could say the same thing: their pricks are the only nice thing about those assholes, whether they're ugly or good-looking, and then, only when they vaguely know how to use it, which is kinda rare. But I don't have any choice in the matter, I take whatever comes my way and it goes as it goes. The only thing I won't do is blow jobs. I only give if I get, and hell, my clit's not in my mouth, as far as I know.

The girl herself says she didn't do anything to get where she is. She didn't even graduate high school. Childhood in Drancy, a shitty suburb, the worst—father's an excavator driver, mother worked in a tire factory at first, then unemployed, at the end a drunk. No brother or sister . . . Just like me, in fact, except I've lived in Val Fourré ever since I was born, and if Mom's an alcoholic too, Dad cut out long ago. And then, me, I actually knew what I wanted to do: Nobel Prize in chemistry. I would've liked that. But, like that girl, I have no high school diploma, didn't even take the exam to get one. I didn't get that far, they sent me to "active life" instead, so I was off to a bad start. And then, chemistry, actually, is a pain in the ass. All those symbols that add up and subtract and the result's never the same . . . What I like in chemistry is the idea that we're more or less a patched-up mix of matter and energy and are basically all the same (I'm not talking about morons)—except, what's crazy is, with exactly the same elements, depending on the mix, you're either that girl or you're me.

Me: 235 pounds, a face to make you think God didn't screw up so bad when he created the duck-billed platypus, flabby skin, flabby eyes, flabby lips—like, they hang down, you know . . . when I'm not paying attention—flabby IQ, flabby nose . . . a total flop, okay? An ode to flaccidity (yes, "flaccidity": I saw the word in a crossword puzzle in *Télé 7*, my TV mag). But if they screwed up my mix, there's nothing I can do about it. That's the way a mixture is: you put everything in a container, you shake, and you see what comes out. Like colors, they're the same for everybody, but depending on the mix, you get Van Gogh or Jeff Koons, the guy who sells his inflatable balloons for millions of dollars—I saw that one night on TV, it made me sick. Even a fluorescent-pink balloon can sell for millions. Me, I'll never be worth more than minimum wage. And that's if I have a job. If not, it's welfare, period. And that's what's disgusting. I can't help it if my mixture's screwed up, but I'm the one who pays for it. That girl's the opposite: she can't help it if her mixture's great, but she's the one who rakes it in.

So there she is, hesitating between a bolero and a miniskirt, and another chick comes in and offers her nothing less than being a worldwide icon. Me, I can stand in a store with a bra in each hand, hesitating between the S cup and the T cup, and the only chick who'll come and talk to me is the one I'm bugging because I'm in the middle of the aisle and there's not an inch of space to get around my 235 pounds; nobody's gonna tell me, "Hey, sit down there, crouch comfortably inside yourself and wait quietly. You're gorgeous, you're smart, you were given everything, you never had to look for anything, and that's why we'll give you still more. Don't worry, it'll rain millions."

God didn't screw up creating the duck-billed platypus, but he did screw up creating me and creating her. He doesn't have a sense of proportion.

The only thing I can do is teach him.

One good thing, though: I don't stink. The mix was bad enough, no point laying it on thick. I don't smell of roses, mind you. In fact, I don't smell. So I'm forced to spray these fucking deodorants all over me—way too expensive if you don't want to stink even more, and really nauseating if you don't have the cash, and that's why, whatever they do, the poor always stink (I couldn't tell you why they're too dumb to realize it). Long story short, I don't stink, and paradoxically, thanks to my 235 pounds, I go unnoticed. In the eyes of a society that sees only what shines, I'm totally invisible. Come to think of it, maybe that's why I don't stink: God wanted to try hatching nothingness out of an individual. He almost made it. Between nothingness and me, there's only 235 pounds after all.

Invisible, odorless, mute ("aphasic" is the word they use in *Télé 7*) . . . The ideal profile to serve those "fancy people," as Mom says. Aesthetically I'm a blot, but ultimately my status as an inoffensive ghost takes over. Mom was proud when I got a job at the Hilton Paris Opera to take care of the dirty laundry of five-star customers. And I was real happy: the hoi polloi don't sack out in the capital, but at least Mantes-la-Jolie/Gare Saint-Lazare is direct by train. I go into the rooms when people aren't there anymore. Invisible, okay—but showing my face when they're having breakfast? You gotta be kidding. Although . . . when Strauss-Kahn screwed that dog-faced Nafissatou, my hopes and the hopes of a whole bunch of chicks went sky-rocketing. Honestly, with all the bread Dominique had, he could've done better than that, and he goes for a Black bitch who's at least forty, completely shapeless, disfigured by fatigue or drug or drink or whatever she might've swallowed . . .

Mom must be right when she says girls believe they're beautiful, but for a guy, a girl's just a hole with hair around it. So yeah, she's not far from being right, but my mom, she's a little behind the times: now they shave their pussies like in porn flicks. I've tried, with the razor Dad left and Mom still hasn't thrown out, but it always tickles me, and then I get excited and jerk off, but in the end I'm too lazy to finish and just lie there on my bed for hours with my pussy full of dried shaving foam. A real pain: I have to cross the hall to go rinse off in the bathroom, and every time, Mom shows up to see if something's finally happening in this fucking apartment— as if something could *really* happen in an apartment perched on the fifteenth floor of a high-rise in the Val Fourré projects in Mantes-la-Jolie! So we start talking shaved pussies, and frankly, it's not a fascinating conversation. Last time, she said: "So now, women . . . it's a hole with nothing around it, is it? Not getting any better, I see!" So anyway . . . I dropped the topic. But what's certain is, anything humid at 98.6 degrees F, Strauss-Kahn can't stop himself from sticking his dick into. So there's hope for a girl like me. A good trial—man, that sure can save a situation for you.

Maybe he won't fall for it again, but he's certainly not the only one like that. The Strauss-Kahn type, there isn't just one model per slice of humanity . . .

Hope . . . I'm such a dope . . .

What lies around in rich people's beds, and what's still there sometimes when I come in to change the sheets, is a fucking nice piece of meat, there in the dirty linen. Fifteen or sixteen, or looking like it. Like the girl they spotted in that clothing store.

I scared the shit out of one, once. I may not look it, but I'm pretty strong—I cultivate my muscles under the fat, and my two arms, capable of lifting 235 pounds in a series of fifty push-ups, can do hard labor—and the kid, well, she was definitely chosen for her build. Not a minor, I don't think—though who knows, I don't give a shit—but from behind she really looked like a twelve-year-old, and given the state of her ass, I'd say that's how they used her. She was spread out naked across the bed, sleeping in her messy hair. A pretty picture against a backdrop of silk sheets. I grabbed the whole thing, sheets, bed pad, and all. At first, the girl wasn't aware of anything, then she started to moan. Little warm cries, the kind old men like to hear, convinced that what young girls really want is to eat their wrinkled dicks. She must've thought the customer was back and it was time to work again. Sometimes, in addition to sperm, they swallow quantities of alcohol, drugs, or weird medicines that can make them think anything at all. Then she realized there was something nonkosher going on. But it was too late. Locked in her silk straitjacket, she couldn't do anything. I threw her into the washer with the linens and I started up the damn thing. Thirty secs, no more. She must've had the scare of her life. Waterboarding is surely nothing compared to that. Thirty seconds must seem a long time when you think death is at the end of it. When she got out of the drum, she spit out her lungs. I returned her clothes and she got dressed, still soaking wet, then she split through the employees' entrance. Naturally, she didn't file a complaint. And if she'd died, I would've thrown her into any garbage dump or into the Seine and nobody would've given a shit. That kind of chick, she lives in law-free zones, just like me in the Val, though it's not the same kind of zone.

The Cannes girl, she's like everybody else. She doesn't see me. She's not even aware I exist. But actually, I observe her. Enjoying her five-star suite, paid for by who I dunno, but not by her. That's the way it is when you're rich. Your food, your clothes, your trips, your car . . . it's always someone else who's paying for them. It's another thing the poor don't understand; they think "rich" means you got what it takes to pay. Well, no. "Rich" is when you got what it takes to *not* pay. In short, the girl's in her suite, and one morning when I come in to take the sheets she's still there. The door is half-open, the sign saying I can come in is hanging from the knob. A mistake. Fine. Very nice, she tells me it's okay, I can do what I need to do. She can't see me, she's in the bathroom. Very well, Mademoiselle, no problem, I shout. Then, without a second thought, with a firm movement, I rip the sheets off the bed (not silk this time, you have to request that), I go into the bathroom masked with those very same sheets, throw them on top of the girl, and wrap them around her. Before she can say anything, I punch her hard on the side of the head. Radio silence. I take the whole thing down to the laundry room, but I don't throw the girl into the washer. I have a half hour to kill. On an impulse, I dart out with my bundle. The boss would yell, but he's never had much to complain about with me. If he did, I'd tell him I had my period and a hell of a headache. Guys always change the subject when we talk about our periods.

On the train, comfortably settled in, my fat ass and my laundry bag taking up two seats plus a bit of the central aisle, I can finally breathe. I look at the huge towers of the Porcheville power station, our very own monument, glowing in the sun, and I smile.

I just realized I'm on my way to restore a little order into all this mess God made.

Mantes-la-Jolie station. Off the bus at Doret, in Val Fourré, the painters' neighborhood. Val Fourré, one of the largest housing projects in Europe. Hey, it's special to live here! Right away, I decide to put the girl in the basement. Mom never goes down there. She doesn't even leave the apartment now. As for the few old things rotting away down there, no way Dad's gonna come get them. On the other hand, for fucking I'll have to go somewhere else. Or stop for a while. Anyhow, that's not every day, and I like it better when I do it to myself. As far as convincing guys, no problem. I'll say I caught a fungus. Fungus is the best antirape medicine I know. There's AIDS too, but the guys got used to it. In doubt, they wear a condom. Fungus, however, works like magic. The idea of sliding their cocks, even protected, into a forest of pustules and dubious oozes turns them off completely, all the more when the whole thing's capped by a big heap of fat. For a moment, I tell myself maybe I could sell the girl to all those assholes, but that might take me away from my goal. I don't want to hurt her. I just want to deal the cards differently. How? I don't know yet. It's all happened so fast. I'm not the kind who weighs the pros and cons before jumping into a project. Otherwise I wouldn't do anything. Once on a scale, my 235 pounds of flaccidity always tilt things to the negative. So I act, and I wait for the projectiles to smash me in the face. Or I do nothing.

I set my bundle down on the gang-bang mattress and poke around the shelves. One day, I decided I was a big girl and took down all my kid games. It should be here . . . Yeah, there it is. The Dumbo mask. Dad thought it was funny. I understood why a little later, when I realized I didn't have the right aesthetic for Sleeping Beauty masks. You don't realize who you are right away. I put on the mask—luckily the elastic still holds—and untie the bundle. The girl's just coming to. I didn't wreck her face: there was a good cushion of linen between it and my fist. Even in the worst situation possible, even with her face ravaged by fear and incomprehension, the girl's gorgeous. So gorgeous you could die. I feel like biting into her. Eating her up. Beating her. But I hold myself back and start to cry. The girl's finally awake. She asks me where we are. She thinks I'm locked up with her. Then she remembers. The five-star hotel, someone coming in, a sheet thrown over her head, bang, and then nothing. Suddenly, her eyes sparkle. Anger brings her to life. She has no time to speak—I slap her. She opens her mouth again, I slap her once more. She seems to get it. I straddle her belly, careful not to press all my 235 pounds on her. I can't stop myself from looking at her again. I have another urge to bite her. I'd like to rip off her breasts with my teeth, lick her pussy, stuff my head inside it to eat up her guts. Jesus, beauty hurts! So much! . . . Quickly, I dig out a piece of rope, tie up the girl's hands, and gag her. Then I cover her with the sheet again—before changing my mind. The sheet, I gotta bring it back. She's naked. I freeze for a moment, arms dangling at my side. Tears flow down my cheeks. My cannibalistic madness is gone, but I'm devoured by jealousy. The rage against injustice, helplessness, a force nothing can contain or appease, because helplessness says exactly what it means: it means you can't. I slam my fists into the wall a few times. The girl stares, terrorized. I throw a greasy blanket over her, leave with the sheet under my arm, double-lock the door. Outside, I'm crying.

Emma, Emma, what've you done?

The only thing that brings me some comfort is eating. I walk over to the plaza to buy a Biggy. The plaza is the huge central square of Val Fourré where there's a market twice a week. It's lined with dozens of stalls. You can find anything there. All kinds of food: Moroccan, Algerian, Tunisian, Chinese . . . Japanese, I don't think so, but I dunno because I know zilch about the Japanese. On market days, there's always guys or chicks selling various stuff that fell from trucks. They display their junk on a board over two trestles. Also vegetables from "back there." Coriander, oxhorns, eggplant, mint . . . offered by handsome old men with dried-out arms. On the way, I bump into Hamid. He walks over to me, looking all innocent and phony. As usual, he's bored and wants to fuck. Bingo! I tell him it's no longer possible, I got fungus. He's turning green and right away asks me since when. I feel like pissing him off so I say I don't know, those creepy things incubate for a fucking long time. But last time? . . . Dunno, I'm not a doctor. He takes off, and I can already picture him in his bathroom, examining his cock.

When I get to l'Étoile de Fes, a fast-food joint squeezed between a halal butcher's and a café where the guys drink only coffee or mint tea—how the owners can make a living with that is beyond me—I see Amar. Now, here's a guy I like. He doesn't ask questions, doesn't give answers; he just waits till it's over. I ask for a "double-double." Amar doesn't ask for details, he knows my order: a double Biggy, ketchup and mayo, two large fries, and a Coke. To go, yeah. Amar wraps up all that and hands it to me with a smile. Jesus . . . Amar's smile . . .

I'm just about to leave when suddenly I stop. The girl's gonna be hungry too. Given her size, a single should do. As I'm opening my mouth to order again . . . I give up. Who the hell could fat Emma be treating to a Biggy, even a single?

So, okay, this time I'm gonna share with the girl. It's not a problem: this double Biggy is a consolation prize, after all. In half an hour, I'm gonna go upstairs to eat with Mom. In a way, this is an excuse to diet.

I stop right in the middle of the plaza. A crow bangs into me with her stroller. A totally black thing, covered with a nightshirt from head to foot and wire netting over the eyes. She apologizes in her language and walks on. If it's a girl in the baby carriage, she must be one of the rare people who know exactly, from early childhood on, what their future will be: something that resembles death and ends in death. An eternity promised to her from her very first day. I stop thinking about the disastrous fate of the baby (a fate much worse than mine; God screws up all the time). Coming back to what immobilized me so suddenly: I'm thinking of him, God. I'm thinking again about how I can correct his work: it's easy as hell; it's based on the principle of communicating vessels. I'm simply going to make the girl swallow everything I'm about to eat. As time goes by, she should find herself with my 235 pounds, me with her 110. I'm fully aware it'll probably take a while. I'm gonna need a lot of patience, and I'll have to be very cautious.

Patience, prudence, and a scale. A scale is indispensable for justice.

"Here, eat."

The girl looks at me, terrified. I've exchanged the Dumbo mask—not very practical and kind of depressing—for a kind of Ku Klux Klan hood that I sewed in no time. I imagine it'll add to the atmosphere.

"What do you want?"

"None of your business. Eat."

"I'm thirsty."

I hold out the Coke. She takes a big gulp and coughs, making a face.

"It's too sweet," she says.

"You gonna have to get used to it. That's all you'll have to drink . . . Hey, I brought you clothes too. They're too big for you, but from now on, you're gonna have to learn to adapt."

"I don't understand . . . What do you want? Is this a kidnapping? You want money? I can give you my agent's number or . . . no, not my parents. I'm begging you, don't say anything to my parents. Take my agent's number instead. It's—"

"I don't want it. Nobody knows where you are and nobody will know. Money's not a bad idea, but it's not my goal."

"S-so . . . so you want . . . what?"

"Bring back a little order to this rotten world. God had no idea what the hell he was doing."

She opens big frightened eyes. Everybody tries to be tolerant with religions, but as soon as God is actually invoked in an action, everybody gets off their chair to make sure there isn't a bomb under it.

"I don't understand."

"That's okay, there's nothing to understand. All you have to do is get into these clothes without swimming in them."

"But . . . they're way too big for me!"

"Don't act dumb. According to the paper, in addition to being gorgeous, you got a Nobel IQ. So take the problem the right way and tell yourself you're the one too small for the clothes."

"You mean . . ."

"Yeah. You gotta swallow all this food. And hurry up, it's gonna get cold."

"But . . . why?"

"You may be pretty bright, but you can't understand the problems we have, God and me. Eat. The sooner you get fat, the sooner you get out."

At eight p.m., the news opens with the girl's disappearance. Just think, the new queen of French cinema! The theories are running wild. From the act of a lone degenerate to a terrorist plot, they roll out every situation you could possibly imagine. They detail the circumstances of the disappearance, relate the girl's last known actions, wonder who last saw her, what she did yesterday, what she was supposed to do today, is it possible to know the exact time she vanished? . . . Her parents, in tears, make a plea to the men who kidnapped her. Of course, they assume the kidnappers are men. It never occurs to them that it might be a woman. They went to see Mylène too. You know, the one who . . . I keep calling her Mylène; they've given her real name on TV but I've already forgotten it. She blabbers on for at least three minutes about the miracle that let her discover the girl and how totally, absolutely perfect she was. As if she were already dead. I zap to another channel and there they go again: they don't understand, a plea to the kidnappers, etc.

Mom is sniffling a little. Like all mothers, she's thinking of the parents. You can do anything to her, but take her children? No, never—if she had the guy who hurt her daughter in her hands, she'd kill him for sure. And she'd take her time! The guy would be sorry he was ever born, believe me . . . A real western!

Hey, Mom, I'm here! You got a daughter, a real one, in the flesh—and not just a little flesh! If you wanna save her, be my guest. And if you're really ready to die for your child, well, go right ahead, croak and leave me the fuck alone!

I jump up from the couch and walk toward my room.

"Emma, what's got into you?"

I don't answer. *I got a mission.*

I come back to the living room, a Tupperware container in hand. I pour the rest of my plate into it—half a pizza and dauphine potatoes. Mom asks me if I'm sulking. I say no, but I'd rather eat outside. The TV's on from morning to night— it depresses me. She's got nothing, really nothing better to do? She looks at me like an oyster lost on a dinner plate on Christmas Eve, and I begin to understand where I get my retarded-cow expressions. No, she has nothing better to do. Or worse. She has nothing to do, period. Nothing at all. That's bull! She could look for a job. Since I got mine, I'm the one who signs all the checks. Bitch! And you're exploiting your daughter on top of it! As I leave, I walk by the kitchen, where I grab the bucket of ice cream I bought yesterday, on sale at the Leader Price.

The girl's having a hard time finishing her double Biggy, so you can imagine her face when I come in with the second course.

"I'll never be able to swallow all that."

"Yes you will. You'll take your time, that's all. What's too bad is it's gonna get cold and the ice cream's gonna melt. And then there's your afternoon snack. If you wanna take a break in between, you're gonna have to hustle."

She begins to whine: "But I can't, I can't . . ." There's real despair in her voice. "And I need to pee."

Shit, I completely forgot that detail. I rummage through

the mess and come upon a pink beach pail with a drawing of a yellow sun on it. The girl gets up, sits on it, and pisses. I can see her tiny legs emerge from the huge T-shirt that's covering her. Her knees are like two flat stones taped onto bamboo stalks—the least beautiful thing about her. Not surprising she always wears jeans. Once she's done with her business, she looks around before I give her the napkin from l'Étoile de Fes. She wipes herself. I'll have to bring down toilet paper. She gets up, takes a deep breath, and turns to me.

"Listen . . . this is totally idiotic. I can't possibly swallow all that, I know I can't. My stomach isn't used to it . . . It's not big enough . . . I have no idea what your goal is here, but you'll get nowhere with me. So here's what I suggest: release me and everything will be forgotten. I have no idea what your name is and I don't know where I am. All you have to do is blindfold me, take me anywhere far from here, and this business will be over with. I go back to my life and you go back to yours."

I let a moment go by and say: "But God . . . if I don't carry my experiment all the way to the end, how is he supposed to understand?"

She clenches her fists. It's obvious she feels like smashing everything. She didn't choose to be gorgeous and end up on movie posters, but as long as things were on a roll, she never questioned anything. When he deals us aces or a royal flush, fate is no problem. We welcome him—*Come on in, pick your favorite armchair!* But if he starts to fart, we ask him what the fuck he's doing here and if he could go have fun elsewhere. All of a sudden, we find him unfair and hold him accountable . . .

I can tell the girl's going to have another fit of hysterics. I slap her again, methodically, leaving her little time to breathe, then shovel the food into her mouth. The remaining Biggy,

the fries soaking in mayo, the pizza, the dauphine potatoes
. . . She hardly has time to swallow the last bite when I put
twice as much in her mouth. And if she shakes her head, she
gets another slap. Finally, everything manages to get in. But
just as I'm about to wash it all down with ice cream, I run
into a technical problem. Since it's melted now, I can't shove
handfuls down the girl's throat. More prospecting around the
archives of the basement, from which a funnel emerges. Not
very clean. It vaguely stinks of gas. I wipe it with a corner
of the greasy blanket. The girl watches me with vacant eyes.
And when I bring the tip of the funnel to her mouth, she
opens her lips. Like a nice little girl at nursing time.

She gets it at last.

And God's in trouble.

When I'm back upstairs, the cops are there. Shit, it's true that
it's pretty quiet now. They have no problem getting into the
Val. One young and one old. They ask if I am Emma Flaubert.
I confirm. They'd like to talk to me inside. They knocked but
nobody answered. Doesn't surprise me; Mom never opens.

"Can't you question me here on the landing?"

My request makes them suspicious. "What's in the apartment that you don't want us to see?"

"Nothing, it's just that . . ."

And I give up.

It's just that it stinks; it's just that the place hasn't been
cleaned in weeks and that everything is ugly, worn out, filthy;
it's just that Mom must be sprawled out on the couch with her
blond-gray hair all sticky, giving her the look of a woman of
sixty when she's only forty-five; it's just that the living room
table must be covered with greasy plates, dried-out spaghetti
dropped on the rug; it's just that all that . . . I know it exists,

but I stopped seeing it long ago; it's just that suddenly I realize how much we've let ourselves go, both of us.

It's just that I'm ashamed.

But the cops don't give a shit about that. So I say nothing; I open the door and they come in. The young one can't help pinching his nose. Then he pretends to scratch it to justify his gesture. The old one merely shrugs. Instinctively, I go open a window. I can see the foothills of Vexin in the distance and the curve of the Seine. Shitty neighborhood but a beautiful landscape. Mom was asleep in front of the TV. She jumps. Me too. I'd forgotten her bathrobe spotted with grease and tomato sauce, her half-open legs revealing a brownish pair of panties stained with farts . . . The old cop understands there's no point going into all that and gets to the heart of the matter: the girl.

"We realized you're very probably the last person who saw her before she disappeared."

We realized . . . I can see it from here. *We* list everybody, *we* question the manager, the bellhops, room service, and then, just as he's going to leave, sitting at the wheel, his hand on the key in the antitheft device, *we* see a furtive shadow slide along an adjacent street and go into the hotel through a little door. *We* then say: "Shit, we forgot the slaves!"

It's natural, guys, that's what slaves are for: to be forgotten. But the chambermaids have nothing to say. And suddenly, a bellhop, or a receptionist, or the manager himself, who wouldn't want them to think he tried to hide something—already, the band of undocumented Black chambermaids forgotten in the basements, that's a blot—exclaims: "Oh, and there's the fat one too!" Plus that one is white and has documents. It would be a shame to waste the opportunity.

"And when am I supposed to've seen her?" I ask.

"Doing up her room."

"The card that said she wasn't there was on the door."

"So you entered the room."

"Yes."

"And?"

"And she wasn't there."

"You're sure of that?"

"That she wasn't in the living room and not in the bedroom, yes, I'm sure. But she might've been in the bathroom, though there wasn't any sound. Who knows? I went in, I took the sheets—my job's to strip the beds and take away the sheets—and I left."

"And between the two, between when you entered and when you left, you didn't see anybody? Neither the girl nor anyone else?"

"Well, no."

"It seems you left your job early."

"I didn't feel very well and I'd finished my work, and then I had hours coming to me . . ."

"Yeah, okay, that's your business. You always leave through the back door?"

Christ, is this cop a moron or what? Does he really think we lug our misery into the hotel lobby? Wretched culturally, financially, aesthetically: three wounds versus five stars, we lose every time. We're so fucking ugly, you have no idea, really . . . That Strauss-Kahn guy's a pure addict, he should be put away . . . But I explain nothing, why bother? It's about time this interrogation ended. I let my lower lip hang to give myself the face of a cow exhausted by the astronomical quantity of reflections she's had to produce in five minutes, and I say, laconically: "Well, yeah." And suddenly, illuminated, with fluttering cow eyes: "You think the girl could've left through the back? To meet a lover or something like that?"

"We don't think anything," the cop says gruffly.

And they leave.

The girl's disappearance made the front page of every paper and the headlines of every news program for at least three days. Three weeks later, they're still talking about it. It's fantastic publicity for the movie. Every day, I see the girl's body—the one she had before, I mean—plastered on the walls of the metro or the advertising panels in the Mantes station. Lounging on a bed, in a rather lascivious pose, she's staring at us with her beautiful eyes and a Mona Lisa sort of smile. She offers us her naked shoulders and a little bit of her small breasts, hidden in the shadow, but you can see their shape quite well. It's crazy, really: we scramble, we sweat, we're stuck together in the metro, we run to go break our asses at our shit jobs, and these half-naked girls in fuck-me positions seem to be taunting us all year long. *Hey, guys, wouldn't you rather be here with your cock between my legs instead of rushing to slave away like assholes?* As for the women—the heteros, I mean—I don't have to tell you they don't have much to chew on. There's another message on the posters of the girl now. Fans or jokers, dunno which, framed her face and wrote *MISSING* underneath, with a marker. Meanwhile, everybody goes to the movies to see the missing girl.

Where she still exists.

"You're the only person who can get this."

Sprawled out on my bed, Amar has a battered face. He's come to leave me one of his suspect packages—sometimes, I help him as a fence, out of pure friendship—but now he wants to talk to me about love. Monster love. Fag love. I'm not the one talking about monsters, it's him. Him, by his attitude, I mean. Being a fag is easier than being fat—after all, there are other fags who love you for what you are, while fat people don't have any choice, they just can't do anything but be together—but in the Val, it's truly hell. So where's Amar going to look for a little comfort? With a soul mate. He likes saying that, "soul mate," just to say that in fact we're equally miserable. You'd think we slit our veins and mixed our blood. And my blood is monster blood. QED.

Like me, he fucks unhappy. On the sly. He goes to the Bois de Boulogne, and so it doesn't cost him anything, he gets someone to pay the price of the train ticket. But he insists he's not a whore. Certainly, getting your ass drilled for the price of a ticket—thirteen euros round trip if you buy them by tens—is not a whore's job! But the real pros didn't take it that way. Because at the price he was charging, he churned the jobs out. Unfair competition. After poking around the neighborhood to make sure Amar didn't have a pimp—practically impossible at that price, but you never know, it could've been a punishment—they jumped him. Beat him good. Spike heels in your balls, sure to leave memories. He almost got cut too, but they finally realized he was just an unhappy kid. Which didn't give him the right to practice social dumping but didn't deserve permanent disfigurement.

All things considered, he thought they were rather nice. Problem: he doesn't know where to fuck anymore. I offer to screw him with a dildo. He says I'm nice, but "it's not the same," and with a dildo he already does it to himself. No, what he likes is to be a little scared, feel a man, his muscles, his hair, his smell, find out what he likes, his demands, his perversions, the size and shape of his prick, the way he uses it (I'm surprised: they know how to do something else besides pound?) . . . In short, all the things that make the man who he is and not just a girlfriend who does him a favor . . . And there, he starts laughing.

"Sorry . . . I'm not saying this to hurt you, okay? But I'm not sure I'd have the strength to . . . ha ha ha . . ."

"The strength to what?"

His laugh breaks up in a stew of phlegm. He coughs to hide his embarrassment and give himself a little time.

"Sorry, Emma, I . . . it's not funny at all."

I can see the state he's in. Put himself down first, then everyone else. Make sure nothing matters anymore, desacralize everything, whack everything, wallow in the mud and boast about it, dirty everything you touch, plunge your hands into shit and smear your face with it . . .

"You see, Amar, the problem is, us, the underworld, us, the not beautiful, the not white, not slim, not cultivated, not hetero, not rich, not married, not parents, not salaried, the only thing we can do is feel like shit together. For you, I'm just a fat cow; for me, you're just a little fag. Why should 'normal' people see us any different?"

"Really, Emma, I'm sorry . . . I'm so miserable . . ."

"You're a pain in the ass, Amar. Being unhappy doesn't give you the right to be an asshole. You didn't even notice I'd lost weight."

Like a three-year-old German shepherd running after the stick you throw, he goes into his total queen number.

"Oh of course I did, darling, of course I noticed . . . You're on a diet? It's funny, I still see you just as much at l'Étoile."

Now there, I realize a change of method is necessary. I'll stick to my theory of communicating vessels, but I'm gonna fill them my own way. That's gonna give me more fucking work. I don't know if God made the world in six days, but to unmake it, I'm gonna need a little more time. And a little more courage.

Amar's one of my rare friends, but if I keep seeing him he'll end up suspecting stuff. So I put on my totally disappointed face and kick him out. He starts crying and finally says it won't last. He's right. I can't picture living long without Amar's smile. Before leaving, he combs his hair and puts on his little-thug-of-the-projects face. That's Amar number three. Not the Biggy's worker, not the fag, but the dealer who had to survive despite being five feet one. The king of rodeo helmet-free wheelies, commonly practiced in the streets of the Val with stolen bikes. And when the cops turn up, he's not the last one to throw stones at them! Amar, my love. But with his disgusting tastes—frankly, what do people see in guys?—even if I had the face of the other slut, he wouldn't see me.

Honestly, God, you're a fucking pain in the ass!

And so here I am cooking. Pasta and crepes. The former with canned tomato sauce or whole-milk sour cream, the latter with sugar or jam. Chicken or pork roast when they're on sale at Leader Price, yogurt, ice cream, or all varieties of pudding, and voilà! Pork roast, sometimes I can get it for two euros a kilo. At that price, I'm surprised there's any meat left in it, but as long as the girl's getting fat, what the fuck do I care? And with this diet, she *is* getting fat, trust me. I don't know if it's the water, the fat, the starch, or the sugar, but all this mixed together sure gets the job done, especially since I'm generous with the proportions.

Mom yells. She says I'm making too much food, it's ruining us. Ruining *us*? Hey, Mom, are you kidding me or what? Who's bringing home the cash? I'm hungry, I eat, that's all. She says it's weird I'm not getting any fatter when I stuff myself like that, and I'm even losing weight before her very eyes; I'd better go to the hospital, I must have diabetes or amoebas or some shit like that. To get her off my back, I always leave a bottle of Port within easy reach. As soon as she starts talking, I pour her a glass. After three drinks she starts nodding off, and after five she's out like a light. Or she collapses onto the couch with her eyes wide open and a dumb smile on her face. And me, I'm off to the basement.

The girl pounces on the food and ingurgitates it presto, then goes to the other end of the basement and curls up. Scale-wise, it's getting there, but not as fast as I'd like, and she too would have liked, I bet. Because this business is getting seriously exhausting. Every morning, I get up forty-five minutes early so I can go down and get her bucket—a new bucket I bought, with a lid—empty it, clean it, and bring it back to her, along with the five sugared brioches under plastic wrap that I usually swallow myself, or a full bag of muffins. That could be done faster, but the elevator's out of order again and probably won't be repaired anytime soon. Lugging two hundred pounds of flesh—I did tell you I lost weight, right?—and a shit bucket up fifteen floors doesn't take five minutes, believe me. It's good for my diet though. With that, I'm sure I've reached my sports quota for the week! But still . . . I start work at the hotel at six a.m. and gotta grab the first train, at twenty past four . . . So usually I wake up at three thirty, giving me time to shower and gulp down coffee. I eat the little bag of muffins during the commute. For the last month, I've been getting up at a quarter to three. Since I bring down the evening soup to the girl only after I'm supposed to have eaten it in my room—let's say around nine—and since, like everybody else, after a shitty day I feel like taking a breather, I rarely go to bed before eleven. Three hours and forty-five minutes of sleep, yes, con-gratulations, you're good at counting. And don't forget the fifteen floors several times a day. I did the math: 975 steps to climb per day.

Luckily, I know someone's waiting for her meals.

It's been going on for three months. The girl now weighs almost 215 pounds . . . With that, I doubt she'll keep surfing the wave of success. Not to mention she has red spots everywhere. Pimples keep popping up, her skin's all scaly and ready to burst, her eyes are glassy, she stinks, rolls of fat have formed under her arms, her neck has broadened out, her chin is resting on a little cushion of fat that looks like a goiter. And I won't even talk about her ass and her belly . . . My God . . . the day she sees herself in a mirror, she'll have a heart attack. Can't happen any other way. God must be wondering by now, or he's looking somewhere else, which wouldn't surprise me; he's enough of a two-faced bastard to do that.

For me, it's simpler: I don't eat but I watch myself eat. Or rather, I watch myself wolfing down food. Without missing a crumb. A ghost sitting silently in the corner, I observe the girl gobbling up everything before her without balking. Probably the only way she found to get it over with.

And after that, I can't swallow a thing: seeing myself eat like that disgusts me.

It disgusts me, but it's terribly effective. I'm down to 150 pounds and I'm totally into sports now, despite the repaired elevator. For one, this prevents me from being a heap of sagging skin, and for another, it helps me explain why I've slimmed down so much. Because everybody has noticed, obviously. The guys want to screw me just like before, but now they don't hide it. And they try to be civil: they comb their hair, put deodorant under their arms, ask me out on dates, take me to the movies.

They know it's not like before. They know I can be choosy now, and in one way or another, they're gonna have to pay. I can do my prude number and I'm not shy about it. The girls understand too: new competition, you have to size it up. I'm not a masterpiece like the girl was: if I stand in the middle of a store hesitating between a G-string and a pair of bras and that woman Mylène appears, she won't see me, but still, she might realize my features aren't so bad. My breasts too. Before, nobody saw them. In the dark, the guys had to plunge their noses in my chest to make sure they were screwing a girl and not a hippopotamus, but nobody could actually distinguish them in the general mass. Now, they make a pretty balcony over a belly that I still hope to flatten in the near future. The ass is still a problem, but it stands out nicely against the mass, and the eyes of the guys pause on it when they're making a vertical sweep over the merchandise. Of course, it's all to my advantage, because now, I go out with nobody. I made my choice long ago anyway, but Amar prefers swallowing pricks. I'm not complaining: I still have his smile, more beautiful than ever before, because it gives him so much pleasure to see what a good fuck I've become.

Long story short, the girls have no choice but to become accomplices, so they invite me for drinks. Downtown, where I never used to set foot. I've discovered that even if it was bombed in 1944, Mantes-la-Jolie—with its helluva collegiate church, its banks of the Seine, its cafés open late at night, and its fancy neighborhoods crammed with breathtaking houses—is a pretty nice place to live. So what's wrong with us monsters? Why do we stay penned up in our projects when we have the right to walk anywhere we want?

On the job front, things have changed too. Between two piles of laundry, the boss tried to assert his rights and I crushed his balls. Presto pronto, he fired me, of course, but I don't give a shit. I abandoned Mom in the apartment with her welfare check and found a studio downtown, where I work in a clothing store.

I've got only one thing to settle now.

Of course it was impossible to do it alone. Over two hundred pounds of fat is hard to move. I asked Amar to help. Nicely, at first, but he was so horrified by my story he wanted to duck out. So I reminded him of Amar number two. The one who's stuck between number one and three. The one who'd be king in the gay Marais in Paris, but we're not in the Marais, we're in Val Fourré, stupid. I also reminded him I still had a suspicious package under my bed . . .

Climbing stairs with a heap of dead meat must be one of the hardest things I've ever done. Though Amar's short, he's very strong too, but it must have taken us a good hour to climb, inch by inch, to the ground floor, soaked with sweat and tears.

Thing is, deprived of physical exercise for four months, the girl was totally unable to walk. Not to mention the obvious: the last time she used her muscles, they'd only had 110 pounds to support. Also, she couldn't understand anything. She'd been in a quasi-comatose state for over a week. She'd be delirious at times, but it sounded more like a series of gurgles than anything else.

We loaded her into the trunk of Amar's car, and then everything happened very fast.

Between Mantes-la-Jolie and Limay, the town on the north bank of the Seine, there's an ancient bridge—built in the Middle Ages, kind of. In the 1944 bombings, one of its arches had been destroyed, smack in the middle. It was never repaired—they built another one farther on—but with its stone arches from a thousand years ago, the broken bridge is very beautiful. Lovers sometimes walk there in the summer, crazies use it as a diving board to jump into the river. Amar also sells his shit to the bourgeois there. But most of the time, especially at three a.m., it's deserted. We dumped the girl into the Seine from this dream spot. She sank like a rock. I really didn't want to hurt her, but nothing very good could happen to her now, and I liked my new life too much.

They fished out the body a week later. No one could identify her. No one ever made the connection between that swollen mass and "such a pretty girl" from the movie, a smash hit at the box office in the meantime. Sometimes, I still hear her howl, imprisoned forever in the heap of fat and guts I bequeathed to her.

Amar remained in Val Fourré, I stayed downtown, and that was it.

But I won.

Fuck God.

[Let's be careful, despite the obvious: any resemblance to actual persons, living or dead, is purely coincidental. On the other hand, the quotations that open this story come from an article by Laurent Carpentier that appeared in Le Monde on May 16, 2013. It was about a film presented at the Cannes Film Festival. It is merely a borrowing, as the people quoted in that article have no connection with the purely fictional characters depicted above. I do not recount reality, I'm inspired by it. I mean, I try to be a writer, that's all. —C.R.]

PART II

ATTEMPTS AT ESCAPE

BENEATH THE PÉRIPHÉRIQUE

BY MARC VILLARD

Saint-Ouen

Translated by Katie Shireen Assef

Lucienne Berthier, fifteen years old, had ditched Ville-momble and her parents. Mainly because she'd had enough of her father and his habit of touching her ass. Lulu doesn't joke around when it comes to that kind of thing. One Saturday morning, she took her backpack and decided to let them waste away in front of *Koh-Lanta*, their reality TV shows, and their *speculoos* ice cream.

Six months later, she's bumming around Saint-Ouen, in the neighborhood near rue du Docteur-Bauer, just beyond the boulevard Périphérique. It's where the rich people live, the types who own massive lofts yet can still afford to rent office space and artists' studios. Here, she's sure to find treasure in the garbage bins: broken cell phones, tattered clothing, strollers with white wheel rims, jeans slightly faded at the knees, and even CDs of Louane and Celine Dion. She piles all her stuff into a caddy and, making her way to the rag sellers' square at Porte Montmartre, picks up a few odd things at Marché Malik. The vendors know her well. She whines, begging them to give her the old clothes no one buys—clunky platform shoes, washed-out military jackets, Obama T-shirts. Then, walking along the Périphérique, she arrives at the square where Fatima Slimani is waiting for her. The fiftysome-thing Moroccan is one of the square's original vendors. A hundred of them—licensed, managed by an association—sell their wares beneath the bridge. With registered stands and all that. Official.

Lulu elbows her way through the shoppers and joins Fatima. Her friend, dressed in European-looking clothes, straightens up and starts to empty the cart.

"Will you go get us a couple of coffees, Lulu?"

"On it."

The day goes by smoothly, without incident. A dozen street hawkers are told to clear out by three cops with hardened faces, and the Turks get riled up as usual. The other vendors surrounding the two women specialize in run-down laptops, cell phone chargers, barely functional electric shavers, sputtering radios, sad-looking shoes, and Tacchini tracksuits on their last legs. Here, it's not unusual for people to get worked up over fifty cents. "Can you give me a discount?" is a refrain that customers hum in every tone.

At six p.m., Fatima and Lulu pack up their stuff, piling everything into two caddies that they push toward rue des Rosiers, where the Moroccan lives. She puts the merchandise away in the building's basement and hands Lulu fifteen euros.

"It's not much, but we'll make up for it tomorrow. I'll clean out Barbès and Château Rouge by eight a.m."

Fatima leans toward the girl and gives her two quick kisses on the cheek. Then Lulu heads back up the main artery through Saint-Ouen to the Chope des Puces, the Roma jazz club. She peeks inside; two guitarists in the left corner are plucking away, playing "Les yeux noirs" for the neighborhood regulars and the tourists, most of whom throw a little change in the hat. From behind the zinc bar, the owner eyes Lulu and shakes a bottle of *limonade* in her direction. She gives him a thumbs-up and elbows her way in. Caught in the middle of a group of North Africans, the girl lets herself be swayed by the songs that Django made eternal. Around nine o'clock, she orders a *jambon-beurre* and devours it while whistling to "Minor Swing." Then, night closing in thickly around her, she ventures out onto the sidewalk and weaves her way through the darkened streets of Saint-Ouen, empty except for a few dealers out for a stroll, night workers, and idlers like her, walking close to the walls with their heads lowered.

The squat is located on a poorly lit corner. It's a small abandoned loft, occupied by three homeless people: a Sri Lankan man, a Syrian widow, and Lulu. The Syrian's sleeping with her fists closed and Lulu creeps over to her corner, where a sagging mattress awaits. She quickly checks to make sure that her few possessions are still in her black backpack, then sits down on the mattress and rolls a joint.

Two hours later, she's dozing off when a fight on the street jolts her awake. She gets up and looks through the peephole of the perfectly preserved stone facade. A man and a woman wearing dark clothes lean over a teenager, who tries to dodge the kicks pummeling his thin body.

"Really, Rachid?" says the woman. "You couldn't do better than that? 150 euros? We're not idiots, kid. Let's see the cash."

"I got jumped at Clignancourt."

In lieu of a response, he gets a couple of hard kicks in the ribs.

The man takes over for the young woman, whose blond hair lights up her face.

"We agreed on two hundred a day, Rachid. Come on, the cash."

But the young man curls up into a ball and clings to the pavement, as if hoping to be swallowed by the ground. The blonde straightens up and, infuriated, lashes out with more kicks and insults.

It's an everyday drama, and yet Lulu is alarmed. She slips through the entrance to the squat and watches the scene, wide-eyed, hesitating to go back inside. She's fifteen, that's the problem. Trying to pass unnoticed, she steps back and knocks over two green plastic trash bins, making a racket.

"What's that?" asks the blonde.

Her partner pulls out a Glock and walks toward the corner of the squat. He glimpses a slender silhouette hurrying toward the nearby square.

"Probably just a junkie."

With these words, the woman pats down the now-unconscious kid's clothes. Her hands find a wallet and remove thirty-five euros. Then, raising her shoulders, she gives the kid one last kick in the temple.

"Let's get out of here. See you tomorrow, Rachid."

Rachid has stopped moving. The neighborhood is as calm as it's ever been. Three windows that had briefly lit up now go dark. Lulu tucks her head into her jacket and hurries toward the cemetery, where the darkness guarantees her anonymity. She's a more or less pretty girl, with short brown hair; her teenage breasts sometimes draw men's attention. She wears a brown imitation-suede jacket and jeans with holes in the knees. She slips into a bar-tabac across the street from the cemetery. The night server, Gorgan, is a friend of Fatima's. He winks at her and points toward the back room with his chin.

At seven in the morning, she heads back toward the squat. She crosses paths with a group of Senegalese men who've just finished their day of work and a few cagey-looking clubbers. Once inside, she immediately runs into the Sri Lankan, who's carrying a small duffel bag on his shoulders.

"You're leaving, Amal?"

"The police came, a kid was killed. They're taking our papers."

She pushes the man aside and takes a few hurried steps over to her corner. The mattress is still there, her backpack too, but when she checks the pockets she realizes her wallet's disappeared. Her ID card too. She runs over to look through the peephole and discovers a crime scene right out of a film: two cop cars, the area marked off by yellow tape, a dead body beneath a thermal blanket, and two bloodhounds pawing the dirt. She turns toward the Sri Lankan as he tries to get a stubborn cell phone to turn on.

"You're sure it's a dead body?"

"The cops said so."

She can't come back to the squat. Suddenly she's hungry, thinks of the flea market, of Fatima. She speed walks down the side road that runs along the Périphérique and enters the city limits. The area just below rue du Mont-Cenis is normally already scoured by Romanians but at this hour they're probably sleeping. And so she stuffs her backpack with all the quality junk left by the neighborhood's residents—a production company has even dumped a good number of CDs. Then, exhausted, she orders coffee and a croissant at a bar that's just opening.

Around eleven, she hides out near the square and scans faces for anyone unfamiliar or suspicious. But no, everyone seems to check out. She weaves her way between the rows of vendors and sits down next to Fatima.

"Well, then, you find anything good?" asks the Moroccan.

"Look." Lulu opens her backpack and pours out her treasures from the morning.

"Not bad. Is something wrong?"

"Someone stole my ID."

"All the better, no? If anyone asks, you tell them you're eighteen."

"You think?"

"Of course, we've all done it. And besides, they can't send you back to your country because you're in your country."

"Oh, shut up, Fatima."

The two friends burst into laughter. They manage to make a few sales, but no one will touch anything over ten euros. At twelve thirty Fatima heads back to her place to make lunch for her grandson, leaving Lulu to work the stand. At one, the caseworker arrives. He's thirty-five, bald, and bearded. He plants himself in front of the teen.

"You know who I am, Lulu? I'm a social worker. My name is Julien."

"Hi."

"Can I talk to you in private?"

"Come over here, I'm running the stand by myself."

Julien clumsily twists his torso and shuffles past Lulu and the mounds of junk.

"You live in the squat with the Syrian woman," he says.

"Sometimes. Why?"

"A young guy I've been working with, Rachid, was beaten to death last night. Right in front of the squat."

"Oh. And?"

"He was seventeen, a dealer, but a good kid. I was helping him get clean; now it's all over. I want to know if it was his bosses who killed him. You happen to see anything?"

"There were two of them, a man and a woman. But he wasn't dead . . . I got scared and ran away."

"Would you be able to recognize them?"

"Maybe. I'd rather tell *you*, though, not the cops. I'm fifteen."

"You can trust me, you know that. If it's okay with you,

we'll drive around Saint-Ouen and I'll bring you to the spots where the dealers tend to hang out. All you have to do is tell me if you recognize one of them."

"Okay. I'll be done here around six."

"I'll come by and pick you up. You're doing the right thing."

At seven, they're still combing the city in a run-down gray Clio. They've checked everywhere except the flea market, which is blocked off to cars, but dealers don't do business around there anyway—it's swarming with tourists. Julien makes one last round and parks some fifty feet from the police station on rue Dieumegard. Exhausted, they sit in the car and smoke Camels, staring into the distance.

"If you're up for it, we can try again another night," Julien says.

But she doesn't answer. He turns to Lulu, who's slid down below the dashboard on the passenger side, ducking her head.

"What are you doing?"

"The blonde on the steps of the police station—she's the one who killed your friend."

"But . . . but that's a cop."

"Don't ask me, but that's her."

Julien's interest in getting to the bottom of Rachid's murder suddenly dwindles. He says he has to think, that this changes things. Lulu understands that he's afraid, and she is too. She jumps out of the Clio and runs off without looking back.

In a panic, she decides to duck into a dark corner bar near the flea market. She sits at an old wooden table and orders a glass of white wine from a tired-looking Arab man who couldn't

care less about her age. Then a second and a third. Now she
starts to see things in a more positive light. And it comes to
her all of a sudden: *Notre-Dame-du-Rosaire. Father Augustin.*
She pays for her last sauvignon blanc, walks out of the bar,
and a few minutes later finds herself in front of the church.
Blasé, she enters the nave without dipping her fingers in the
holy water—she's careful about germs—and slides onto a
chair in the back row. She has a perfect view of Father Augustin, who's whispering to an eighty-year-old member of his
flock. He regularly checks his watch, but the old lady keeps
talking. Lulu decides to give him a hand. She stands up and
silently approaches the pair.

"Father, please, if I may?" she says in a flutelike voice.

The priest raises his head, mouthing a few last words
into the old lady's ear. Lulu sits back down and the priest approaches her.

"Father Augustin, will you give me some communion wa-
fers?" she asks. "I love the taste."

"I've got a pack of thirty, but they're all expired and stale."

"Aw, that's gross."

"True. No one cares much for the body of Christ anymore."

"I like you, Father Augustin. You're legit—the direct line
of communication with God and all that. I feel like I'm in the
front row at a Booba concert. Do you iron your own jeans?
The crease is so neat."

"I'm a man of God, not a hobo. What are you doing here,
Lulu?" Father Augustin talks straight with the girl; he saved
her life, after all. The day of her first epileptic fit, he was the
one who found her, laid her on her side, and held her tongue
out so she wouldn't bite it.

After that, she would have readily offered him her body,
but the man of God isn't into girls. Father Augustin, forty-five,

wears ironed jeans and a green down jacket, his long hair tied back in a ponytail. There's something of the mystified Mormon about him.

"I have a big problem," she says.

Understanding, he pushes her gently into the confessional and takes his place on the other side of the wooden lattice.

And she tells him the whole story.

"There it is. I don't know what to do, Father Augustin."

"The police took your ID, you're a witness to a murder. It doesn't look good for you. You have two options, Lulu. The first is to take the legal route. You file a report, the cops will hate you, there'll be a trial, and they'll win because they never lose this type of trial. They prefer to keep their dirty laundry in the family. And of course, since you're fifteen, you'll have to go back and live with your parents. And then one day, you'll be walking along, minding your own business, you'll cross a street and a car without plates will run you down and you'll be dead."

"I don't like that plan too much."

"I know. The second route is both simpler and more complicated. You don't say another word to anyone about what you saw. You throw your stuff into a bag and you go anywhere, as long as it's far from the neighborhood. And that's how you'll survive. You're too young to get caught up in a case against the cops. And anyway, you don't really think it'll go anywhere, do you?"

"You're right. I'll go away, like you say. Thank you, Father."

They step out of the confessional and Lulu suddenly throws her arms around the priest's neck, crushing his mouth with her trembling lips.

"Goodbye, Father Augustin."

"Come by and see me in a few months. And stick to hash,

no needles. Hold on, I think I have a little change on me, if you want to take a train."

As he says this, he holds out three twenty-euro bills and some coins. She takes the money and, to please him, says, "I'll keep God in mind."

Then she remembers: Fatima. She pulls her gray knit cap over her ears and hurries along the winding little streets to rue des Rosiers. She stands in front of her friend's building and looks up to the third floor. The Moroccan passes in front of the window screen, busy preparing a meal in her kitchen. Lulu, who knows the code to the front door, steps into the narrow entryway. She scans the mailboxes, finds the Slimani family's, and quickly removes the little Saint Christopher medallion from around her neck, then slides it through the slit in the box.

Now she heads toward the Porte de Clignancourt metro station. Spring is on the way, but it's still chilly. She zips her jacket up to the neck, makes her way across the square beneath the glaring lights and down into the station. She sneaks through the turnstile behind a dazed Black man and walks up the platform to the second metro car. At Gare du Nord, she gets lost in the corridors—she never takes the metro—stares in the windows of the luxury shops, takes the wrong escalator. Finally, she makes her way up to the departures hall. She'll leave, go somewhere far away.

Lulu wanders around the station and, trying to get in the right mood, reads the destinations on the boards at the end of each platform. She takes in the jumble of strange names, the unknown territories: Calais-Fréthun, Chambly, Lille-Flandres, Persan-Beaumont, Liévin, Dunkerque, Hazebrouck, Crépy-en-Valois. When you've never been to any of them, they sound scary.

With Father Augustin's money, she buys a *jambon-beurre* and a small bottle of sparkling water, then leans against the wall of a closed shop. She scans the station and slowly takes in the comings and goings. Young dealers constantly moving around, bums huddled in dark corners, SNCF security guards escorting pickpockets outside. And the whores. Three blondes—Ukrainian, maybe—pretty good-looking and modestly dressed. Lulu follows them out of the corner of her eye and sees them go into the women's restroom, a few beats ahead of their customers. As easy as that. She finishes her sandwich and throws a last look at the exotic destinations written on the illuminated boards. "What a shitshow," she says under her breath. Finally, she decides on a fiftysomething man with a potbelly and a weak look in his eye. She takes a few steps over to stand in front of the guy in his raincoat.

"Hey, what's-your-face. Want to see my shaved little pussy? You'll think you're fucking a silk glove. It'll be around thirty euros, what do you say?"

She stands there pouting while he thinks it over. Around them, the world distorts and warps. Night's shadow is settling over the station. On the staircase leading to the Eurostar platforms, a few squatters are setting up for the night. The Relay shops are starting to close and a beer-drenched soccer team heads noisily toward the metro. It's only later, around two in the morning, that despair starts to sink in.

With her second overdose and his first stroke.

THE DONKEY CEMETERY

BY JEAN-PIERRE RUMEAU

Fontainebleau

Translated by David Ball

Alec Martin lowers the metal shutter of his little bike-repair shop in the tenth arrondissement of Paris, two steps away from the Gare de l'Est. It's mid-September, and hot. In the last rays of the sun, Alec carefully puts up the sign he wrote in fancy letters and laminated: *Closed Saturday afternoon September 15, reopening Monday 17.* He backs off to check his work and then contemplates his shop window. He opened two weeks ago. At thirty-two, he's finally his own boss and his real life has begun.

Alec is of average height with an oval face and big, gentle brown eyes. He has a shaved skull, with only a little tuft of hair on the front. That's why people call him Tufty. His skin-tight tank top hides nothing of his big biceps, and molds his impressive pecs and abs like the squares on a chocolate bar. Under his Bermuda shorts, you can make out his prominent butt and enormous thighs while lower down, robust calves bulge above his slender, muscular ankles.

Alec pumps iron assiduously, but his real passion is biking. He proudly looks at his Moulton Campagnolo Chorus 22 leaning against the iron shutter of his workshop. This folding gem of a bike, handmade in England, equipped with a revolutionary suspension system and small wheels, cost him thirteen thousand euros—that is, two years of savings, moonlighting during his vacations.

He straddles his thoroughbred, and with a few pushes on the pedals he's on rue du Faubourg Saint-Martin, sprinting all the way down to the corner of the *grands boulevards* where he stops. With a few precise motions, he folds up his bike, tucks it under his arm, and climbs the six flights to his walk-up studio apartment.

No sooner has he opened the door than his inner calm disappears, replaced by a pang of anxiety.

Tonight, he'll be out in the unknown, in the middle of the forest; he'll sleep under the stars with Sandra. His best friend, Jeff, who manages the convenience store on the corner, got all excited when he heard the news: "Oh, man! You're gonna fuck her in the wild! Too cool!"

Alec played the macho who's sure of himself, but he's kind of scared. This trip into the wild is Sandra's latest idea. And she's had plenty of ideas since they started going out, each nuttier and more uncomfortable than the last. It began the second he met her, during an "open doors" event at the firemen's barracks. Sandra was waiting near the rollover test car. They needed one more passenger to start the demonstration. Alec was walking by and looking at it curiously. She pointed at him with an imploring expression on her face.

"Monsieur! Come on, be the fourth, please!"

Alec hesitated. She didn't.

"The prize is a kiss when it's over! If we get out alive."

Alec is afraid of dogs, lizards, crows—everything. He gets dizzy. He's claustrophobic. Allergic to pollen, the leaves of tomato plants, mosquito bites, sunlight, and seafood. But Sandra is so gorgeous she takes your breath away, along with your ability to think. A little taller than he is, sculptural, with jet-black hair, enormous green eyes that seem to be permanently asking for help, a big mouth bordered by lips that make you want to bite into them like a ripe peach: Sandra is irresistible. Alec got into the rollover car, hypnotized. Three minutes later, he came out pale and nauseous. She laughed and kissed his cheek.

For five months now, Alec, madly in love, has taken it upon himself to follow the young woman and her insatiable thirst for new thrills. After horseback riding came hot-air ballooning, parachuting, and scuba diving. Alec paid for them with tremors, anxiety attacks, and nightmares, which he carefully hid from her. He did try to redirect the adventurous course of Sandra's caprices by introducing her to his Moulton bike. No use: biking didn't tempt her at all. She passed definitive judgment on it.

"That's for the doped-up assholes in the Tour de France!"

In principle, a night with her under the stars in the middle of a forest seemed a lot easier on the nerves. Except that she decided to make a long night march before camping on top of a butte that would give them a spectacular view at sunrise.

Alec sips a glass of carrot juice. As usual when he's worried, he wonders why this magnificent woman goes out with him. She has no lack of suitors. Everywhere they go, men take advantage of the slightest occasion to try and pick her up. She charms all of them. She's everything he isn't: bold, artistic, cultivated, funny, resourceful, always ready to do something wild. Alec ruminates for a moment and then resigns himself. In a bit, they'll leave for a new adventure. Direction: the forest of Fontainebleau, forty miles from Paris. At the end of the world.

At that same moment, Sandra claps her hands and cuts off

the music, dripping with sweat. The students in her hoop-
dance class crowd around her to talk about the lesson. It's
not easy to keep your body in rhythm while twirling the Hula-
Hoop around your waist. Still under the spell of that excitement, the girls follow Sandra to the locker room and the
chatter continues under the shower. They can't stop checking
out their teacher's body, whether they're admiring or jealous.
Slender, muscled, toned, with lovely breasts and a round butt,
Sandra is a dream girl. Only a big scar on the side of her knee
mars the perfection. In any case, it's impossible to guess that
she's moving gaily into her thirty-nine springs, not counting
the winters.

Sports bag slung over her shoulder, she leaves the space
in the Belleville neighborhood where she teaches and pauses
on the sidewalk to think. She doesn't feel like walking all the
way to Alec's; her knee hurts too much, and the metro at this
time of day is sure to be crowded with assholes trying to rub
up against her. She opts for a taxi and its fifteen minutes of
air-conditioned peace.

Sandra rests on the backseat, closes her eyes. Little by little, a mask of sadness covers her face and a bitter crease appears at the corner of her mouth. It's always like this when she
relaxes for more than three minutes. She thinks of the failure
of her life. At twenty, she escaped the fate her hairdressing
certificate promised her. She left everything to follow a guy
who was a trapeze artist and a clown. Ten years of mad love
all over the world under the big top, during which she learned
the art of Hula-Hoop and was able to put on an excellent
circus act. One day, he left with a woman who ran a cabaret
in London. Totally lost, she joined crappy circus companies
on their wretched tours before hitting the jackpot—a season
with the Cirque du Soleil in Las Vegas. Until that stupid ski-

ing accident in the Rockies, two years ago now. Her dreams in pieces, depression, unemployment, back to home and square one. Now she's a part-time hairdresser who also teaches hoop dancing, the only vestige of her former glory.

As for love, the available guys her age are either second-class or morons, and the others, married with children, are only after her ass. But there's Alec. In love like a teenager, eager to please her, he's respectful, generous, nice, *very* nice—and compared to the others, that gives him real advantages. All the more so as, contrary to the legend that gives a little soft noodle to men with hypertrophied biceps, Alec has a fat cock that hardens on command, as often as she wants, and it makes her come like mad. The only problem with Alec is he's *very* boring, and she doesn't love him.

Once she gets to Porte Saint-Martin, the young woman can enjoy the warmth of this Indian-summer evening. She smiles as she climbs the stairs. A month ago, blushing like a virgin, Alec asked her to shave around her pussy and just leave a tuft of hair. She burst out laughing. "In other words, you're my Tufty and you want me to become your little Tufty too!"

She complied chop-chop. And he licked her till she came. Before she fell asleep, completely satisfied, the idea dawned on Sandra that tuft over tufty, Alec got off on licking a sort of twin, licking himself.

She catches her breath on the sixth floor and rings Alec Martin's bell. He opens the door immediately. She puts her forefinger on his chest and assumes a dramatic tone.

"Tufty and Tuftette meet in the dead of night in the middle of the forest . . . That's the beginning of the story. You better rack your brain and find a way to make the rest a little sexy!"

* * *

That evening, a little electric car goes through the village of Noisy-sur-École, south of the Seine-et-Marne department, forks out to the left to leave route 16, goes along the cemetery, and silently parks in the Roche aux Sabots parking lot. It is seven thirty. Night is chasing away the day under a nice round moon. There's just one other vehicle there, a van, parked a little farther away. Sandra rushes out, bent in two, squeezing her thighs together. She runs to hide behind a big boulder right in the middle of the lot.

"If anyone comes, direct traffic!"

Alec stations by the rock near an old fountain no longer in use. He sneaks a look at the white buttocks coming out of the jeans as Sandra squats. The gurgle of a copious pee precedes a sigh of relief. Suddenly, voices break the silence and three silhouettes come out of the forest twenty yards away. Alec hides a little more behind the boulder, signals Sandra to be quiet, and watches. She tiptoes up to him and climbs the boulder to get a better look. One of the men, a rifle strapped over his shoulder, leads the way to the van; another, strong and stocky, carries a deer on his shoulders. The third, the tallest, follows them calmly and waits, with hands in his pockets, while the game is loaded into the vehicle. The man with the rifle counts some bills and hands them to the tall one, who salutes him with a finger to his forehead. Motionless, he watches the van start up and its rear lights disappear behind the cemetery. At that moment, Sandra's foot slips from the rock and crunches dry leaves. The man whirls around abruptly. Alec draws back his head. He puts a finger over his lips for Sandra. They wait a whole minute with beating hearts, listening to the night, to distinguish a human sound. Alec dares to look. No one around. The man has disappeared. He sighs deeply and speaks to overcome his fear.

"We're okay. We can go back to the car and get our things."

They've walked three steps in the open when suddenly, a deep, hoarse voice rises, slow and threatening: "What are you looking for in the forest on a night with a full moon?"

Sandra gives a surprised cry, and Alec's heart stops. As if by magic, the man is now next to them. The light is so good they can see the flame shining in his eyes. Youngish, around forty, bony with a rugged face, he looks relaxed but you can sense he's ready to spring. His whole person exudes extreme animality and danger. Sandra steps in front of him and looks him up and down with astonishing calm.

"We've come to listen to the stags belling. Got a problem?"

The man sniggers salaciously. "The cry of the male in heat interests you?" He comes so close he could touch her. She can feel his breath. "The stag makes that groaning sound, half roar, half moan, when the does give off their pheromones. Mad with desire, he follows their trail with his muzzle close to the ground, his upper lip lifted and his tongue hanging out." The man frowns and raises his lip slightly. "Impossible to escape him, and at the same time, that's exactly what they want."

Sandra backs off, troubled.

Without even glancing at Alec, the man turns around with calculated slowness. At that moment, a far-off deathly howl rings out. He freezes instantly, raises a finger in the air, all ears but staring at the moon. "He's back!"

Sandra forces herself to laugh. "What? That dog we're hearing?"

"No, not a dog . . . The wolf."

Sandra explodes: "Cut the crap! If you think you can scare us with kids' fairy tales, we've been there!"

The man remains motionless, rapturously listening to the animal's howl.

"There are three wolves in Île-de-France, two in the forest of Rambouillet and one in the Fontainebleau massif. I haven't heard that one for a few months . . . Listen to his song . . . He's sick of being alone . . . He's looking for a fellow creature . . . He's waiting for an answer."

The man resumes his walk at a calm pace until he disappears in the darkness of the forest. His voice again, from behind the trees, like a warning: "Be careful."

Leaning against the boulder, Alec is still paralyzed. Sandra walks up to him, falsely relaxed.

"Okay, let's cut out."

Alec breathes out in a tiny voice: "You sure?"

Sandra cracks like a whip: "Shit! We're not gonna let a fucking poacher doing his Indiana Jones number bring us down!"

She walks to the car with a firm step. Alec runs after her. They silently put on their backpacks and their headlamps. He locks the car, checks the screen of his GPS, and points in one direction, looking like an anxious ox scenting the slaughterhouse.

"We have to go right. Then, in two or three hundred yards, we should take the circuit of the twenty-five mounds. It's marked with a red bar." He turns his headlamp on.

"Put that out, we can see plain as day!" Sandra is annoyed.

They take a sandy, moonlit trail. Anxious, Alec says, "You told me it was full moon."

"Isn't it obvious?"

Above them, the moon is shining, round as Alec's fearful eyes.

"Yeah, it is, but . . . well . . ."

"Well what?"

"Well, they say lots of weird things happen on nights when there's a full moon."

Sandra bursts out laughing. "You're kidding, right? Don't tell me you believe that crap!" She puts an arm around his neck and rubs his chest, mockingly. "Dunno about you, my little Tufty, but me, with all those muscles to protect me, I feel safe."

She kisses him on the corner of his lips and he agrees to cheer up. She spreads her arms open to the sky and sighs loudly with happiness. "Breathe in, Alec! Open yourself up to nature! Let's forget our petty little lives and get drunk on this perfection!" She jolts, lets out a yelp. "Shit, something touched me!"

She flips on her headlamp. An air ballet is flying low over them. Alec's scared voice cuts in.

"Bats. It's their moment."

"How d'you know that?"

"I read about the place. There's lots of stuff . . ."

"What kind?"

"Poisonous mushrooms, vipers . . ."

"Man, you're *so* negative!"

After a few hundred yards, they find the first red mark on a tree and begin to climb a steep slope. It's hard going up because the sand slides from under their feet. They stop to catch their breath. Alec takes advantage of the pause to display the fruits of his careful preparation.

"In my opinion, we have to walk along mound number fifteen, the Justice of Noisy. The name comes from the fact that they put the gallows up there back then!"

Sandra sweeps the obstacle with her headlamp. She seems to be gripped by a fit of madness. "Wow, we managed to escape before they could hang us! The hangman's running after us! Quick, Alec!"

With no warning, she begins to run and boldly tackles the

almost perpendicular terraced trail with high wooden risers on each step to block the sand. Alec catches up to her on a rough slope covered by a mass of tangled roots. After a few seconds of sprinting alongside her, he stumbles. Breathing heavily and happily, she reaches the summit first, gives a triumphant shout, sits down breathlessly, and rubs her knee. He limps over to her slowly, visibly worn.

"I bruised my shin," Alec says.

"With my aching ligaments, we make a fine pair!"

He plops down, removes from his bag a bottle filled with some kind of alcohol, and applies it to his shin, massaging for a long time. "Shit! That really hurts."

"Wait, I'll give you the kiss of the witch!"

She runs her lips lightly over the wound and gets up chomping at the bit, without an ounce of compassion. "There, it's over!"

Alec stands up, making a face. And they keep walking under the trees by the faint light of their headlamps. When they reach a big flat rock, the trail stops at the edge of a precipice. Taken aback, they walk in circles before discovering a red mark on the sandstone at ground level. Under it, the startling spectacle of a big gap going straight down, winding inside a scree. They stare at each other, dumbfounded. Sandra makes up her mind. She's the first to go down, carefully, using her butt and her hands.

"Don't worry," she says. "If you fall, I'll act as a mattress!"

Alec follows her, terrified. Fifteen minutes later, dripping with sweat, they're relieved to find the trail below. Licking the scrapes on his fingers, Alec points to a sign on a tree: *Chemin des Sables du Cul de Chien*—"Sandy Path of a Dog's Ass." Not reassuring.

"That's where we're going."

Sandra gives him her cell phone and goes to stand under the sign. With her arms around the tree, she arches her back so her butt sticks out. "The bitch's ass! Right now, it's the only thing I got that's presentable!"

Alec takes the picture and the flash goes off. Laughing, they set out again. Little by little, the path gets wider and gives way to a lunar landscape, a sea of white sand forming a huge dune, bordered by pine trees that stand out in the distance. They stop, enthralled by the beauty of the spot, which they imagine more than they see. They shine their lamps again to make sure they're not dreaming. Sandra shoves her hands into the sand, letting the grains flow between her fingers. Alec proudly shows off his knowledge again.

"Thirty million years ago, a warmwater ocean covered this site. It withdrew, leaving the sand, which is among the finest in the world. Venetian glassmakers used it at one time. Today, it's used to make optical fiber."

After consulting the GPS, they walk toward a huge sandstone block emerging from the dune. It looks like a dog sitting on its haunches. Alec points to the forest ahead, a dark, impassable barrier. They feel their way along in a wooded funnel the moonlight hardly penetrates, until they're able to make out a lighter gap that opens onto another stretch of white sand.

Just as they're about to proceed into it, an explosion of electronic music rips apart the night. Sliding notes and deep percussion rush down the dune and submerge the space in a terrible roar. Alec and Sandra prudently retreat and hide behind the trees. A hundred yards away, right in front of them, in the middle of the sand, a campfire is burning. Around it, thirty-odd young people are wiggling around hysterically to hard-core techno and its earthshaking bass.

Sandra squats down, fascinated. "I can't believe it! A party in the middle of the desert! It's totally loco!"

Alec squats beside her, studying his GPS. "They're blocking our way, but no problem. We'll veer east into the forest and go west again after the sands."

Sandra stays motionless for a moment, biting her lips as she stares at the scene. "What if we join them?"

He almost chokes. "You crazy? We don't know those guys; they must be totally wasted and drugged out of their minds!"

"No big deal . . . Just for a minute . . ." She raises her eyes, tantalized.

"We didn't plan for this! Let me remind you, you wanted to hear the stag belling. It's got nothing to do with this pathetic music!"

"Well I'm going, you do what you want!"

She gets up and walks determinedly toward the campfire. Alec jumps up and grabs her arm.

"No! No way!"

She jerks her arm away and looks at him furiously. "Nobody gives me orders, not you or anyone else! I'm free, got it? You can't accept that, get the hell out of my life!"

She walks toward the party without even glancing behind her. The revelers hardly notice her arrival in the light of the flames. The guys are wiggling around, stripped to the waist, with piercings and tattoos; not to be outdone, the girls are dressed like Gothic punks or hard rockers. Sandra mixes in with them and begins to dance. Someone screams in her ear so she can hear above the music: "Welcome to paradise!"

The poacher is facing her. The shadows of the flames dance over his hatchet face, and he's smiling. The light reveals gray, expressionless eyes and a messy shock of red hair.

He holds out a bottle of tequila-spiked beer to Sandra and raises his in a toast.

"To our reunion."

A girl comes over to them and hangs on to his arm nervously while smoking a joint. She's completely spaced out, her eyes popping. She gives him a twenty-euro bill.

"Another, Rob."

He frowns. "You sure you can take it? No ambulance here."

She laughs hysterically, stroking his crotch. "I swear! I'll do anything you want!"

He takes a pink pill with a smiley face on it out of the bag slung across his shoulder and gives it to her. Then he kisses her right on the mouth and fondles her breasts. She leaves to join her friends, dancing and twisting around in an erotic trance.

Sandra cups her hands like a megaphone. "What is it?"

"Ecstasy. Pure MDMA with no junk added."

She nods her head like someone in the know and downs her beer.

He taps his bag casually. "You wanna swallow some?"

She wags her hand to decline and points to the wild assembly. "You're the one organizing this?"

"Whenever I want, wherever I want. I provide three top-of-the-line speakers, and alcohol's included in the price." He strokes his bag with a big smile. "You pay for dessert separately, of course!"

Sandra drops her backpack and takes out a small purse. She comes back to Rob's ear and shouts, "How much do I owe you for admission and the beer?"

He brusquely swivels his head around. His lips brush over Sandra's for an instant. A greedy gleam flares up in his eyes.

"You're a guest! The beer's over there, all you want, you can just help yourself without asking."

Sandra can't help looking flattered. He draws his head near and grabs her delicately by the neck to bring his mouth to her ear.

"What's your name?"

"Sandra."

"I'm Rob. You're hot, Sandra, you're giving me a hard-on."

He sucks her earlobe and she pushes him away with a nudge of her shoulder, unafraid. He holds another beer out to her. She gets up with a funny smile and joins the others to dance. He stares at her with the keenness of a predator. Then he spots a walker coming out of the night. He sniggers.

"The stag—or the fag—on the trail of his doe . . ."

Alec comes over to Sandra, his head low. He talks into her ear while she's dancing. She tells him something. He walks over to Rob, who's sitting on the rock, and stops in front of him.

"Where's the beer?"

Rob motions that he can't hear. Alec repeats, yelling at the top of his lungs. Rob looks him up and down with amused insolence.

"Who for?"

Alec points to Sandra. Rob flips him a beer and he catches it on the fly. He goes back to the young woman and stays next to her for a moment. She dances and drinks without giving him a glance. He returns, dragging his feet, and sits down on the rock near Rob. He drops his backpack on the ground with a weary, submissive air. The other man holds out a beer, with a crafty look.

"Where you goin' like that?"

Alec takes a big swallow and points with his thumb. "To spend the night outside, on a mound that way."

"Which mound?"

"The Jean des Vignes boulder."

Rob appreciates it like a connoisseur. "Great view from up there!" He sweeps the air with a broad gesture, like a proud landowner presenting his domain. "All those beautiful land-marks: the Pignon des Maquisards, the Pignon Poteau, the Donkey Cemetery, Tortoise Rock, Great Mountain, Potala Rock, Cathedral Rock . . . That's the view you'll have tomorrow morning, when you wake up."

He comes close enough to Alec to touch him, shoulder to shoulder.

"If you manage to sleep, of course! Because comfort-wise, it's the bed-of-nails kind. To fuck, you gotta be a fakir! Unless you took what you need!"

He holds out another beer to Alec.

"Come on, you're gonna need it!"

A sweaty young man comes over, looking high. Word-lessly, with jerky movements, he holds out a twenty-euro bill to Rob. In exchange, he immediately gets an ecstasy pill.

Alec points to the bag with a disapproving look. "It's illegal." He points to the fire. "So's that."

An inexpressive mask falls over Rob's face. He sizes up the young man from the corner of his eye. "Illegal's my specialty."

Alec shrugs and drinks sadly. He begins to talk without forcing his voice, in a confidential tone. "See, me, what I like most is biking. On my Moulton, I go through city streets, roads, little paths, I feel happy . . ." He indicates the young people getting high as kites. "Far from that shit. So as you can see, me and Sandra, we're not the same. I love her, but she—"

Rob interrupts him, signaling he can't hear a thing. Alec makes a vague little gesture with his hand, as if to say, *Doesn't matter.*

Sandra comes over to them, dancing, a wild gleam in her eyes. She's sweating. *"Cerveza y tequila, por favor!"*

Looking delighted, Rob gets up and hands her an open bottle, which he pushes gently against her lips. She throws her head back and opens her mouth, guzzling the liquid that he slowly pours. Rob lets the last drops fall on her T-shirt, between her breasts. She straightens up, facing him, provokingly. He takes a little amber vial out of his bag, opens it, and puts it under the young woman's nose.

"Take a whiff of this jungle perfume, Sandra."

She inhales. He keeps holding it there. She inhales again. He waits a few seconds, then presses up against her and kisses her right on the mouth, sticking in his tongue. He strokes her thighs, her groin, her breasts. When Alec realizes it, he gets up looking dumbfounded, grabs Rob by the arm, and yanks him violently. The other man steps back, offers no resistance. He keeps staring at Sandra, motionless, with saliva gleaming around his mouth. Staggering, she looks at Alec with desperate eyes.

"Take me away, Alec! Please, please! Let's go!"

Alec frantically picks up the two backpacks, slings them over a shoulder, and guides Sandra out of the circle of fire, noise, and furor. They head in the direction of the Jean des Vignes rock, Rob sees. He raises his upper lip, canines ready to bite. He takes out an envelope full of white pills, each stamped with a half-moon logo, and downs one with beer.

Sandra is still staggering. After an hour of arduous walking in the sand, now they've been climbing the rock for twenty minutes. She's exhausted, but is spurred on by shame. Cold sweat flows down her back and floods her belly. Alec pushes her butt hard to help her climb the endless labyrinth of rocks. Their rhythm slows. Finally, completely drained, she sinks to her knees.

"My head's spinning. I feel like vomiting."

"Throw up, it'll do you good."

Their first words since they left the sands behind. Sandra puts out her headlamp and kneels down, hiccuping.

"I can't do it."

"Put a finger down your throat."

"Oh, no, not that!"

With no warning, he puts an arm around her waist, holds her head by the hair, and squeezes hard on her belly, almost lifting her from the ground. Sandra expels a gush of vomit, followed by a few aftershocks. Alec turns his head away, disgusted. Finally, he sets her back on all fours and lets her catch her breath. She stands up, trembling, and leans against the wall of rock.

"Can you give me some water?"

He opens his canteen and lets it flow over her hands. She washes her face and rinses her mouth. Finally, she sucks on the pipette and straightens up.

"Thanks."

They start climbing again without another word. Fifteen minutes later, they reach the summit. She sits down in a daze. Far off, they can make out the gleam of the fire through the trees and faintly hear the music. Alec chooses a large sandy space surrounded by stone blocks, and unrolls the ground cloth and survival blankets. He lays out their packs for pillows. It is eleven forty-five and the night is unusually mild for the season.

"With the survival blanket, we can strip naked . . . if we want to."

He brushes his teeth and gets undressed, keeping only his underpants on, then he turns off his lamp and lies down on the cloth.

Sandra, in a small voice: "Alec."

"Yes?"

"Thank you."

She takes off her clothes, only leaving her panties and bra, and lies down next to him. She takes his hand. Their fingers intertwine. He draws closer to kiss her. He hears a slight snore; she's already asleep. He stays a moment with his eyes open, gazing at the moon, before he sinks into his own sleep.

At 1:36 a.m., Sandra wakes gently, purring. A finger is caressing her clitoris. Her belly slowly begins to respond, undulating more and more. She opens her eyes and looks at Alec. He's asleep. The finger becomes a hand that grabs her thigh and pulls it to the other side. Sandra's heart jumps in her chest. She turns her head. Rob's face is right next to her, his beery breath. She howls, pushes him away, and jumps up, wrapped in her survival blanket. Alec wakes with a start.

"Sandra! What's going on?"

He grabs his headlamp and switches it on, trembling. In the beam of light, he discovers Sandra standing, her back to a rock. Rob grabs the blanket she's pressing to her chest and rips it violently out of her hands. His voice is hoarse and calm.

"Come on, don't make a fuss. You know what I want, and I know you want it too."

Alec rushes forward, wearing only his underpants and his watch. His muscles are impressive. He grabs Rob by the shoulder, shining his lamp on him. Rob slowly turns his head. His bloodshot eyes are flaming, his twisted face menacing.

"It won't take long. I screw her and I give her back to you. Get lost."

Alec's features decompose. He looks like a child who's

going to start crying. His voice breaks on the high notes. "No. I won't let you do it!"

"Defend me, Tufty honey! Hurt that fucking bastard!" She's both enraged and pleading.

Rob faces Alec with a carnivorous grin and starts moving slowly around him with his knees bent, ready to leap. Words whistle through his clenched teeth.

"Ever seen two stags fight? Eyes bulging, heads up, mouths foaming, antlers whipping the air and plowing the ground. At some point they stand sideways, and in a split second they start fighting with extreme violence. *Boom!*"

"Hit him, Tufty honey! You're stronger! Crush that pig's face!"

Rob laughs hysterically. "The goal, *Tufty honey*, is to break through the enemy's flank with his murderous antlers!"

He unsheathes a hunting knife and slowly approaches Alec, who freezes, a pale moron incapable of reacting, hoping a heart attack will free him from this nightmare. A hard kick to his chest sends him to the ground. The lamp goes spinning off; they hear it bounce on the rocks below. Rob kneels, grabs Alec's ear, and puts the blade under his throat.

"Fuck off before I kill you."

He forces Alec to get up, and with a kick in the kidneys, pushes him down the rocky slope. He comes back to Sandra, who is again wrapped in her blanket, eyeing him furiously.

"If you touch me, you son of a bitch, I swear I'll find you and make you eat your balls!"

Rob doesn't seem to hear. He rips away her survival blanket, grabs her throat, and knocks her over. He straddles her, tears off her bra, licks her breasts, unaffected by her punches and scratches. Suddenly, she stops defending herself and folds him into her arms, draws him close, and nibbles his lips.

"Fuck me, you bastard! I'm horny! Fuck me hard!"

Rob quickly rises and drops his pants, she removes her panties and spreads her legs, he lies on top of her, she pulls his hands toward her breasts. Rob puts his dagger down. He positions himself to enter her—and at that instant lets out a terrible scream, rolls on his side while grasping his thigh. Sandra gets up with the bloody dagger in her hand.

"You piece of shit. I would've liked to shove it up your ass to hurt you even more!"

Blood is flowing down Rob's thigh. He's writhing in pain.

"I'm gonna kill you, bitch!"

He tries to stand, dives to grab one of her ankles. She jumps back, picks up the survival blanket, and disappears down the slope. He howls.

"You're dead! You're fucking dead!" He takes out his cell and taps out a number.

Lower down, huddled against a rock and shaking all over, Alec hears Rob's hate-filled voice.

"I'm on top of Jean des Vignes! Bring my first aid kit and fast! The whore cut me, I'm pissing blood! Move it, for Chrissake! I need to find her and kill her ass!"

Alec hears a sound right next to him. He throws his arms forward in defense. "No! No!"

Sandra's naked body appears, the knife in one hand, the blanket in the other. "You little sissy, you make me wanna throw up!"

Alec stares at her in a daze. "Sandra . . . forgive me."

"I don't wanna hear your fucking faggot voice anymore!"

She continues her descent into the night. Alec straightens up. He's covered with wounds and terrified, but follows her like a little abandoned dog.

"Sandra, wait for me!"

He runs down the slope like a madman. Two minutes later, he finds her at the bottom of the mound, sitting on a boulder. She's examining the sole of her foot, which is bleeding profusely.

"Shit. Fuck!"

She cuts up the survival blanket with the knife and makes herself slippers. Alec looks at his own feet; they're also slashed up. Ripping the blanket, he, too, makes a sole that he ties around his ankles.

Sandra gives him a dirty look. "You got any idea what direction to take?"

Alec shakes his head pitifully. "The GPS is up there with the phones. And we don't have clothes or shoes."

"Whose fault is that, you ball-less bastard? Shit, you should call your mother so she can make you over again! God, I can't get over it. You would've let me get raped without lifting a finger!"

Alec takes his head in his hands. "I hate myself, Sandra, you have no idea . . . It's horrible what I did, I know . . . I never could fight. I get scared."

Sandra makes a weary, disgusted gesture. "Okay, the hell with it, we'll deal with that later. Now, we gotta get out of this fucking forest . . . Would you know how to read the stars, by any chance?"

Alec dives down, then holds his two hands out and deferentially presents his treasure. "I found the headlamp. It still works."

"Yes!" Sandra shakes a fist in the air. Her eyes sweep the surrounding darkness. "We came from up there . . ." Her voice is firm, her face determined. "So, we go that way!"

She gets up wincing with pain and takes a few steps, limping. She bends double, holding back a groan, and then gives the knife to Alec.

"Cut a branch to make a stick for me. Move your ass! They're gonna be after us soon!"

He complies, breathing heavily. Sandra sets out again, doing her best with her improvised cane.

"I can help you if you'd like."

"I'd rather die!"

They walk for a long time in the soft, loose sand. Suddenly she stops and listens, her finger pointing to the sky.

"You hear that?"

Alec listens. A sort of snoring sound is rising from the night. "Cars! . . . The A6 highway! It's the right direction! We have to get there! We'll ask for help!"

They start walking again, as fast as they can, full of new hope. The path goes down into a sandy hollow. Then something moves, two yards ahead of them. Alec shouts. Sandra raises her stick to strike. A wild boar trots out of its den, dazzled by Alec's lamp. It smashes the cluster of trees and disappears in a noise of broken branches. Sandra gives a sigh of relief.

"And to think it was my idea!"

The sound of the highway gets nearer. Alec spots a red line on a tree.

"It's the trail of twenty-five mounds! We have to go to one side . . . or the other . . . and then turn into the first trail that goes toward the sound of the road."

Sandra exhales wearily, at the end of her tether: "I say left."

Alec draws close to her. "Lean on my shoulder." He puts his powerful arm around her waist. "This time I won't let you down, Tuftette honey. We'll make it together, I promise."

Sandra's eyes are staring at a dot in the night, to the left. She seems submerged in despair. "Oh no! It can't be!"

A ray of light is filtering through the vegetation. Sounds of voices. Sandra leans on her stick and puts her arm around Alec's neck, her fingers tensing on the handle of the knife.

"They're coming this way! Put out the light! We have to hide."

They flee to the right, blindly scrambling over an unpredictable scree of slippery, cutting rocks. A big stone starts rolling under their efforts and bounces farther down with a deafening crash. They progress on all fours, crawling, pursued by voices drawing nearer, looking for them. At last a narrow plateau comes to rescue them and a breeze cools them down. They've reached the summit and can't go any farther. Exhausted, they hide behind a big block of sandstone. Sandra takes Alec's face in both hands.

"You won't leave me?"

The young man doesn't hesitate: "No, Tuftette. That's all over with. I want to be someone who deserves you."

A tear flows down Sandra's cheek. She kisses him full on the mouth, then abruptly lets go. "I love you, my Tufty."

He raises his eyebrows, flabbergasted. "You've never said that to me before."

She hands him the knife and her stick. "Sharpen it on one side to make a pike."

He gets to work. She looks at him, her jaw tensed.

"If they come, you charge and repel them with that. You up to it?"

"Yes, Tuftette," he says, checking the sharpened point of his weapon. "If they come, I'll hit them."

"No, you stab them with the point to stop them from advancing! Got it? Like a goad for cows. Even bulls don't like it."

"I'll do what you say."

"Shit, they're coming closer . . . They're almost here . . ." She kisses him. "Go on, my Tufty!"

Alec jumps up, and with all his strength plunges the sharpened stick into the body of the first one there. The blow is so violent that the point shoots out the victim's back, and Alec's hands hit his belly.

In the beam of a flashlight, Alec's face emerges above the shoulder of the park ranger, who's holding on to him and vomiting blood. The sergeant of the gendarmerie, who's lighting the scene, feverishly takes out his weapon, almost drops it, and, using both hands, shoots at point-blank range. The nine-millimeter bullet enters Alec's forehead, under the tuft of hair. He collapses, taking the ranger with him in his fall. A second gendarme rushes over and kneels next to his partner, completely panicked, on the verge of tears.

"No, it can't be! It can't be!" He grabs his radio and calls in a shaky voice: "Night Patrol Echo Charlie . . . Send a copter immediately with a doctor for a helilift. One man seriously injured, in critical condition . . . Attempted murder . . . Neutralized the aggressor . . . We're Lot 126, at the top of the Donkey Cemetery . . . Communicating our GPS coordinates . . ."

Meanwhile, the first gendarme is taking care of the wounded man. He cuts his clothing to view the damage. Blood is oozing from both sides of the wound. The victim's eyes are wide open, and the gendarme strokes his pale forehead.

"You'll be okay. We'll evacuate you very quickly. The spear is blocking the hemorrhage. We can't take it out. You're gonna be okay, don't worry. Hang in there."

He glances with disgust at the muscular body of the maniac, cut, bleeding, wearing just a pair of underpants and his watch: 2:51 a.m.

At that moment, a strange sound rises from behind a rock, something between a hog squealing and a puppy yapping, finally giving way to a human groan. A woman's voice, broken and quavering.

"Tufty honey?"

Approaching cautiously, not at all reassured, the two gendarmes point their guns in the direction of the noise. In the beam of their flashlights appears a naked young woman, wounded and bruised, waving a bloody knife. She's hunched up on the trail of the southern access point. They pin her to the ground on her belly and handcuff her. Then they drag her roughly to the corpse and force her to sit next to it.

Sandra falls flat on her belly, pulls herself over to him, kisses his face. A cry comes out of her twisted lips, an unbearable scream growing stronger and stronger, reaching a high-pitched crescendo. From the depths of the forest, a deathly howl echoes the grieving female. The wolf is answering.

PANTIN, REALLY

BY TIMOTHÉE DEMEILLERS

Pantin

Translated by David Ball

B
ekim came to get me the day after. I don't know who
warned him. He'd driven all day and night from Pantin to Kukës. Then with me the other way. With me
sitting next to him. The French passport borrowed from one of
his friends who looked vaguely like me squeezed in my moist
hands. Confused thoughts after that glacial night. Scared stiff
at the Croatian border. The European flags looking at me from
the other side of the sentry box. No problem. They hardly
checked my borrowed papers. Distractedly leafed through the
pages and glanced at the car registration, then waved us on.
Entering Schengen. For the first time. Europe.

Bekim didn't say a word throughout the trip. He drove
fast on the highways. He would yawn, and his head would
droop, then jerk back up as if he'd had an electric shock. I
was thinking back to what I'd done. It was tiring. Exhausting.
I tried to get Bekim's eye, so we could have a conversation. So
I could explain, make him understand what had happened.
I stared at him and told myself I'd never been so close to my
cousin. To that famous cousin. So close, but separated by
mountains of incomprehension. In the silence inside the car.
The silence filled by tunes on the radio, and whichever borders you crossed, they always sounded the same. We reached
Paris—well, Pantin, really—by the end of the day. He set me

up on the couch of his apartment. It was smaller than what I'd imagined.

"I'm going to sleep because I have to get up early tomorrow; I'll be back around four o'clock," Bekim said as he closed the door of the living room. It was the first time he'd spoken since we'd left Kukës the night before.

"Thanks," I murmured, but the door was already shut.

Kukës

My father's the one who'd told me they were looking for me. The *gjakmarrja*. The day after it happened, one of the Kastriotis showed up while I was still hiding out in one of the bunkers at the entry to the village, where I had spent the night, naked and surrounded by the smell of piss. They were granting us a twenty-four-hour guarantee of safety. But after that, you had to make retribution—in blood. We had twenty-four hours to leave our lives. My parents had to flee too. Hide elsewhere. On the other side of the border, in Kosovo. In an old farm, near my mother's family in Gjakova. The Kanun was clear: the crime had to be avenged by the murder of a man in the guilty party's family. It could be me, or my brothers, or my father. Especially me. The culprit. They surely suspected I'd left for France. They knew Bekim. Everybody in the mountains knew him. They must have told themselves it was the most likely haven for me. They'd end up sending someone, for sure, or they'd come themselves. They'd take as long as they needed. All the time in the world. Time was on their side.

Pantin

Pantin wasn't Paris. Even if I only understood that later: for a long time, they were the same thing to me. Anyway, at the beginning, I was shut in at Bekim's. Behind the curtains he always wanted closed. It was one of the first things he said to me—"Never open the curtains." The day after we got there. When I was just discovering his apartment. I'd imagined marble, antique statues, massive stairs, a flowering garden; I thought you'd see the Eiffel Tower from his balcony, but man, was I wrong. It was a little gray building with blistering paint and windows decorated with satellite dishes, over a garage. It smelled of paint in auto-body jobs, it smelled of oil for oil changes, it smelled of cold cigarettes in the dark, dirty stair-wells. You could hear the neighbors' TV. The yard was full of rusty bikes, old tires, and bulky objects left by successive tenants.

Bekim told me I had to stay closeted tight at his place, I shouldn't show myself outside alone; it was dangerous and he was risking a lot too, therefore I had to do what he said. He wanted to respect the Kanun in the strict sense, or whatever he'd read or understood of it, so he locked me up in his place as in the tower of a prison. Paradoxically, he thought going out in his company was okay, and so, after a few months, I could go from the apartment to the front seat of his Mercedes, then from the same seat to the wooden chairs of his favorite bar. At that point, the only things I knew about France were what I could see from the interstices in the shutters and the path we took a hundred times from his apartment to his favorite café.

Today, I think Bekim really liked my story of the Kanun and all it evoked, and that's what drove him to help me. He'd lived in the West for so many years that he'd more or less forgotten us, all of us over there in Albania. He'd been away from his culture for so many years but now, with this vendetta, he found a way of reconnecting with the purest Albanian tra-dition, one of the most ancient and striking. I also think it helped him with the guys he knew here, making him look tough. He often talked to Mehdi, the only friend I ever saw him with. "Shit, brother, it's my cousin who's getting death threats, see, they're all nuts back home in Albania," he'd say in his café, in front of a Coke, surrounded by men playing the horses. "Albania, it's all traditions, bro, honor—see, it's really hot for him over there," he'd say proudly, putting on that accent they had there in the outskirts of Paris, and discreetly nodding in my direction. He thought I didn't understand and I acted that way. I would stare into space, smile when there was nothing to smile at, watch the entrance: I was waiting. And Bekim would go on: "See, it's all medieval traditions, bro, the Kanun thing's at least a thousand years old, and it's still around today because Albania's one of the oldest countries in the world. It's a country of traditions, and the thing is, see, if he gets whacked here, well, it'll be my turn to avenge him, I'll be the one taking vengeance again." Mehdi would agree without seeming particularly impressed, and would outdo him with facts about his own home country: traditions being lost because of globalization, consumption, money, and a bunch of other theories he explained in detail. Little by little I lost him, I would turn off, maybe because, after a few minutes, conversations in French demanded too much attention. I slipped back into the role of decorative spectator, which was what Bekim wanted me to be.

And gradually I became Bekim's mute companion. Or his dog. The one you'd always see at his side but never spoke to. I'd go out with him two or three times a week. Go with him to the Vieux Père Lolive, where he met up with Mehdi or the guys he did jobs with. Cars to pick up in Germany and resell here, cigarettes from Montenegro, sporting bets. I would follow him, always silent. Well behaved. Transparent. And at some point I started listening very carefully. I'd listen to the words that came out of their mouths. So carefully that I finally learned the language without ever speaking to anyone from France.

Sitting at the back of the café, I would look at Paris—Pantin, really. The little big shots outside hanging around the tables, over empty espresso cups, murmuring with their hands cupped around their mouths to blur the conversation, rolling thick, spicy-smelling joints, and then sometimes, if they didn't like the way the discussion was going, they'd grow threatening, like they'd seen in movies. Leave dramatically, elbow their way out, and throw threats into the air as if they were Sicilian godfathers. Inside, graying drunks crowded around the dirty zinc counter, because the house charged fifty cents less for a beer if you drank standing at the bar—"Come on, let's have another one, and one more for the road," patrons inevitably said. The crowd of bettors, a scribbled-on copy of *Paris-Turf* in their hands, their heads nodding to the rhythm of the horse races on the screen over the entrance, swearing they'd picked the outsider, the upset in the third at the Chantilly racetrack. On the other side of the bar, a family of Asians who ran the joint conscientiously, tallying every order on the cash register so nobody could get away without paying. And then a few old guys, out of breath, resting at a table with their hands on a shopping cart overflowing with brightly colored products from the nearby Leclerc supermarket, because Leclerc had "*a-ma-zing* sales!" every month, they'd exclaim, accenting every syllable to the waiter who came to ask if they wanted something and they'd only answer no, they'd be leaving soon, they were just catching their breath because their pins didn't carry them the way they used to, and when would the city put in benches for seniors? ever since it went Socialist the city only cared about the bougies, the Parisians, and young people with kids.

For months, I thought the Vieux Père Lolive was the center of cultural life in Paris, the heart of nights in the French capital—a capital that eventually seemed so disappointing. And Bekim and I were part of that small world, always silent in the back, holding on to our glasses of Amstel or pastis, wearing the shadiness of shifty guys from Eastern Europe, perfectly blending into this kind of tableau—"You're what, exactly? Polacks, Turks, Yugos?" they'd ask us, as we weren't too disturbing, too offensive, or too suspect, but still, a little bit of all that.

Bekim, my cousin from Kukës, at least twenty years older than me, who'd left a long time ago. Bekim with his fancy looks, prewashed jeans, leather jacket, gym-built body. Bekim with his beard impeccably trimmed, his hair like slick dark waves perfectly in place. Bekim, the example of success back home in Albania. When we'd talked about him, we'd tell ourselves we'd like to leave too, try our luck in Germany or Switzerland or Sweden, we'd gladly leave our mountains and kick prosperity in the ass, make it spit banknotes so we wouldn't always be the last in all of Europe to hit the jackpot, yes, we'd think of Bekim at the dinner table, we'd tell each other we'd love to live the life Bekim must have in France, in Paris, and as we pronounced that word, *Pa-rri*, those two soft syllables, with that mispronounced *rr*, it was like boatloads of romanticism, marvels, and enchantments were engulfing the dark space around our old wooden table, and our eyes would turn almost unconsciously to the white surface of the fridge door, where we had stuck colorful magnets of the Eiffel Tower and the Arc de Triomphe and an old Citroën 2CV Bekim had brought back when he came for a visit in his Mercedes with a French license plate, and he talked about the avenues planted with flowering trees, the perfume wafting out of stores, sidewalk cafés where people drank wine and smoked cigarettes like in our Tiranë, but with so much more style, elegance, and refinement. "I couldn't tell you what's different; it's just that the French, as soon as they do something, they do it with class," he'd told us that day, in the black night of those cursed Albanian mountains, as we sat on plastic chairs on the patio of our farmhouse, around a barbecue sizzling on the embers.

I remember it well. I must have been thirteen or fourteen. They were building the highway day and night at the end of our land in a chorus of metal and blinding headlights, and I was still far from suspecting that my illustrious cousin Bekim would be interested in me except as a distant audience for the stories he was telling. Far from suspecting that a few years later I'd be sharing a space with him in his little Pantin apartment, and that after a few more years I, too, could tell the same stories to my family, to my mother, about the *bouquinistes* along the Seine, the parks where women tanned themselves in bikinis, the bakeries that gave off the smell of buttery croissants browning in the oven—but I wasn't there yet. Because back then, the rare times I succeeded in talking on the phone with family, it wasn't Paris or Pantin we spoke about, nor was it Gjakova. Words, already rare, had given way to the curtness of bitterness and the shame of dishonor. So we were silent, and we silenced my responsibility. We'd call for a minute, or thirty seconds, to listen to each other's silence, to the sigh at the other end of the line, the sigh that meant vengeance had not yet been taken, they hadn't yet "taken back the blood," and my family and I, lying low on opposite sides of Europe, were still waiting, and maybe there was some hope it would stay that way for a few years, for a few months . . .

Certainly, I hadn't imagined back then, when I was writhing between the clumsy certitudes of adolescence and the fe-

verish threshold of adulthood, that my life in France would
be this—this, the filthy interiors of the Vieux Père Lolive
in Bekim's company. But above all, I hadn't imagined that
Paris—Pantin, really—would be so close to me, within my
reach, within reach of flight, within reach of a simple blunder.

Kukës

The Kastriotis lived down below the village, in the valley.
That's where the best soil is, the most fertile, where you don't
break your tools by hitting chunks of stone. That's where I'm
from, Albania, the cursed mountains, an austere little village
not far from Kukës, an old stone sheep barn separated from the
city by enclosed valleys, exhausted torrents, and centuries-old
silences. We didn't talk to the Kastriotis. Part of our heritage
as we grew up. My family and the Kastrioti family were at war.
It was never really clear why, but you had to respect that ancestral sentiment. You had to accept that silence, accept that
no one spoke of the reasons for it. So I grew up avoiding the
Kastriotis, even if they lived in one of the farmhouses closest
to ours.

The Kastriotis repeated to anyone who would listen that
they were direct descendants of Skanderbeg and the Albanian royal family. Maybe that's what irritated my family, even
if, according to my great-uncle, it actually came from an ar-
gument over the ownership of a parcel of land. Centuries of
enmity were finally swept away by something else. By a huge
construction site. A line that came to separate our two farms,
our lands, our conflict. Two hundred kilometers of gleaming
asphalt between Tiranë and Pristina reuniting us with our
brothers from Kosovo and opening up our village, isolated
during the long winters, at the edges of the trails that wound
over the mountain, at the edges of those icy roads cut off by

fallen rocks, all the way up to the formidable pass that sent cars tumbling down the dizzying precipice. My brothers and I used to go down there when weather permitted to look for valuable objects, or a few lekë in a wallet, or maybe jewels.

The national highway, Rruga e Kombit in our beautiful language, was on everyone's lips: it had almost become a close relative, a cousin we were summoning, who would bring us modernity, bring us prosperity, bring us foreign investments, lift us out of our underdevelopment and medieval customs. And it was, in fact, that long band of asphalt carrying hope with it that ended up smothering our ancestral grudge against the Kastriotis, as if, by separating our two sheep barns, hatred had been buried under the tons of earth turned over by big machines, by the power shovels plowing through that earth hardened by frozen winters and crushing summer suns, that earth darkened by the blood shed by our Shqiptar brothers, fallen on our many battlefields—that stony earth of cursed mountains, so terribly cursed, especially for me, God knows.

Pantin

The familiar *tweet tweet* of the swallows woke me up. To the boredom and the darkness of Bekim's apartment, I responded with a considerable amount of sleep. But that morning, I was pulled out of bed by this familiar song, like a thrill in the monotony of my life, stuck in waiting, in this fantasized West, in this country of liberty where I was living like a recluse. Like in prison. Like in a nightmare.

I was waiting.

I was waiting for Bekim to take me to the café so I could finally get out of his place.

I was waiting, immersed in my medical textbook, telling myself that maybe I could resume my studies and become a doctor here, when *all that* was over—before I got hold of my-self: *But if all that were over, you'd no longer be in this world, you idiot.*

I was waiting for Bekim to come back, concentrating on the small screen of my phone. Checking out the sports re-sults, the news from AC Milan, my favorite team. The latest news from Albania, the scandals of a local reality TV star, the weather forecast for Gjakova. To bring me closer to my family, also shut up between four walls in my maternal uncle's farm, also waiting for the blood to be taken back.

Waiting for the situation to change, at last.

Waiting for one of them to finally find me, seize me, and shoot me. Or miss me—and my life, now between parenthe-ses, would go back to normal.

But on that sunny day in May, I'd heard swallows, the springtime *tweet tweet* of migratory birds back from their long African journey, the arrival of fine weather, the arrival of heat. It reminded me so much of Albania, of the mountains, but above all it made me realize the poverty of my life here, in captivity, behind shutters I couldn't open. The swallows were an excuse and I knew it, they were an excuse to go look around outside, an excuse for recovering a bit of the freedom I'd abandoned since coming here, since Bekim locked me in his two-hundred-square-foot apartment, since I left Kukës so quickly. Above all, it was an excuse to hasten my fate. Give the finger to the Kastriotis. *Go ahead, kill me. Go ahead, show yourselves.*

I went out and randomly walked the streets, passing through places that looked strangely familiar. One-way streets, deserted, lined with little workers' houses hidden be-hind metal gates and hedges, big industrial sheds, a textile warehouse, a garage in the recess of a building. Nothing so very different from Albania. I could have been in a residential neighborhood of Kukës or Tiranë. The smell of melted plastic soon replaced by the smell of a gutted garbage can lying between two smashed-in cars. Where was French romanticism? The opulence of the West? I found Paris—Pantin, really— very different from what I had imagined. I found Pantin ugly. Ugly as the thoughts going through my head.

The swallows had disappeared from the soundscape. For a moment, I told myself maybe I'd imagined them, they were only a sign, an omen that soon the Kastriotis, too, would appear and take what was theirs by right.

Finally, I came upon a big park that was something between a forest surrounded by modernity and a garbage dump taken over by nature. A few families were picnicking on old worm-eaten wooden benches, and groups of nervous teenagers were smoking joints behind a thick bush. I tried to walk up to a futuristic construction—it could have been a control tower, or an airport from far away, or who knows, the Eiffel Tower even, since at the time I had no idea what it really looked like—but then I got lost in the little trails in the park. They could have made me think for a split second I was back in my cursed Albanian mountains. It was nice out. It was hot. I wasn't dressed for it, with my denim jacket and sweatshirt. I was sweating and out of breath from boredom and all the cigarettes I smoked to pass the time in Bekim's apartment. In the park, two guys hiding behind their sunglasses were staring at me. Suspicious. And then farther on, that guy walking behind me. *They found me, it's over*, I began repeating to myself as I quickened my step on the steep paths. *They found me, it's all over*. The path gave way to a vast clearing with a synthetic soccer field in it. Around it, big housing projects and prefabricated homes. The place seemed to come out of nowhere. On the field, a girls' soccer team in fluorescent yellow shirts was standing in a circle with their arms on each other's shoulders, listening to their coach. I sped up to cross the field. The team froze, watching me zigzag between the orange pins and bags of training balls. I ran like that for a long time, sure that my time had come and Pantin was full of Albanians out to get me, sent by the Kastriotis. And the whole city wanted to take back the blood, take back *my* blood, apply the Kanun over here. I ran until I found myself by the delicatessen where Bekim parked his car. I was able to get back to the apartment safely before his return.

I had forgotten the swallows, but not the oppressive feeling that my time had come.

Kukës

It was before the highway, before the big construction project. A long time before Pantin. I was still a child, hardly a young man. For the first time, I was taking the 6:50 a.m. bus, which stopped at the end of the village and took me to middle school in the city, far from the rural life I had always known. You had to ride for a long time, pass all the little localities as you wound over the turns in the mountain road, going from a view of the border down into the valley again, pass the electric dam and the outskirts of the city before reaching the bus station, where everything got lively, cars honking loudly as they tried to make their way through the crowd, thick black smoke coming out of the exhaust pipes and dissipating into the mountain air, peasants camped on the roadside with vegetables in the open trunks of their old cars: peppers, big white cabbages, pickles, or tomatoes, depending on the season. The crowd at the station, where people only spoke in shouts, insults, and spit, contrasted with the early hour and the quiet of the village I was coming from. From there, I had to walk another kilometer to get to school, in a classroom much too big and full of books, which really shocked me, coming from a narrow world governed by traditions, the heritage of the past, and the happy archaisms that prevailed in the village.

The teacher did her roll call, and after my name came *her*: Arjana Kastrioti. Arjana Kastrioti. That name—I'd heard it so much, and so much venom had flowed over it that I stiffened, terrified at not knowing what to do or how to behave.

So for the first months, I put a mental patch over her, as if she'd never existed; in my childish naivete, I would turn away from her, as if looking at her could contaminate me and wither the immaculate reputation of my family. To compensate, I absorbed myself in stories of our modern world, in math, geology, and the great history of Albania, of our people, and I let myself get carried away by the fate of our ancestors, my compatriots, and didn't even hear the teacher say her name anymore, Arjana Kastrioti, immersed as I was in the dates, heroic battles, and lives of the fathers of the nation, who made us in their image, proud and noble.

But at that age, taboos exist to be broken, so curiosity took over and I ended up dropping the Skanderbegs and company to check out Arjana from the corner of my eye. Furtive glances which, when I was caught, hid under a mask of hatred, but then became more insistent, prolonged glances that could no longer dissimulate my interest in her, the female offspring of that nefarious family, that great-looking girl over there. I could no longer take my eyes off her, nor my heart, until we finally managed to exchange a first word on the bus, "Hi," then another later, before we sat down together, sharing the long trips, and then sharing the heat of our hands, of our mouths, of our tongues, those illicit kisses of adolescence that filled me with burning euphoria, hidden from our families and our history.

The year after, my twin brothers started going to the school, so from then on we couldn't show ourselves together. Then the highway was built, and just when it seemed to have reconciled our families, it finally separated us, Arjana on one side and me on the other, Arjana still going to our school and me, cut off from it by the four-lane highway, forced to enroll in a new one.

So I was obviously surprised to see her that Saturday night years later, in that café in Kukës. I was celebrating the end of high school with my friends. It was summer, the last week of June, a hot, dry day. My head was filled with plans for the next year: studying, leaving the mountains and the village, leaving for the city, Tiranë, and med school. Everybody at the bar was in a good mood. We were dancing, singing, drinking, the sweat of our overheated bodies beading up on the windowpanes to the point where, from the outside, you would have thought we were spending the evening in a tropical hothouse.

Arjana came in late, with two girls I didn't know. I hadn't seen her since middle school. I'd be lying if I said I'd forgotten her and didn't think about her anymore, or even that I didn't know what she looked like now. I spied on her avidly. Secretly. On Instagram, Facebook, and other social media. I followed her posts. Her and her friends. Her and the different clothes she wore. Her at home, in her room, posing in front of her mirror. At the Kastriotis'. And now her in the bar on this June night. I'm not sure she saw me, but I thought I saw a smile appear on her face, as if to say, *Here I am at last, here we are at last, side by side, nothing stands in the way of us being together anymore.* Then the crowd. Friends toasting each other. The music getting louder. I only found her again later, sitting outside with a glass of mineral water, a long, slim cigarette between her fingers. In the midst of that generalized drunkenness, Arjana. No one there knew the story of our families. No one knew *our* story. I watched her from a few yards away.

Her friends left and she stayed, drinking her glass of sparkling water while people all around were getting drunk. I didn't dare come near or speak to her. But that's all I could think of—her. The shadow of our history. I still don't understand why she came. If it was defiance or chance.

After a while . . . the alcohol . . . I sat down at her table. I was drunk. I wasn't used to drinking that much and my head was spinning. Those brandies we'd emptied in a gulp, inhaling them to show that, from now on, we were grownups, strong like our fathers. Real men. She didn't say anything. She remained silent. She didn't even look at me. The silence between us could hardly hide the violent storm bursting inside me. Everything was seething. I felt myself growing hard against my thigh. Burning. I tried to squeeze my legs together, to press it against the icy surface of my glass of beer. Finally, in that silence lasting an eternity, she said a word, then another, then everything went back to the way it had been before, naturally, as if we'd never left each other. We moved away from the others. We walked, as if guided by fate, toward the parking lot, a little farther, plunged in the dark night of the Albanian mountains.

The darkness of night and our naked, intertwined bodies, in the back of Arjana's car. Our bodies. Our breath mixing. Our groans. Discovering pleasure. Love. And then suddenly, knocks on the window, *BAM-BAM-BAM*, the brutal drumming of an enraged beast, the body of the car buckling under the shock of fists. And then the face deformed by fury showing itself in the window frame, red with blood, red with hate, red with rage, in the black night. I was too drunk. For a brief moment, I was almost proud that he'd surprised us there. As if it were a game. As if those things in Albania were only a game. Proud I could prove my virility and my power of seduction before a witness. But it was Arjana's horrified look that ripped away my pride. Her face livid, staring at the face of the monster on a rampage, still hammering on the car, blindly striking out in all directions. "Shit, my uncle!" And then the glass broke, and the shouts and blows, and the door that managed to open, and my flight, naked, in the black night of Kukës, running like a madman, the howls of my pursuer echoing against the mountains, breaking the majestic silence of that summer night woven with stars and forcing me, that night and forever, into the darkness of vengeance, honor, and blood.

Pantin

I didn't know much about the Kanun, actually. Of course I'd heard talk of vendettas and distant relatives who had a stake in those bloody settlings of scores, but I had no idea that my story, what happened to me, was included in that ancient code. I didn't know you could be condemned for that, didn't know people took blood for that.

My last day in Pantin was heavy and stormy. For a month now already, I'd been sneaking out of the apartment as soon as Bekim left. To explore the surroundings, but above all to face down my fear, to thumb my nose at the anxiety that never left me. Even shut in at my cousin's. Even watching TV, the characters seemed to be carrying messages predicting my death. I even came to think the Kastriotis had made a deal with Bekim for him to take back the blood without arousing my suspicion.

My outings really amounted to provocations. So the torture would stop. So the affair would be settled as fast as possible. I strolled around all over, but within a perimeter conditioned by the length of Bekim's absence. That day, I was exploring the nearby canal, which gave me a kind of rural escape from that stifling urban universe. Along the landscaped banks of the motionless body of water, like a long shimmering ribbon of cellophane on which waterlogged chunks of bread, plastic bottles, and corpses of pigeons were clinging, as if stuck in ice, as if stuck in time. As for me, I was stuck in my line of thought and hadn't noticed that I'd gone well beyond the time limit I usually set myself before returning to Bekim's. The landscape around me had changed, the dusty construction sites and half-finished buildings had given way to quays lying fallow, abandoned warehouses, and persistent silence. A silence so noisy it pulled me out of the peaceful flow of my thoughts and brought back that oppressive anxiety in full force.

So, in that atmosphere of neglect and decrepitude, only interrupted from time to time by a reckless jogger—each time I was convinced he was coming to settle my score—I'd turn around and avoid the same path, just in case, taking instead the grim boulevard parallel to the canal. Not that this was necessarily more reassuring: old, squalid buildings camouflaged by the sickly branches of plane trees, fast-food joints selling smoky barbecues, and grocery stores displaying various strange-looking vegetables. But here, at least, I wasn't alone. I was lost in the crowd. Other people were walking down the same sidewalks deformed by the aggressive roots of the same plane trees. Others were loitering before the used-car dealerships, whose prices, all negotiable, were scribbled in white paint on the windshields. Still others were hurrying toward something else or to a metro entrance.

It had begun to rain. The storm that had been on hold since morning had finally burst. I started walking fast toward Bekim's. I had never gotten back so late. Night had come in with the storm and was covering the streets with a strange, mournful softness. At the intersections, the streetlights poured their orange halos over sodden sidewalks, crossed by the innumerable shadows of passersby. At the corner of a street a few blocks from Bekim's, a small cluster of people were muttering excitedly about something. Rough, hard syllables. Which sounded like Albanian. Yes, Albanian. As I drew near, the plotting stopped short, heads turned toward me one by one and then assumed a natural posture, which seemed forced. I quickly turned on my heels and disappeared into an alley. Old, battered little houses, reduced to ruins to make room for modern constructions, with strips of flowery wallpaper still sticking to the adjacent buildings—the only relic of the past. Thunder was rumbling and the power went out, plunging the city into unusual darkness, so dark you felt like raising your head to make out the stars. A car was parked on one of the sidewalks, blocking the passage completely. An old Fiat. An Albanian license plate. The plate . . .

KU 6749 B.

KU.

Kukës.

It was them. I turned around, but then thought that the little group at the intersection had gone into the street and was charging toward me. I jumped over the car. Then I ran. Ran. My steps stumbling over the slippery asphalt. Behind me, a car roared into action. My assailants, for sure. I ran in one direction, then another. Bumping into people. My heart knocking against my chest, knocking as if it wanted to rip itself out of my body. The *BOOM BOOM* in my temples, in my thorax, in every one of my limbs. As if by miracle, I reached Bekim's street. Breathless. But here, too, another parked car. An Alfa Romeo, this time.

KU 319 M.

KU.

Kukës.

Kukës again.

And behind it, the revolving lights of the first responders flashing in the Pantin night, whipping their beams of blue into my eyes. Ambulances, firemen. Gathered in front of Bekim's building.

So I kept running. My sweat and the rain indistinguishable. Like dream and reality. The rain lashing my face, lashing my skull, lashing my ideas, mixing my vision with my fantasies, scrambling my thoughts.

But I kept running. Far. Farther. The farthest possible from Kukës. From Pantin.

And then, for the first time, I crossed the beltway into Paris.

And the cars had disappeared. Like the group of Albanians. The ambulances, too, had surely left.

PART III

SCARFACES OF THE SUBURBS

TO MY LAST BREATH

BY RACHID SANTAKI

Saint-Denis

Translated by Nicole Ball

I
Péri Projects

The face of the northern suburbs has changed. It expanded a lot with the plan for Greater Paris. Transportation now connects them to the capital, but also to the other suburbs. Despite this new face, Saint-Denis is blighted by the refuse of Paris. The more I see it, the more it disgusts me. I get on a big fat bike with Sprite driving, we zoom from the entry to Paris, the motor roars on boulevard Marcel-Sembat toward the station, and we stop in front of the basilica across rue de la Rép'. This commercial thoroughfare is infested with illegal street peddlers: guys right out of their Maghreb "bled" selling smuggled cigarettes, yelling "Marlboro, Marlboro bled!" and picking the pockets of vulnerable passersby; or Black women selling roasted corn while trying to dodge the municipal police. A restless crowd, moving quickly, like in an anthill. Welcome to my home, the city were everything is possible. And yet, it used to be a fine kingdom.

They call me Burnup because of my ability to do crazy things, never calculate, and above all go further and further. I've done everything in this city: stealing, dealing, loving. From the first day I talked to her, I immediately understood why I love this city so much. You can experience the best and the worst here. She's the best, I'm the worst. If the best is never certain, the worst is certainly the best way to survive in a city like Saint-Denis.

I raise the visor of my helmet and look at my smartphone while my buddy checks out the horizon. A two-wheeler approaches and stops alongside us. The biker takes off his helmet. Average height, stern face: it's the boss, Saïd Bensama. He manages the most important turfs, has become the most dreaded, most formidable drug dealer in the district. He shows up in the crime section of newspapers and in court records. Holds people hostage to get heaps of dough, murders to get rid of competition, uses pressure to tamp down ambitions. Saïd Bensama is ruthless and everybody knows it. And yet, he needs us for this job: he gives us a high-caliber and we help him with the cleanup. With Bensama, I'm already in the starting blocks of crime.

I'm aware I have a card to play, something to get out of him: I'm the type of lieutenant who's never afraid of a dirty job. I'm on fire, more and more. I'm hungry, I can hurt, play dirty, fast. My buddy Sprite needs me and so does Bensama. I'm determined.

"You okay, Burnup?" Saïd asks with a smile.

"Yeah, you?"

"No, not really. I can't wait for you to get on with that fucking cleanup. Hassan, he's had it, and people must know it."

"I'm on it. We'll get rid of him once and for all. He acted too crazy here."

"I can't stand his mess anymore. We're not even home here no more. Can you believe it? I fed the guy and now he wants to eat me up! . . . You know what you have to do, brother."

"Consider it done," I tell him.

I signal Sprite to start. The TMAX roars through the street. My buddy slaloms between cars and pedestrians before we get to the plaza in front of the station. Here, too, the crowd is restless. The "bled" guys hold the street and carry on with their business. Most of them come from Barbès and have nothing to do with my city. After glancing at this mess, I stare at the place where my target usually hangs out.

Hassan is well known in Saint-Denis, the city of the French kings. He's from another project. Violence is his thing, that's how he made it here. Close to forty now, he's a loud-mouth and beats up everyone. With him, you got to act fast to stop his senseless brutality. I spot him in front of a bar; he pulls out a smoke and watches the horizon. Our two-wheeler rushes toward him, and he understands that our TMAX can be the end of him.

I reach for my caliber. Hassan drops his cigarette. I shoot several times but miss, and that dog runs inside one of the bars and gets away. A guy got one in the mug and lies on the ground, pissing blood. I get off the bike, rush into the bar, and see Hassan bolting through the yard. I chase him but the ass-hole runs away fast. Now he's on boulevard Marcel-Sembat, but I won't let go. I run as fast as I can; I can hear his Nike Airs pounding the asphalt and fear drumming inside his thoracic cage. We run along the quays, Hassan already well out of breath but death giving him wings. The son of a bitch keeps doing these zigzags. He's taking refuge in a street when my accomplice appears on his bike and rams into him. Now he's on the ground, moaning from pain and fear. I get there and stick my piece right in his face. I've already shot somebody but I've never killed. When a guy sees his whole life passing in front of him and he's completely helpless, it's so crazy. After a few seconds, he understands there's no way out. Hassan brought crack to the station, he destroyed lives with absolutely no remorse, he killed other guys, and he keeps escaping the grim reaper, but this time his luck has turned. And that big fat shit is begging me: "No, no . . . Please, I'll give you anything you want, brother . . . everything. Saïd's the one who sent you, I'll give you twice as much, twice . . ."

I still have my gun pointing at him. I hesitate a few seconds, enough for him to kick me, make me lose my balance and drop my arm. He takes advantage of that to rush toward the canal. I pick up my piece and run after him. I'm enraged. Detonation. Dodging. He jumps into the canal and swims to escape. I aim at him. He tries to go underwater but the first bullet makes his skull explode and another goes through his right shoulder. He's stopped moving. His blood runs out of his body and sinks into the filthy water. My breathing gets heavier and heavier, I've gone further on the road to crime: I just whacked my first guy. Sprite's staring at me; he gets on his bike, starts it, says nothing. I look one last time at the canal and get on behind him. Sirens are blaring. We disappear. Then I glance in the rearview mirror: witnesses are walking over to the water.

It's a sunny day, magnificent even. But to me it's really dark. The harm you inflict is like throwing a boomerang: it comes back one day and hits you right in the face. I know I'm sinking a little more into crazy stuff, but I have no other choice than getting my balls over to Saint-Denis. That's how you get to be somebody.

After this punitive expedition, Sprite suggests we go up to Hassan's building. We find three girls and Didier, a guy who worked for Hassan. My victim made girls work for him and advertised them online. His lieutenant understands right away that things are getting hot for him. Sprite explains that he can either work for us or get a hole in his skull.

"Take the girls, you're all coming with me," Sprite says. "Let's move it."

"Where's Hassan?" that little punk Didier asks.

"In the cemetery. Wanna join him?"

"No, no. I'm really with you, guys."

Back in the hood, I don't know what to make of all this. Sprite apparently has no feelings for the girls he's put in the apartment we use to fence our stuff. He lays down the rules with this irritated tone he sometimes has.

"With Hassan, it's over. Now I'm the one who protects you, but if you try to fuck with me, you can't even imagine what crazy stuff I will do to you. I want my dough, and as long as I don't get it, I won't let go of you."

Then he picks up a designer scarf and uses it to strangle Didier. The guy struggles to free himself, but Sprite holds tight. I don't react; never seen my buddy like this before. The girls beg him to stop. He releases his hold on Didier, who has trouble catching his breath.

"Mecca, you try anything, and I mean *anything* . . . I'll whack you," Sprite concludes.

Then I examine the group of babes. Two, Sprite explained, are runaways from the provinces who got trapped in Saint-Denis. The third one is called Nina; I know her, ran into her by chance in a nightclub. There's something mysterious about her and she's very beautiful. Sprite and I, we split. I go home, all confused.

But the night is agitated. I keep thinking about Nina, her voice, her magnetism. She's made a tremendous impression on me, I'm obsessed. I'm sad she had to fall into this; she doesn't deserve it.

I won't admit it out loud, but I fell in love with her right away. Love at first sight. I'm disgusted to see her in this and to see Sprite exploiting her. I imagine myself with her, but to make this happen I have to move my ass. I'm seriously thinking of getting her out of all this. How?

2

When I wake up, I have a weird taste in my mouth. I'm not proud of myself. But it's the price I have to pay to be in the game. My phone vibrates, I pick up: it's Saïd, wanting to see me. Smile, hope. I had the guts to do it, after all. When you kill a guy, you're scared, but once you've done it, you tell yourself you're strong, more than the day before but less than the next day. It's as if there were someone else in me planning jobs. The old-timers here call me "everything right away," but if I had to define myself, I'd say all I want is to "steal it all." At fifteen I was a lookout, at sixteen I did my first muggings, at twenty I'd already done time but not much. I'm less dumb than the others; I'm hungry and act with determination.

When I see Saïd, he says he's happy with my work and gives me new responsibilities. I have every intention of pulling in lots of cash.

Next, I'm busy recruiting teams, lookouts, and dealers. As for Sprite, he manages his own business. We get together to count our cash and tell each other our dreams. I've got a plan: to leave Saint-Denis, but to go where? On my turf, I ask my lieutenants to keep quiet and check the movements in the housing project. I may be paranoid, but I don't want to lose that turf, I'm making a lot of bread, more and more.

In the projects now, I'm the one managing the shit. My guys are serious and not too greedy. From my car, I see the base of the towers where I distributed my employees and all the areas of activity. They're all efficient in their field. Look-outs watch the surroundings, orient clients. One team gets the cash and helps them. When there's a problem with the cops, we clear out the shop in a matter of seconds and go back to work as soon as they're gone. When you deal drugs, you treat the residents well, carry their groceries, smile at them—but with people we don't know, we have to do a little snooping. We do everything to avoid being wiretapped or caught in the act, so we search anybody who's a stranger to the projects: they could be undercover cops infiltrating our system to take pictures of us, learn details about our business, and bring down our whole network.

Two weeks are enough to have the turf running at full capacity. The clients are happy and business is growing super fine. I've just doubled the number of dealers. I'm enjoying my fate and already thinking of my next step: inject coke into the operation. Right now I only sell weed.

While I do business, Sprite makes his girls work in an apartment he sublets somewhere in Saint-Ouen. He developed his operation through social networks. He's got his audience—young kids, old guys looking for sex. On other sites, you see him with big cars; he puts on a show, picks up girls, and asks them to work for him. That's how he started making cash without getting his hands into drugs. He's far from stupid, he's a manipulator, he's narcissistic. His only concern is himself, and I find him fucking boring, more so by the day. Yet I tell myself we're childhood buddies and have to keep our friendship. Whatever the price. He has five girls in the apartment now, including Nina. I like her more and more, and to be honest, I love just talking with her. Her delicate voice gives me goose bumps. She's gorgeous, enchanting.

* * *

One day, Sprite arrives looking like hell.

"What's the matter?" I ask.

"We've got a job to do."

"Like what?"

"You know—Didier. He wants to fuck with me. He took one of my girls, Nina. He offered to protect her and now he keeps her in some slummy place near the station."

"Yeah, but your whore business, it's not exactly my thing . . ."

"Relax, I'm not gonna whack him, I already took risks with Hassan . . . But I need to get rid of that guy and I can't do it alone. I just want to scare the son of a bitch, I want him out of Saint-Denis. You in, bro?"

"About Nina, you serious?"

"Of course—look."

He shows me a text Nina sent him: *I'm scared, Didier wants to make me work somewhere else.*

"Yeah, okay . . . When do you want me to do it?"

"Now. But just put a scare into him."

On the way, I think of Nina. Anger is coursing through my veins. We arrive at the station. In the middle of the plaza, a few junkies are hanging out. I spot the guy, I call out to him.

Didier turns toward me and laughs. "How you doing? What d'you want?" He looks weird.

"I want you to get the fuck out of here. But first, tell me where Nina is."

"You're the one who's gonna get out of here, mother-fucker."

"Oh yeah?"

When I see the guys he's with, I understand right away he's become a fucking druggie. I look around, pick up an iron rod, and hit him with it. The guy's really skinny, and with his weak physique and sagging jaw, he starts bawling and making a show of himself.

"Go on, hit me again, you fucking piece of trash, hit me. I can't die, I've been dead for years! Think I'm scared of you and your pal? I'm not Hassan, man. Get the fuck out of here."

"Shut up and tell me where she is!" I yell to intimidate him, but it's no use.

"Hit me, hit me, it doesn't even hurt!"

"What's this motherfucker made out of?"

I beat the shit out of him and a whole crowd of druggies forms around me. Can't get him to talk. The junkie's on the ground, crying. His hair's standing on end, his face is swollen and bloody, his eyes are all red too, and streaming with blood. His lower lip is burst. He's a complete nutcase, but mostly he's totally stoned. He's having a mental breakdown. The guy's tearing off his clothes to impress me, but I'm out of my skull with rage. More and more insane, he throws his shoes at me. They're caked with filth. I see his feet, covered in scabs. His blood spatters me. I'm alone, disgusted, and start feeling a bit helpless.

"Nina's mine!" he screams. "I won't let go of her!"

As he's bawling, there's a bang, and Sprite takes me by the arm. I understand nothing. I just see my buddy motioning me to get on his bike. Groggy from the detonation, I get on the TMAX and it all goes too fast.

When we're back at the projects, I question Sprite. "Are you serious? Why did you shoot like that? What's happening to you, man?"

"Listen, he had Nina," Sprite says.

"But where is she?"

"I found her. It's settled."

"What's your game, brother? You understand what's go-ing on?"

Sprite's not clear and I find his story real fishy.

Not too long after, he calls back to tell me he's sorry but he's happy Nina is safe. Something's bothering me in all this. But what?

My phone rings again: Saïd's waiting for me.

I leave the building and signal to the lookout slumped over his scooter to come over. I get behind him and we speed along. We get to the entrance of the project, watched over by two kids. I get off the scooter and walk. Saïd's leaning on his fat car, a German one. He greets me coldly.

"Everything okay?" he asks.

"Super, bro."

"Great. Except you can't have the turf anymore. I learned from your pal what you did at the station . . . You've got some nerve, man. What's wrong with you? Stop managing my business."

"But . . . the turf's mine . . . and at the station, that was Sprite's problem. Not mine."

"What d'you mean *your* turf? Thanks to me, you made some dough. If you want the turf, you've got to pay now, and above all, be discreet. What's the matter with you? Don't make like you don't know the rules."

"Saïd, I know what we need to do to last . . . You told me that if . . . that if I did the job, you'd let me manage it. That thing with Sprite, it was just an accident."

"You're nuts, man! You think that's what life is like? Stop thinking you can do whatever you want!"

"But Saïd—"

He grabs me by the neck and stares at me without pity. "When I tell you something, you shut up!" He's squeezing harder and harder. Suffocation. Blurred vision. Then he releases his grip. "Got it?"

"Yes, I got it." Tears flowing, pressure going down.

Saïd doesn't take his eyes off me. He gets in his car. He looks at me again through the window and says, "Get the fuck out of here."

I nod, contain my anger. "Yes, Saïd . . ."

His tires screech loudly and his car zooms off. I'm enraged like never before, with a furious urge to kill the motherfucker.

3

The suburbs brought sex back to the towers of the projects, and young girls fuck or give blow jobs in apartments, cars, or hotel rooms in exchange for designer bags.

I'm thinking of my buddy and that new business I could try, but I have a hard time accepting that I lost my turf and got screwed by Saïd. When I ask Sprite about Nina, he offers me some time with her.

"Bro, I know you just want to fuck her . . ."

"No, I'm just curious about that chick."

"Know what? All the guys dig her, she's like . . . mysterious. It's crazy . . . She's got style. Okay, I'll give you a moment with her."

"Yeah, but it's not what you think."

"I'm not thinking anything, bro. We're together."

I have no idea how we got to that point; it's as if nobody has any feelings for human beings anymore. I'd like to go backward, before things went to shit. But in the end, I tell myself that's how our lives are. This is life.

When Nina's with me, I talk to her and enjoy it, I want to know who she is. She seems to be a decent girl. We spend two hours together, I fuck her, then she lights a smoke, inhales the nicotine, puffs out, and stares at me.

"I can tell you're not a thug. You're a cute guy."

"What're you talking about, you don't know me . . . Cute? You make me laugh."

"You're not like the others."

"You serious?"

"Yes, very." Then she shoves me, cracks a smile.

"I'm hotter than your pimp."

"Forget him. He's got no brains, all he can do is beat up girls."

"Why're you so cold?"

"I don't wanna talk about it."

Her silence fills the room. She slips back into her clothes to get on with her day. Sprite comes to collect her. I'm disgusted for her.

"Where you taking her, Sprite?"

"She's gonna spend the day in Paris . . . What's your problem, man? You in love with her or what?" He snickers.

He's ridiculing me.

Days pass. I wander around the projects. From time to time I go all the way to the top of the tower and watch the turf roll. The whole team's doing business without me.

One evening, my phone rings. It's Saïd.

"Can I see you?"

"Yeah, sure."

"In an hour. Stay awake, man," the pig adds.

An hour later we meet. He explains he's thought it over: he needs a lieutenant to put coke and shit back into his turf. He thought of me and I grab the opportunity. He entrusts me with the biz. My job is to prepare the stuff to be sold: cutting and wrapping it at the fence place. I've got work again. Once he's gone, life smiles at me. I'm gonna make tons of cash once more, and I'll be ruthless.

The next few days, I listen to rap and relax. Sprite calls

and I ask him for a favor: to drop Nina off at my place. In return, I give him some cash. He's okay with that. That's how she gets to stay with me while I package the stuff.

After I've done the job, I undress her and take advantage of that intimate moment with her. Then we nap. In bed with her, I rehash what Saïd said and did. Nina keeps quiet. I examine her without appearing to, and I see myself as her when Saïd bosses me around, and that feeling of being his dog is raising my blood pressure. It sucks to have come to this.

"You okay?" she asks.

"To be honest, not really. I've got a few problems I have to take care of."

"Relax, it's gonna be okay. Everything's gonna turn out fine. You know what? It's weird, but I don't do it with Arab or Black guys normally . . ."

"So . . . what's different?" I reply with a snicker.

"They're dogs, aggressive . . . forget it."

"What about me?"

"You? I'm not sure. You're weird."

"You want a line?"

"No, never touch the stuff. I work for my little girl, not to do stupid things."

"You've got a kid? How old?"

"Twenty months."

She pulls out a picture, smiles. I feel sick: a mother who has to prostitute herself for her kid. I stare at Nina, get back in my shell.

"You're right, it's shit. All I do is show off my ass."

She laughs. Her innocence is catching. I take to the game. We talk a little about our lives. She tells me about her parents, about her life before Vivastreet, the website where she lures her customers; she feels bad about it. Then she leaves.

"See you," she says.

"See you."

After she's gone, I light up a smoke and think. And I go downstairs: business is rolling, customers come to pick up, teams are on the turf and deliver. I ride my bike around the projects and at some point catch Nina on a street corner. What's she doing there? All of a sudden, she's joined by Saïd. They leave together. I follow them.

After a short walk, they stop at the foot of a building and enter it. Me, I stay not too far away, chain-smoking, with this voice in my head: *What the hell are they doing together?* Then she exits, alone, heads quickly toward Paris, and goes down into the metro. I leave my bike and follow her. She's waiting on the platform, direction: Saint-Ouen. The train arrives, she boards, so do I. She's sitting there with headphones over her ears. Her neighbor has his eye on her, but she's too into her world to notice. I wait and observe her. She gets off at Garibaldi. I do the same.

"Nina?"

"What are you doing here?"

"What about you?"

"Nothing."

"Where you going?"

"I'm gonna pick up my kid. And you?"

"I'm gonna see a buddy of mine . . . Listen, you know Saïd?"

"Yes, he's one of Sprite's buddies."

"And you see him often? I thought you didn't do it with Arabs."

"Yeah, I was with him . . . Hey, you been following me?"

"No, no."

"He's nuts. Don't do anything stupid. He doesn't kid around!"

"But why're you so upset?"

She has tears in her eyes. She finally shows me her thigh covered with bruises. I'm not surprised. And she runs off through the corridors of the metro.

Saïd Bensama has no limits. I already knew that.

I go back in the other direction, angry as hell.

I don't understand. I feel something for that girl and can't stomach the fact that Bensama is hurting her.

I spend the evening thinking about Nina.

I call to see how she's doing but only get her voice mail. I worry about her.

About her life.

I go around in circles and contemplate every possibility.

4

Saïd Bensama is pissed: he hears Burnup has been mixing work and his personal life. He summons Sprite and puts the squeeze on him about Nina: he wants her to stop whoring in the neighborhood and not disturb Burnup. Meaning, he wants her out of Saint-Denis. Sitting inside his fat car, Saïd won't let go of Sprite, who's standing outside. Nina's in the backseat, scared.

"I don't want to see her here no more!" Saïd says harshly.

Sprite nods. "But she has a kid . . ."

"I don't give a shit." The boss gets out of the car, grabs Sprite's hair. "Who the hell are you, talking to me like that?"

"Sorry, sorry, Saïd."

The boss looks at him, lets go. Then he gets back into his car and starts the engine.

"Burnup, he's what to you?" Saïd asks Nina all of a sudden. "That guy, who is he?"

"No one."

"Oh really? Let me ask you differently: he's in love with you?"

"No . . ."

"You sure?"

"I think so . . ."

"You wanna play that game? Okay, let's play then."

Saïd takes a pipe and a rock from the glove compartment, lights up the end, and holds it out to Nina. "Smoke."

"Why? I can't—"

"Smoke, I said!"

Nina refuses, but Bensama's slaps quickly convince her to inhale the crack. She complies. She's starting to transform, is off elsewhere, into another world. She's flying, laughing, babbling away about anything and nothing. Bensama stares at her, smiles, enjoys watching her lost like that. Then he drives a small distance and throws her out at Porte de la Chapelle, in the middle of the junkies.

Nina's on crack. She wanders around and gets hit on by mean, aggressive dudes who spot her as a cash opportunity. Bensama watches. What he loves is humiliating people, lording it over them.

His phone rings. He answers and tells Sprite that they need to take care of Burnup.

A few days later, Sprite's at my place. I ask him how Nina's doing. He tells me she's busy but will call me. Now Saïd shows up, with his air of superiority. He's even more agitated than usual. He walks nervously around the room for a while, then sits on the couch, staring at the prepared packages of drugs.

And that's when the shit hits the fan.

Saïd throws Sprite out but orders me to stay.

He looks at me and suggests I could buy back part of his turf and become his partner, but on one condition.

"Know what? Your buddy there, he's a total loser. He doesn't listen, and I'm fucking sick of him. I want you to bump him off. He's nothing but trouble. This guy's not your buddy, he's a useless wimp."

"I'm gonna talk to him," I say.

"No, you don't talk. You act."

"You want what, Saïd?"

"You're tough, right? So whack that pig."

Then Saïd leaves.

I think for some time, several hours. I have a plan. My conscience speaks to me and reminds me life is priceless. So is friendship. But if I don't do it, I'll be doomed too. So when my cell rings, I've already made my choice.

"So you're good with it?"

"Yes, Saïd. I'll do it."

I go downstairs, walk through the neighborhood to meet with Saïd, who's waiting in his car. What he doesn't know is that I told Sprite everything. Together, we're gonna trap Saïd.

While he drives, I keep silent. I think of Sprite. My childhood friend's nickname comes from his green hair. He was the first one to dye his hair a weird color, and he spent all his time at Groomers, a barbershop in the city center that sold haircuts like hotcakes. In the hood, the owners of that barbershop embodied entrepreneurship. "They'll say we did it" was their catchphrase. Sprite liked to repeat that. My buddy doesn't deserve to be betrayed. Our plan can't fail, and Bensama has been polluting us for too long.

What's even worse is I cried when Sprite's dad died. I felt so bad for him. And now Bensama wants to take his life by using me? It's crazy it's come to this. I don't want to croak with that weight on my conscience. His words resonate in my mind and I hang on to them.

"What you thinking about?" Saïd asks.

"I'm thinking of Sprite; he really became a big piece of shit."

"You seem to get along fine with him though."

I feel a lump in my throat. Words don't come out easily. "No, I'm determined. Sprite's a friend from the past."

"Yeah, the famous buddy you end up zapping. By the way, you know about Nina?"

I get scared as soon as Saïd says her name.

"He got rid of her because you liked her. He gave her to a bunch of junkies. I was there, and believe me, it was ugly."

"You can't be serious! You're lying!" I scream.

"Let's ask him . . ."

We're in front of Sprite's building. We go up. My legs are like gelatin. I knock. Sprite opens the door and Bensama punches him. His nose explodes, and he's hit with another right; he sprints straight toward his bedroom. Saïd and me, we run after him. My heart goes *boom boom* . . .

"So . . . about Nina . . . you didn't tell him?" Saïd says.

I feel dizzy, but a powerful surge of anger rises from my guts. I know Sprite's jealous of me. I know it.

"What you talking about, Saïd?" says my pal, who's scared to death.

"Oh Jesus . . ." I start. "Oh fuck, man . . . You did what to her, Sprite? Answer me!"

"Nothing. I dropped her, that's all."

"He dropped her and asked me to get rid of her," Saïd says. "I took her to the junkies' hill and left her there."

"What? For fuck's sake, you're outta your mind!" I yell.

"Calm down, Burnup . . ."

A few seconds later, I completely lose it, but Sprite pulls out his piece and shoots. Saïd collapses to the ground. And Sprite splits.

"Take me to the hospital," Saïd moans. "Come on, man, move your ass."

But I leave the apartment; I'm running from this guy, from this city, from all this trafficking. I need to get Nina first, and as fast as possible. I'm in my car, and while I drive an idea pops in my head: go to the fence place, grab the money, then find Nina. Yes, it's my only way out of this shit.

5

I rush inside the apartment, to the bedroom, and fill up a sports bag. In a few minutes I've swiped hundreds of thousands of euros, then I get the hell out of the building. My heart is beating up my torso. At the end of the block, someone hits me on the head; I stagger but keep my balance; my reflex is to start running. My attacker throws himself on me but I push him away, grabbing his arm as I fall. It's Sprite. I punch him in the face, over and over again, keep hitting until my hatred calms down and he's in a daze. I'm furious. I feel for Nina and hate my buddy. He turned her into an object.

He screams: "I knew you were crazy about her! And she was about you, you knew it, right? But what about me? I'm what? Me, your friend?"

"Shit, man, why did you do that?"

"She's just a chick, she's just a chick," Sprite says.

"What the hell are you talking about? Calm down."

"A chick, who gives a fuck about her?! It's you and me, brother."

I throw him to the ground and his head hits the pavement. He's unconscious—that's what I think, anyway. I run to the car and drive. Porte de Paris, avenue du Président Wilson, and finally Porte de la Chapelle, where I park in the lot of the bowling alley. I run to the hill of la Chapelle: a squat filled with junkies, where humans are no longer themselves.

Through the heart of the hill, I walk slowly, among the junkies, the homeless, the whores, the migrants. All I want is to find her, to run away with her . . . I keep yelling her name; no reaction from these zombies. The clock is ticking: if I don't find her, Sprite, my so-called buddy, will. My legs feel heavier and heavier. With a lump in my stomach, I push my way through the crowd; they all have eyes infected with crack.

I finally spot her, not too far away. Five feet seven, notably thinner, her clothes filthy. I take hold of her shoulder. When she turns to me, I see rotten teeth, a face covered with pimples; she's a shadow of what she was before. My whole body is shivering.

"Sorry, Nina, I'm so sorry . . ."

"Where were you?" she asks. "He told me you didn't want me anymore . . ."

"That's right, that little shit didn't want you no more," whispers someone behind me.

And then, I feel something pierce my lower back: I turn around and am face-to-face with Sprite. How'd the mother-fucker get back on his feet and show up so fast? I grab his knife, punch him twice, spit at him. Struggling, he pushes me, I'm bleeding. I push him back; enraged, I send him to the ground and hammer his face right above the eyebrows, then his nose. Covered in blood, he begs me to stop but I don't. Nina screams and runs away. I stand up, I'm fucking banged up. I don't want her to escape, not in that state. Words ring in my head: *Run after her, catch her, catch her.* I see her scramble to the middle of the street—cars slam on their brakes to dodge her, but then a scooter hits her. She's sent flying and crashes down, hard. I feel my heart exploding in my chest, I rush to her. The biker's in shock, and Nina's moaning on the ground. I take her in my arms. She has trouble breathing.

I don't take my eyes off hers. Her breath is rumbling louder and louder. Then stops. I try to keep her awake.

"Nina, stay with me! We'll go far away from here, Nina, hang in there."

But she doesn't hear me. Her eyes are wide open but don't shine anymore.

"Nina, Nina . . . No, Nina, hang in there, hang in there!"

I'm exploding inside. She's unconscious. People gather around.

I get up, and I realize all my hopes for the future have just crumbled. My eyes sweep the horizon, and I catch Sprite across the street, limping and trying to hide his face with his hand. Right away, I run after him, reach him, and kick him hard: he collapses on the pavement. Standing over him, I unleash.

"Here, motherfucker, piece of shit! Me, your childhood friend?"

He screams with pain. "Please, Burnup, please!"

"Fucking pussy. Be a man!"

A surge of hate, of blows and insults, pins him to the ground. I go at him like never before. His blood's dripping on my face, spreading on the sidewalk. I'm out of breath but keep clobbering him. The pain intensifies. I lose consciousness. My God, this whole stuff is so ugly . . .

Images file past. My first class with Sprite. Our friendship sealed by theft. Our first bike in the hood. The first time we made some cash with our turf. Why did I do all that? Why did I believe in street life so much? Regrets are settling in and multiply. I launch a series of hard blows into his face again, then stand up with great difficulty. I head for the lot and get in my car. Cops approach, yell at me to raise my hands. I start the car and speed right at them. But they shoot and I lose control. The sound of sheet metal, of tires screeching and glass breaking. The car flips over on its roof. I'm in pain. Voices of cops all around me, all over.

THE BARONESS

BY MARC FERNANDEZ

Neuilly-sur-Seine

Translated by Katie Shireen Assef

She still looks good, the baroness, in spite of her seventy-two years. You'd think she was at least twenty years younger. It's true she's never lifted a finger in her life except to tend to her appearance. An early marriage to an aristocratic heir she met at a ball in a western suburb of Paris, two children—a boy and a girl she spent little time raising, having left this lowly task to a Colombian nanny, and who soon fled the nest with the help of Daddy's money—countless dinners, trips, spa treatments, a few lovers, a little weed or coke now and then at private parties. A rich woman's existence, luxuriating in the wealth built on the backs of others. The only sweat she ever breaks is the stream that trickles down her back during fitness sessions. Joséphine de Sainte-Croix squeezes all the juice out of life, as they say. She goes by Jo and everyone in Neuilly knows her. Always smiling, always in a good mood, always generous toward her neighbors and the local shopkeepers. From avenue Charles-de-Gaulle to rue du Château, they're all perfectly fond of her. She's never stingy with tips or small kindnesses, always ready to open her wallet and fork out a few bills. Some would say that people in the neighborhood take advantage of her and her money; others, that we've all got to do our part to help one another out. A widow for five years, she's fallen for a younger—much younger—man she met very soon after her husband's death. Pablo Torres, a thirty-eight-year-old Colombian. Classic. "The baroness turned out to be a real cougar," people whisper at dinners around town. Their upper-class grooming doesn't make them any less bitchy than the rest of us. If there's one thing all of humanity has a knack for—the rich and the poor, the common man and the grand bourgeois—it's judging other people and talking trash about them. In Neuilly, just like in the projects.

The two cops from the drug squad, sitting together in an undercover car parked on avenue de Madrid—a few yards from the entrance to the baroness's *hôtel particulier*—are bored stiff. They've been waiting there for three days and three nights. And if it's questionable that all cats are gray in the dark, in Neuilly it's true that all of them are in bed. Nothing is happening. *Nada*. Zero action. Not on the street, at least. What goes on behind the walls of the posh apartments and villas is another story. One that the man at the wheel would know something about. Police Chief Alexandre Marcial, forty-one years old, nicknamed the Prince by his fellow squad members, comes from this world. His dad's a doctor, his mom a housewife. The youngest of four brothers, he's the black sheep. The one who didn't go to business school or to Sciences Po. The one who became a cop—by choice. To his parents' great disappointment. He was born here, in Neuilly; he went to Lycée Pasteur, known for its long list of famous alumni, and he knows every corner of this town in the Hauts-de-Seine, so often mocked and caricatured. Pasqua and Sarkozy fought fiercely for the mayorship here in the eighties. It was how the young de Nagy-Bocsa got his start in politics. He'd cut his teeth on the wallets of the residents of Neuilly before scamming the entire country. Alex has kept all his real friends from those days, and they weren't bourgeois kids, but rather the sons and daughters of concierges, housekeepers, nannies. Spaniards, Portuguese, Italians, Algerians, Moroccans. The kids from wealthy families, he hadn't heard a word from after he graduated. He ran into a few of those assholes at his university in Nanterre, but all the others have disappeared. They don't move in the same circles. Don't share the same interests. They lead different lives, plain and simple. And for that matter, it's thanks to one of his childhood friends that Alex is here now.

He's never forgotten José, who he first befriended in preschool. Their paths diverged in early adolescence, when one went on to high school and the other took vocational training to become a mechanic. When Alex was promoted to police chief, José wasn't able to attend the party; he was behind bars. A murky story of a few stolen cars. "A real idiot move, but I won't end up back there again." If the cop is one of the pillars of the drug squad, the mechanic has a deft touch and is known all over town for the miracles he works on engines. A certain number of his customers are well known to law enforcement, as they say. And these guys talk. A lot. Too much, sometimes. José talks too. To Alex, when he thinks he has a tip that might be useful to him. That's what he did a few months ago. Came to him with a tip that was easy to confirm. A dangling thread Alex has been pulling and that he'll follow until he finds his way to the truth. At least he hopes so. He can already imagine the headlines if the rest of the picture comes to light. For the moment, things are at a standstill. And Alex is starting to get impatient.

Jo is still in bed. Having just finished breakfast, she turns on her tablet and opens FaceTime. A few seconds later, her lover's face appears on the screen. It's the middle of the night in Bogotá, but Pablo is wide awake. He rarely sleeps, does business practically around the clock. Time is money: it's a cliché, sure, but he's made this motto his own. If you really want to rake in the dough, you've got to work across time zones. Especially in the import-export business. The owner of a shipping company, he has clients on all five continents, speaks six languages, and uses three cell phones and a satellite phone. He's a member of the Colombian capital's chamber of commerce, and of all sorts of private clubs for the country's elite. His address book is filled with everyone who's anyone in Latin America: politicians, CEOs, cops, lawyers, magistrates—connections that help him eat away at his competitors' market shares, boost his revenues, and make returns on his investments.

"How's my darling baroness?"

"I'm bored, my love. I miss you."

"I'll be there tomorrow."

"I know. I can't wait any longer, I want you."

"Me too, but I still have some things to finish up here. I'm flying out tonight, and when I get there, you can do what you want with me. In the meantime, you remember you're getting a package today?"

"Yes, yes, don't worry. I won't leave home."

"It'll come by UPS this time. I'm done dealing with those idiots from Chronopost."

"I'll send you a text when I've received it."

"And don't forget: tonight, you don't go out for any reason."

"I know, you've told me a hundred times!"

"Okay, okay, don't get upset. Love you, my beauty. See you tomorrow."

"Love you too."

A long sigh. Jo stretches, decides to get up, pulls on some leggings and a T-shirt, and walks down to the basement of her *hôtel particulier*, where she's had an ultramodern gym installed. An hour of cardio should be enough to quell her desire. On the stationary bike, she can't help but smile.

Alex and his deputy didn't miss a second of the conversation. The couple's phones have been tapped for several weeks already. It hadn't been easy to convince a judge to let them plant mics in the home of a Neuilly baroness. Technological advances might be good for society, but they don't make cops' lives any easier. Especially since their targets tend to be tech savvy, communicating in ways that are difficult to trace. There was nothing like the good old methods. With well laid-out arguments and a bit of smooth talking (not least in regard to the potential image boost for law enforcement in the media), the chief had managed to get his way. Just as he's getting out of the car to stretch his legs, two lieutenants from his squad arrive to relieve him. They'll take over until tonight. He heads toward the new police headquarters in Batignolles without stopping by his place, even though he's exhausted and needs a shower. He senses that the case is coming to a head and that the next few hours will be crucial. When he gets to 36, rue du Bastion, he calls the rest of the team into his office. He hasn't yet had time to unpack his boxes or decorate. Only two photos are tacked up on a wall: one of Joséphine de Sainte-Croix and the other of Pablo Torres. The main targets in the case. The case that's about to be closed. And then Alex can go on vacation. But first, they have to make some adjustments to the plan. He's already sent two more men to Neuilly, on a mission to discreetly intercept the UPS delivery guy before he rings the baroness's doorbell. And to confirm the contents of the package, even if there's no doubt in his mind as to what they'll find.

"The delivery's set for today. And Torres leaves tomorrow. We'll arrest them as soon as he's set foot in de Sainte-Croix's place. Do a thorough search and bring both of them here."

Everything's about to start moving quickly. He's been on the drug squad for ten years, worked hundreds of cases. He goes over all the elements of the investigation to make sure he hasn't forgotten anything and, most importantly, that procedure has been followed to the letter. He doesn't want some lawyer to undo months of work on a formality because he forgot to initial a form or put the wrong date on a document. Alex has never cared much for red tape, and he's always railing against these politicians who have no idea what it's like on the ground, who go around changing laws without considering the consequences. Paperwork will be the death of law enforcement.

Two hours later, a phone call snaps him out of the tedium of administrative tasks. His guys have just intercepted the UPS deliveryman on the corner of avenue de Madrid, and confirmed the contents of the package. Soon, finally, there will be some action.

Joséphine de Sainte-Croix is oblivious to the police activity taking place near her home. After her workout, a bath, and a phone call to her wealth manager to make sure the money is rolling in as usual, she decides to plan an exotic getaway for her and Pablo. They'll have earned a few days' vacation after this delivery. The last of the month, one of the most important of the year. The advantage of not having to work or worry about money coming in is that you can act on your every whim. And Jo does. One of her favorites: fleeing winter weather. As soon as the temperatures start to drop, she takes off for somewhere in the Southern Hemisphere. This time, she's set her sights on Argentina. She's heading to Mar del Plata next week. Ten days of basking with her man at this posh beach resort, a kind of Argentinean Saint-Tropez, where the continent's jet set comes together for epic parties, where the liquor flows freely and drugs are exchanged faster than the speed of light.

The front doorbell rings. She hurries toward the intercom. A man in a brown uniform and UPS cap appears on the screen.

"Don't bother, Maria, I've got it!"

The housekeeper doesn't even respond. She's grown used to her boss's whims in the fifteen years she's worked for her. At first, she found it strange that Madame would want to open the door herself to plain old deliverymen two or three times a month. But eventually she stopped thinking about it. After all, she can do as she pleases, if it's her idea of fun . . .

The baroness asks the courier to leave the heavy brown package in the immense entry hall. She holds out a hundred-euro bill that he hurries to pocket, trying not to show any sign of surprise at this lavish tip. Once he's gone, Jo paces around her package, taking care not to touch it. She leans in to check the labels. Everything seems in order. *Fragile. Handle with care. Mochilas de La Guajira Inc.*: the name of the sender, a cooperative in eastern Colombia, reassures her. She's still a bit stressed at these moments, and astonished that it took only five days for the package to cross the Atlantic and make its way to the Parisian suburbs. She goes into the kitchen to pour herself a glass of water and sends Pablo a text to let him know everything's okay.

* * *

Once his team confirmed the contents of the package and his contact at the Bogotá airport told him that Pablo had boarded the plane, Police Chief Alexandre Marcial shut down the stakeout in front of the baroness's place. Now they just have to wait for his arrival tomorrow to set things in motion. He's sent everyone home. A natural leader, he knows it's important to allow moments of calm before an operation. And no one's been slacking on this case. Tomorrow, everything will come to a point, the climax of a monthslong investigation. Easing the tension a bit before the adrenaline burst of breaking down a door and arresting two big targets: that's the secret of a successful operation. He's confident. This is a drug bust in Neuilly, not in some slum in Hauts-de-Seine or Seine-Saint-Denis. Normally, they shouldn't find anything in the tastefully decorated, modern five-bedroom mansion apart from the couple, the maid, and the package. No arms. Only paintings: Mirós, Picassos, Basquiats. All originals. There's tens of millions of euros' worth of property on the walls alone. Not to mention the baroness's jewelry. If everything goes as planned, it will all be seized. To gather dust in the basement of the Palais de Justice while they await a trial, a verdict, and the endless disputes the couple's lawyers will undoubtedly pursue.

In the meantime, after stopping at his apartment in Clichy to shower and change, he decides to head back to Neuilly and join his parents for dinner. They live on rue de l'Église, a few blocks away from the baroness's place. They would never suspect what's going on in this house with its white walls, hidden from traffic and the outside world by trees and a black picket fence. Since their son's coming by on short notice, they plan to meet at Madame Yang's, one of their favorite dinner spots, on the other side of avenue Charles-de-Gaulle near rue de Longchamp. The excellent Asian-fusion restaurant is always packed with regulars from the neighborhood and everyone else in town who shuns the fancy pizzeria across the street, a hub for stars of the big and small screens, where a basic margarita costs as much as three pizzas in a normal restaurant.

Alex's mother looks lovingly at him, says nothing. Even if she's ultimately supported him in his career choices, she can't help worrying about him sometimes. Ever since he received his badge and arm, she's become an expert of sorts in police-related matters and spends a good deal of her time watching and listening to every local crime report. His dad glances at his menu, then smiles.

"So, what's new? Are you on a big case? We don't see you as much lately."

He'd had a harder time than his wife accepting their son's decision to become a cop. But over the years, he's gotten used to it. He'd never admit it—showing his feelings isn't easy for him—but he's proud. Not everyone has what it takes to be a police chief. His son has a good career going and seems happy. That's what really matters, after all.

Their meals have just been served when a deafening sound breaks out. Like nearly everyone, Alex jumps in his seat. Instinctively, he puts his hand on his belt, grips his service weapon, heads for the door. On the street corner, a car horn blares endlessly, seemingly coming from the Porsche Cayenne stopped at the light. It turns green but the car doesn't move, prompting a line of furious backed-up drivers to honk their horns.

He goes back into the restaurant and tells everyone to stay where they are, then runs back toward the car, only a few yards away. He pulls out his Glock, thumbs off the safety, and approaches the driver's-side door. No need for his gun. The man at the wheel is no longer a potential threat. His head lies on the dashboard and a stream of blood flows from his temple.

In ten minutes, the place is flooded with onlookers and the police backup that Alex called in. He's also called his deputy. This looks like a case of score settling between drug dealers. But the results of a quick license-plate search send a shudder down Alex's back. The victim, Rachid Ben Mabrouk, forty-one years old, is well known to law enforcement, particularly the drug squad. A big-shot dealer from Nanterre, who ruled the cocaine trade throughout the department and in the chicest parts of Paris. He'd managed to slip through the cracks until now, but he'd been on the squad's radar, especially since they discovered he was in regular contact with Pablo Torres. If dealers start killing each other in Neuilly . . .

Sitting cross-legged on her leather sofa, a glass of champagne in hand, several women's magazines lying open around her, Joséphine de Sainte-Croix is bored. An evening alone in front of her big plasma TV screen. Maria made her a microwave dinner and shut herself up in her room. The baroness lets out a long sigh. She doesn't like being stuck at home. Pablo told her to lie low tonight and she obeyed, even though she's used to giving orders rather than receiving them. The truth is, he can ask anything of her. Does she love him? She doesn't know. Or doesn't really want to ask herself the question. One thing's for sure, they're very compatible. In every sense. On the business side, he's helped her increase her capital significantly. As for the rest, she feels like a young thing again in bed—and it's true he makes her laugh and knows how to show her a good time. What more can she ask for, at her age? Her children are annoyed by her younger lover, but she doesn't give a damn. She has the right to have a little fun.

She surfs channels, looking for a film or program to watch.

Then pauses on the news. Though she doesn't care much for the nightly news, she recognizes that it's the easiest and least boring way to keep herself informed. The ten p.m. broadcast is starting. She half listens, distracted, until her eye is drawn to a banner at the bottom of the screen. Red letters on a white background: *Murder in Neuilly. A man was assassinated at the wheel of his car tonight . . .* Her blood turns cold. She jumps up and moves closer to the screen, as if to see better. Or to better take in what she's read. Just two lines that send a shudder down her spine. No images yet, but the first thought that comes to her is terrifying. What if Pablo is mixed up in this? He wouldn't have asked her to stay home tonight without giving her the least explanation. She didn't ask for one either . . .

Jo grabs her cell phone. No point in sending him a text; at this hour, he's already on the plane. She logs on to Twitter to try to glean some more information, but the Twitterverse has other fish to fry. People are riling each other up over the usual fare: sexual harassers and victims, Jews and Muslims, fascists and bobos. The blue bird is flapping its wings, carried along on a wind of hate and insults. A steady stream of bullshit sent straight to her phone. She turns on the radio. No news on France Info yet. Nothing on RTL, Europe 1, or France Inter, either. All the journalists repeat the same terse phrases into their mics in the same monotone voice, reading a dispatch from the national press agency before they announce that a special envoy is headed to the scene to bring you more news in a few minutes, dear listeners. She paces around her living room, swallows a mouthful of Ruinart that leaves a steely taste in her mouth. Finally, BFM arrives on the scene. Barely twenty minutes after the murder. Always the first in line, when there's blood and gore to be shown. There's shaky footage of a car in the distance. Yellow tape, uniforms. Just like on TV shows, except real. And happening right in front of her apartment. She recognizes the sign outside Madame Yang's and decides to go see for herself. Pablo won't have to know, after all; she won't tell him anything and will be careful to avoid cameras.

She makes her way to avenue Charles-de-Gaulle, not far from the Pont de Neuilly metro exit, where a kind of organized chaos reigns. Cops try to keep the onlookers at bay, but struggle to maintain the security zone. The TV satellite trucks are arriving and parking every which way. Mics in hand and earpieces on, a few of the reporters are already going live. They've got to hurry if they want to be the ones to break the story. Sure, they might not have the details straight yet, but what matters is getting on the air before the competition. They can always go back and fact-check later, even if it means spouting nonsense in the meantime. Joséphine de Sainte-Croix stays far from the spotlights. She runs into the manager of the nearby sushi restaurant, who tells her that one of his deliverymen had seen everything. The motorcycle that stopped next to the Porsche. A man in all black—jacket, helmet, and pants—at the handlebars. On the seat behind him, a double who took out a gun and shot once. And then the roar of the motorcycle as it sped off. Like that. All in under ten seconds. The delivery guy is at the back of the shop, waiting for instructions from his boss, who will, he tells the baroness, negotiate the best price with whichever pathetic news channel is ready to pay.

"If we can make a little money and get some airtime, why not?" he says as he walks away, a smile on his lips.

Jo approaches, wary, and tries to get a glimpse of the crime scene while keeping her distance from the cameras. She stands on tiptoe to steal a look at the victim's car. Then, trying to look detached as her stomach roils, she retraces her steps back home, not sure she'll be getting any sleep tonight.

It'll be an all-nighter for Alexandre Marcial and his men. Once the identity of the victim was confirmed, he'd called everyone in. For a few moments, they'd considered the question of whether to abandon the operation set to take place at the baroness's. Huddled at the back of Rush Hour, an Irish pub close to where Ben Mabrouk was killed, the team starts in on its second round of pints while going over the new plan in detail. Drinking to prepare for a police action isn't necessarily recommended, but the circumstances call for a swift reaction. Two cops from another drug squad will assist them, heading to the airport in Roissy to "meet" and monitor Pablo Torres. They'll tail him until he gets to Neuilly. If his previous trips are any indication, he shouldn't make detours. He'll want to see the baroness and have a proper reunion right away. But they won't give him the time—they plan to bust the place as soon as he arrives.

A few hours later, everyone's in position. The target has landed and gone through passport control without a hitch. Now he just has to grab his luggage and hop in a taxi and he'll be there in no time. Bulletproof vests on, guns safety-checked, battering ram at the ready—everything's set to go when Pablo Torres arrives at the doorstep of the *hôtel particulier*.

"We give them five minutes," Alex says into the mic.

"Okay."

A cop is positioned on the roof of the building across the street and describes what's happening: "Okay, he's inside. They're kissing. But the lady looks angry. She's waving her arms around, it seems like she's yelling at him. He's trying to calm her down. They're still in the hall."

"All right, we're going in!" Alex shouts.

It's the ideal moment to take the couple by surprise. They won't have to scour the house to find them. A row of men in black, a special unit in charge of assisting the squad with this type of operation, appears as if by magic at the doorway, followed closely by the drug squad. They break down the door with a single blow, yelling at the top of their lungs, a technique that serves more than anything to boost their courage and startle the people they're about to arrest.

"Police! Don't move! Get down! Get down on the ground!"

Jo and Pablo have no time to react. They're handcuffed and brought into the living room. It all takes less than a minute. Alex is satisfied. The package delivered to the old lady is still in the same place. Pablo throws his mistress a look of contempt that says volumes about the turn their relationship is about to take. As for her, bizarrely, she doesn't seem to understand the gravity of the situation. She looks spaced out and can't stop herself from smiling. She gives the cops the name of her lawyer. One of the best in the country. It already looks like the legal process is going to be long and complicated. Even if Alex is confident in the verdict. Inside the package, twelve kilos of cocaine are stuffed between traditional cloth bags. A fine interception.

"The Baroness of Coke," "Jo the Narco," "Neuilly-sur-Coke," "Joséphine Loved Snow." The papers are having a field day with the arrests the next morning. The story's remarkable, after all. It's not every day the cops dismantle a drug-trafficking operation on this scale, let alone in a chic suburb like Neuilly. But the bourgeois like coke too. And this coke was of the highest quality. Not like the stuff that dealers from the ninety-three sell, a disgusting powder cut with who knows what and that causes countless overdoses. Here, among the bourgeois, it's first-rate blow. Higher than the average market price, but they can afford it.

Pablo Torres talked a lot during his time in custody. He ratted out Joséphine de Sainte-Croix and blamed her for everything. She kept her cool and didn't speak to the investigators, simply smiled and invoked her right to remain silent. In this case, appearances were deceiving, to Alex's great surprise. He'd assumed that the Colombian was the mastermind, and he has to face it: he was wrong. It was Jo who ran the whole operation, who first had the idea and manipulated her lover. Before meeting her, he was keeping his head down, making decent money with his import-export company. She'd seen the opportunity to use him to import coke to the Paris suburbs. The idea came to her when she saw how quickly the baggies circulated from hand to hand and from nose to nose during the posh parties she was invited to. And she had a knack for it, Jo—hundreds of kilos were delivered to her place every year. She wasn't in it for the money, she had more than enough. The baroness was bored. A curious motive. It was the only thing she said to the examining magistrate.

"I wanted to spice up my life."

MEN AT WORK: DATE OF COMPLETION, FEBRUARY 2027

BY GUILLAUME BALSAMO

Ivry-sur-Seine

Translated by David and Nicole Ball

I've always hated photos of myself. I have a massive V-shaped chin under a mouth that grimaces more than it smiles. A dark face and light-gray eyes in a luminous horizontal line—the sign of my Kabyle origins. The kind of face you'd remember. And remembering me is kind of a handicap in my line of work.

I was looking at the photo on my smartphone, my feet propped up on what I used for a desk. It showed me next to a girl with a Colgate smile; I didn't even remember who she was. The tag said *Jennifer*. One of these days, that girl Jennifer's going to have a real hard time. Because if there's something I hate more than photos of me, it's selfies of peroxide blondes identifying me . . . I mean, really, in what world of egocentric idiots do you tag your fucking dealer on Facebook?

I deleted the tag on my Facebook name—*The Spade*—with a few taps on my Nokia, and at that exact moment Jose opened my door. It squealed like an old shopping cart.

"The cops just found a body on the quays."

Jose thought following the comings and goings of the police gave him an advantage as a delinquent. You had to know the enemies' moves, he'd say. Be an urban ninja. Discreet like Don Corleone and implacable like Scarface. In reality, he was just lucky he never got nabbed: the day the cops thought to interrogate the little redheaded punk who was always at their heels, they'd learn an awful lot about the ecosystem of dope in Ivry.

"So? Do I care?" I asked.

"Looks like it's the Chinese guy."

"What Chinese guy?"

"You know, Truc. The Chinese guy who disappeared."

I sighed and grabbed my leather jacket. "He's Vietnamese, Jose."

I had squatted an abandoned factory not far from the Pont d'Ivry and made it my center of operations: having an office makes you look more like a pro. Leaving the ruined building, you'd pass through old quays that used to load trucks. In the distance, when the air wasn't too hazy from pollution, you could see the top of the Chinagora pagodas.

Night was beginning to fall. I followed Jose on my scooter to the concrete silos opposite the Hôtel Mercure. Four or five cop cars were parked in front of it, their lights dancing and flickering on the piles of sand. The hotel and the offices were still lit, and crowds of curious people were pressing against the panes to glimpse the scene. I motioned Jose to follow me and went over to my buddy Doudou, who was standing off at a distance.

"The cops identified the guy?" I asked. "Is it Truc?"

"They didn't say anything about a truck. They're just saying it's an Asian."

I nodded. Doudou was a massive Black man with a square face, not unpleasant to look at, who pumped iron while bingeing complete seasons of American shows. The girls hinted he also had a cock like a horse. So, a classic Greek beauty, with the counterpart inherent in democratic civilization: huge prick, tiny brain. You meet a lot of people in my line of work: bankers from high society, druggies with burned-out neurons. Once, I even met an old lady who thought she could buy ecstasy pills from me and resell them in front of le Palacio by hiding them in her pill case: her second customer ran away with the whole stock and her walker. But never, and I mean never, have I met anyone as dumb as my pal Doudou. Seriously, if evolution had done its job right, he would have dried out on his mother's thigh instead of existing.

"They found him in the Seine?"

"No, I don't think so. On a sandpile."

While we spoke, a van left the cement factory, probably taking with it the body of our valiant Vietnamese comrade. If it was really him in the bag, I just lost my best salesman. Because the two others, Jose and Doudou, were my childhood buddies, meaning I'd killed more time watching movies with them than jerking off by myself in front of porn flicks. Really, my small operation brought in cash mostly because of Truc. Precise like a Swiss accountant, with an incredible business sense.

The cops kept fussing around the trucks. Couldn't really tell what they were looking for, but it was strangely soothing to see them gesticulating from far off, lit by blue flashes of light. I got lost in the contemplation of the spectacle, so it took me a minute to realize that one of the cops was walking over to us. A short Asian man wearing a Canada Goose down jacket.

"Seriously?" Jose said. "A Chinaman investigating the murder of a Chinaman? You'd think it's a John Woo movie."

"Shit," Doudou whispered, "I got meth in my pockets. What do I do?"

"You came to a crime scene with meth?" I said. "Seriously,

Doudou, you're really fucked up. Don't budge. That's not why he's here. Let me do the talking." I tried to relax while the cop was covering the distance that separated us.

When he reached us, the cop lit a cigarette. "Lieutenant Kong. The guy we picked up, you knew him?"

"Hard to see from here."

"Truc Nguyen. That ring a bell?"

I acted like I was thinking. "I'm pretty sure it's a Vietnamese name. I got that right?"

"He's mostly a corpse at the moment. You from around here?"

"No. I actually live in the neighborhood of the RER station."

"And I'm from the Maurice Thorez projects," Doudou intervened.

"You're from Ivry?"

I grunted my assent. Ivryen all my life, though not from the station area. I lied, of course. But not Doudou, no. All he had to do now was give him his real name and tell the cop he dealt under the railroad bridge.

"The victim was selling grass, visibly."

"How awful," I said without blinking. "He had his visiting cards on him?"

"Almost. Bags with the price carefully labeled in his jacket pockets. His murderer didn't even bother taking them. It could be gangs settling scores. But three good boys like you have nothing to worry about, right?"

I assured him we did not; my friends and I were honorable osteopathy students. But from the little we heard in the shady circles of our pleasant housing projects, there was no gang war in the drug milieu. (That last part, at least, was true.)

"Maybe this is just the beginning," the cop said. "Or maybe not."

"What do you mean?"

"Listen, you three. I'm just saying it looks like it's a gang thing, okay? Because the murder was staged and it looks like a warning."

"You mean someone cut off his balls and put them in his mouth?" Doudou asked.

"What? No!" The cop looked disgusted. "He was strangled. But the murderer taped his mouth, his eyes, and his ears. And strangely, aside from the mouth, it appears to have been done *after* his death."

"That's a typical *Dexter* thing," Doudou said.

"A *what* thing?"

"What my friend is trying to say," I cut in, "is we've entered the world of Patrick Bateman."

"Patrick Bateman . . . ?"

"The hero of *American Psycho*."

"What kind of pompous ass are you?"

"When you're an osteopathy student, you have time to watch movies."

"So now you probably think we have a serial killer. And I suppose you already got his profile in your head?"

I shrugged. "I can't do your job for you. But good luck anyway."

He threw his cigarette away; it whirled in the air before crashing on the asphalt. I had clearly put him in a bad mood. I decided to pile it on.

"Wait," I called out as he was walking away. "I don't have a psychological profile, but if I were you, I'd ask about monkeys."

"Hilarious. I've heard that one a thousand times."

It took me a second to get it. Lieutenant *Kong* . . .

"No, no connection at all," I said. "Your victim was Asian.

And that bit with the tape . . . Long story short, I'm thinking of those Asian wisdom monkeys, because I'm a supereducated young student. It's just to help you out, okay? But you can do whatever you like."

He stopped short, took out his phone, and typed something. Then, without saying goodbye, he headed back to the ballet of twirling lights.

A few days later, I was waiting for Jose in the cold, in the vacant lot where the BHV warehouses used to be. The place had been a gigantic ocean of earth, debris, and broken beer bottles for seven years. I was stationed in front of the place where the store used to sell electric gates, also long abandoned. But that always got me: it still had electric power, and in the store window, two demonstration gates opened and shut in silence every thirty-eight seconds on the dot. Thirty-eight seconds per cycle, day and night, for nearly seven and a half years; counting leap years, these gates had opened and shut about 6,129,000 times.

Which inspired in me two very deep thoughts.

Number one: sometime soon, I was going to leave Ivry. With all the bread I'd have put aside by then, I'd buy myself a nice villa somewhere in the sun, like a hacienda in Colombia. I'd have the hot tub Katia wanted, a tennis court, a gym with exercise machines, and a collection of sunglasses. I'd be a member of the local golf club and host barbecues for my buddies. Lots of barbecues with lots and lots of buddies. If I had this kind of electric gate that can open and shut 6,129,000 times without breaking down, they could come and go as they pleased.

Number two: one day, Électricité de France was going to discover the abandoned meter, and someone somewhere would get a giant, Bill Gates–size bill.

"You know they found two other bodies?" Jose's voice pulled me out of my daydream. "They were strangled too."

"Yeah. I heard. A worker in a squat not far from the mosque. And the second one, I dunno where."

"A guy from city hall. They found him in the cemetery."

In the cemetery? Saves time for what happens next, but still, what disrespect. I liked the Ivry cemetery. Sometimes I went there just to forget everything and watch the baby foxes. The poor animals had asthma attacks from living in the city, and now they could bump into corpses when they turned a corner, like in a horror movie. Poor little foxes.

"And their eyes, ears, and mouths were taped shut?"

"That's what they're saying. Three—that's already serial, right?"

I nodded, while he casually slipped a roll of bills into my hand. Then I led him into the warehouse site. Jose was supposed to give me a hand that day.

Question: what's the best spot to stash a gun and be sure nobody comes across it? Answer: a big construction project in Ivry. Seven and a half years that thing had been abandoned, planned date of completion: maybe February 2027. Meanwhile, a machine came in from time to time and moved a heap of earth from point A to point B. And then to point C because they'd come upon some archaeological stuff. Then point D, but nobody knew why. And so on, all the way to Z, and they'd start over again. After all, they had sixteen years of work to kill.

Long before, by pure chance, I'd found a weapon with the serial number filed off. It wasn't as if I needed one, so I hid it in a metal cookie box and buried it in the back of the construction site. But then, between the Roma who were settling permanently in the former warehouses, and the Ivry Strangler who attracted half the region's cops, who themselves inter-rogated the Roma three times a day—I told myself the spot wasn't very safe anymore.

"Two guys over there are giving us weird looks," Jose said as I dug up my treasure with a pickax.

Dirty kids in ragged pants. We were on their playground. Little modern-day Goonies, but I was the one digging up One-Eyed Willy's gold.

"We better get the fuck out, and fast," Jose said.

"You scared they'll beat you up? The oldest one isn't even eight."

"You didn't see *City of God*? Those kids are potential killers."

"In the favelas, maybe. But in Ivry, normally, no one has the balls to bump off their neighbor."

I stopped short. I had an idea, but I put it away in a corner of my brain. Jose leaned over the hole and took out the box of cookies, which I then slipped into my backpack. We were nearing the exit when we spotted Doudou's silhouette climb-ing the fence. He was cursing because barbed wire had torn his jacket.

"Didn't we say ten thirty?" he asked.

"No. Ten. We're done now. But nice of you to come, Doudou."

"Shit. I put down ten thirty. Plus, I had to hurry up just when I was getting laid. I'm fucking pissed!"

If the Ivry Strangler had whacked Doudou, the average IQ of the city would have gone up a few points. I wondered why I still saddled myself with this idiot when, on top of it all, he was the worst dealer in the city. Since the Blue Sky episode, nobody wanted his meth anymore. Let me recap: Doudou is a huge fan of *Breaking Bad*. One day, he set up

his own methamphetamine lab in his mother's kitchen. He
wanted to make blue meth and sell it on the streets at twice
the normal price. Except Doudou is not Walter White. No reaction with methylamine to give a sky-blue color to his prod-
uct. All he did was melt candy Smurfs and incorporate them
into his mixture. Result: the druggies on rue de la Baignade
repainted their squat with fluorescent blue vomit, and half of
them re-upped with the competition. That fat prick Loukoum, my competitor at the Jeanne-Hachette mall, sent me a
montage of Mendeleyev's periodic table with an extra little
square: *Sm.*

"No big deal, Doudou." I sighed. "We managed without
you."

"The kids saw you?" He pointed to the Goonies.

"Yeah, but we don't give a shit. They probably don't even
speak French."

"And the guy in the excavator—he saw you too?"

I turned around. Sure enough, about thirty feet away,
there was this bulldozer with a vague shape slumped in the
cabin.

"What do we do?" Jose asked.

"Let's check what the hell he's up to. First time a worker
shows up here on a weekday."

Jose went ahead of us, planted himself in front of the
guy, and let out a loud "Holy shit!" I understood why when
I walked up to him. It's funny, because in the movies, when
you come upon a corpse, there's always that old trick to make
you jump: two hundred musical instruments start all at once,
producing a sudden swell of sound as violently as possible,
while the mutilated face of the unfortunate victim appears in
a close-up. Here, it was just a paunchy fifty-year-old guy, his
back partly turned, a black strip taped to his face. Jose tried

to whistle, but his chapped lips only gave out the sound of an anemic pressure cooker.

"You know him?" asked Doudou.

"Yeah," I said. "He buys smack from me about once a month. He works at the mall—I mean, *worked* . . ."

"I thought the Strangler was only after Arabs. This one here looks kinda white."

"You think Truc looked Arab? Me, I think the Strangler doesn't give a shit if you're an Arab or a pure French asshole."

"Or slant-eyed," Jose said. "Plus, I heard yellow guys have less peripheral vision because of the angle of their eyes. It must be easier for a killer to take them out from behind. Sometimes Mother Nature plays us some nasty tricks."

"Shit, Jose. You're Portuguese and a redhead! You shouldn't make fun of people based on genetic traits."

"So, what do we do?" Doudou asked. "We leave him there? Sooner or later, the little Roms are gonna find him."

"Exactly. We have nothing to worry about. We call the cops before the little Roms spot him. Anonymous call."

Doudou took out his cell and I smacked it down into the mud.

"Anonymous, I said!"

"I'm not dumb, I wasn't gonna give my name."

I raised my eyes to heaven, the time for him to get it. Or be touched by grace. Or whatever, as long as he shut up.

"Okay," he said, after too long a wait. "Gotta find a phone booth then."

"A phone booth, right. And then we'll go wait in a nice warm arcade and listen to MC Solaar. Seriously, you think you're in the nineties or what?"

"Okay, so *you* find something! You're seriously stressed right now."

"Maybe because the cops are gonna show up and I've got a piece in my bag, Doudou."

They followed me to a café on the other side of the street, where I asked for a phone, a greasy old Bakelite model. I left a short message with the operator—purely informative. The sirens started up as we were leaving the crime scene.

"Maybe I should go fish out some info," Jose said as he skipped along beside me. "They must have leads to find the killer."

"Better not."

"I think like the Spade," Doudou said. "The cops won't do squat. We have to find him ourselves."

"I never said that. We shut up and wait."

"Seriously?" Jose said. "There're so many cops in the city, I have to make home deliveries like a fucking delivery boy for Deliveroo. We can't just do nothing!"

"Well, yeah, exactly. You really don't understand a thing about how this city works. Hear no evil, see no evil, speak no evil. That's the way to wisdom and the recipe for happiness, guys. And me, I'm the happiest fucking man in the world."

Naturally, telling them to forget about the Ivry Strangler was like farting into a xylophone and expecting Tchaikovsky. Over the next few weeks, Jose posed as a Communist reporter from *l'Humanité* to snoop around. The cops spotted him quickly and tased him three times. But what's really weird is, they clearly didn't give a shit. I mean, in *Seven*, the serial killer stumps the cops who're after him exactly the way Jose did. Except now, the cops only seemed interested in picking up the corpses without looking for the Strangler.

As for Doudou, he reasoned that, since the killer was a random man on the streets, the thing to do was to ask questions to random passersby on the street. He didn't find any clues, but he did collect a few hits from handbags—one with a big stone in it. So then he refocused on the development of his smartphone app: Amphetahome Deliver. When he'd asked my opinion, I told him the concept was so disruptive it would even disrupt its creator. He looked delighted and redoubled his efforts. I consoled myself by thinking that, after all, Doudou didn't even know how to tap his password into an ATM. He's too fucking dumb even for that.

As for the murders, I followed the events on the Internet, and my customers texted me every time a corpse popped up. You'd have to be totally blind not to notice: the pace of the killings had accelerated exponentially. From a corpse a day, it rapidly went to twelve the next week. The news guys who crossed the beltway said the killer was trying to break a record, and a sociologist blamed consumer society, speaking of "Instagram murders." The phrase quickly became fashionable.

And then, who knows why, the Strangler really went to town. As if his sudden notoriety had energized him. And he'd become incredibly effective: recently, he had moved up to five or six corpses a day. Even better than the Americans in Iraq.

There was no shortage of abandoned places in Ivry, and it seemed every time a kid tested his courage in an industrial wasteland, he came across a body. The Street Golf Association of Ivry warned its members not to practice until the situation became normal again. Stores closed as soon as night fell, at five thirty.

The rare cops who took the affair seriously were totally clueless. They couldn't understand how a murderer could strangle 137 victims in less than two months and nobody in this fucking city heard or saw anything, or talked.

204 // PARIS NOIR: THE SUBURBS

That Saturday, I was having my usual postcoital kebab with Katia at a dive on rue Molière. She had this habit I hated of putting a few french fries aside to soak in the white sauce. She would then eat her sandwich before finishing off the mushy fries with great relish. I was trying to block out her presence by browsing Wikipedia on my phone when Jose opened the door of the fast-food joint.

"I think I got something," he said. "I marked the spots where they found the 139 corpses on Google Maps, I connected the dots, and it makes a drawing."

I glanced at the scribbled piece of paper he was holding out to me. "Looks like an octopus being raped by an iron. What's that supposed to say about the murderer?"

"You think that because you don't read Klingon."

"Klingon?"

"Klingon. Like the Klingons on *Star Trek*. Look, if you connect all the lines, you get letters of the Klingon alphabet one over the other. And it makes the word *maghwl*."

He took on a mysterious air, awaiting my reaction. I gave him one—an exasperated sigh.

"It means *traitor*," he said. "In other words, we're dealing with someone taking revenge for betrayal. And he's a geek. And so I can already predict that the 140th corpse will be found around allée Gagarine."

My cell vibrated. I read the message.

"Promenade des petits bois," I said laconically. Loukoum's little sister, apparently. "I wouldn't say I'm sad for him."

Jose got out a pen, traced the last line, frowned, and crumpled up his paper, which landed next to the spit of the kebab.

"Did you know that *Star Trek* was the first to show an interracial kiss on the screen?" I said, just to fuel the conversation.

"Seriously? That's fucked up."

"Why? Katia's Spanish and I'm Kabyle. With us, French-kissing is interracial."

"Yeah, but with you it's different. And in an SF series, it's just not right."

"I'm like an SF character," Katia said between two fries, "My name on Instagram is Katniss, like in *Hunger Games*."

"Yeah, I know," Jose said. "They shot part of the last film at the Étoiles project right next to me. My little sister went completely bananas."

Jose ordered a Greek ketchup harissa. He'd obviously decided to stay. That didn't bother me: Katia was starting to get on my nerves, and I needed to think aloud.

"My father told me he saw Terry Gilliam in the flesh," I said.

"Terry who?"

"He was shooting scenes for the movie *Brazil* in Ivry. Doesn't that seem super weird to you, Jose?"

"What?"

"Every time a big-budget American movie is shot here, it's an SF dystopia."

He looked like a deer caught in the headlights. *Dystopia*.

"It's an SF technique," I went on. "A nightmare future. It often describes a society where useless people and dissidents are simply eliminated by the regime."

"So why should that seem weird to me?"

"A hundred and forty . . ." My cell vibrated. "A hundred and forty victims in a city of unemployed and ultra-left people. It's kind of the Ken Loach version of a dystopian film."

"Ken who?"

"What I don't get is the tape. And why the monkeys?"

"The monkeys? What monkeys?"

A platter materialized in front of my buddy Jose. On it,

grease, meat, and french fries. Everything was getting mixed up in my head. As if I had the answer to a question I wasn't asking myself, and I couldn't put my fucking finger on it. Terry Gilliam, *Brazil*, Instagram, *Twelve Monkeys*? *Seven*, *Hunger Games*, a worker slumped on the seat of a bulldozer?

And the innocent, naive eyes of my buddy Jose, hesitating, unsure whether to wait politely for me to stop talking or pounce on his fries. I suddenly understood everything. Instantly. The Strangler, the monkeys, Jose, everything.

"I thought you didn't want to know about the Strangler," he said.

"I wasn't trying to know, but to understand."

"Oh, okay."

For some reason, he thought my last reply authorized him to dig into his kebab. I watched him voraciously devour his stuff, lick his fingers. My little Jose. Full of contradictions, absurdly racist, almost as dumb as Doudou—but how I loved the guy!

Chinagora in the fog is my private little bit of exoticism. Concrete in the shape of the Forbidden City inside an ocean of concrete in the shape of hideous buildings. Bertolucci could almost have shot a sequel to *The Last Emperor* here, and to feel connected to the Japanese, he could have had sushi every night in the streets of Alfortville.

As a kid, Doudou once went to eat at Chinagora. He was invited by an uncle or something like that. The next day at school, he told everybody he really went to China just for a meal in a restaurant. The east of Ivry was the limit of the world for a kid who wasn't the brightest bulb to begin with.

It was even colder that morning in my factory-office, and that's why I'd asked Jose to move his ass. I didn't feel like spending the whole day on this business. Especially since I'd already had to show up at the Leroy Merlin hardware store when it opened and wait in line for a purchase of just seven euros and ninety cents.

True, to console myself, I spent twice as much on fucking candy at the stand beside the registers. Artificially colored, carcinogenic junk. I dug into the paper bag like a junkie who'd discovered his dealer's stock. I found a Smurf-blue one and threw it negligently behind me. A groan told me I'd hit my target.

A noise in the hallway. Jose coming in. The sliding door opened and his mug appeared.

"Sorry, I'm in a big hurry. They found the corpse of the old lady—oh."

Abrupt pause. Silence. I sure had managed to shut him up.

"Shit, what the fuck are you doing?" he finally asked.

"I need help, this prick really has the neck of a bull. You gotta hold him for me."

The good thing about Jose was his phenomenal ability to adjust to anything. Throw him into a squat full of punks with dogs, and two days later he'd be playing craps with them, telling them stories about his grandma in some village in the Portuguese mountains. Provided, of course, the guys weren't Asian. Obviously, holding a tough, half-unconscious, tied-up Black guy while I was strangling him with wire was no big deal for him.

So Jose complied, if a little grudgingly. Did his best to hold Doudou against the iron bench to stop him from bucking too much, took one or two hits from his knee—gotta admit, it's not easy to tie a guy up while threatening him with a gun. Me, I picked the easy part. I put the wire around his neck, twisted it around a piece of copper piping, and turned like it was a steering wheel in *Need for Speed*. Three turns, hold it a little, release the whole thing when you feel resistance slackening, when the yelps, muffled by tape, stop. Killing a guy is as simple as that.

When I had finished, I collapsed on the ground in front of the big window. Jose just stood there, motionless. Visibly shaken.

"Can I ask why?" he said after a long pause.

"Why do they give honorary Oscars? Not for just one movie. Well, here, it's the same idea—it's for his lifetime achievement."

"I get it."

Jose pronounced those three words with the tone of a guy who really doesn't get it at all. I dug my phone out of my pocket and opened Facebook.

"Okay, here's the straw that broke the camel's back."

I showed him my screen. Me and that bitch Jennifer in close-up. Behind us, a little blurry, Katia is pulling that asshole Doudou out of the party, pointing to me. I shouldn't have handled the delivery myself that night. For weeks, I'd tried to ignore the whole thing and play the fucking wise monkeys by closing my eyes, my ears, and my mouth. But I guess I was far from being as zen and detached as a little statuette in an old Chinese restaurant.

"Relax, Jose. I'm not a psychopath. I taped his mouth, his eyes, and his ears just to act like the Strangler."

"You didn't kill the 364 other people?"

"Stop talking bullshit. You know that's not what happened since I obviously didn't kill Truc."

He sat down next to me and remained silent, our asses in the dust of the abandoned factory.

"Tell me," I said, "the Asian wisdom monkeys—you did that on purpose?"

"Shit, man, I don't even know what you're talking about. Most of the time I can't understand a thing you say."

"The tape on Truc's face."

"On his mouth; it was to stop him from yelling. And then, when he was dead . . . Well, the eyes of a guy you just strangled aren't a pretty sight. And I didn't want to touch his eyelids directly. For the ears, I dunno what the hell came over me. An inspiration."

"In any case, it was a real hit. The whole Internet loved it."

Jose turned around, probably to look at Doudou's corpse. Something was finally percolating in his mind.

"Shit," he said. "It's not a serial killer, right?"

"No. I think it's another phenomenon. I'd call it a series of killers. The proof is, this morning I got the last roll of tape in Leroy Merlin. The guys don't even have time to restock."

"So when's that gonna stop?"

"No idea. When Leroy Merlin exhausts its suppliers? When the population of Ivry is cut in half? How should I know?"

"What about the cops?"

"They must know already. But they'd rather see no evil, hear no evil, speak no evil too. Anyway, they're not going to bust half of Ivry, right?"

I was famished and craving a bo bun. But I owed Jose an invite after the help he'd given me. And Jose hated Asian food.

"Maybe it'll stop once they're done with all the construction," Jose said.

"Yeah. When there are no more vacant lots, it'll be harder to scatter corpses around."

I got up and brushed off my jeans.

"Come on, Jose, I'll buy you a pizza."

PART IV

Ghosts from the Past

THE SHADOWS OF THE TRAPÈZE

BY ANNE SECRET
Boulogne-Billancourt

Translated by Paul Curtis Daw

Prologue

It's him. I'm almost positive.

It's not that I recognize his face. After all these decades, he's changed way too much. But I know the voice. That high-pitched quality, so distinctive, coupled with an accent of the Parisian suburbs that you heard back in those days.

The blue band at the bottom of the screen reads, *Roland, Boulogne-Billancourt, ex-Renault worker*. Roland. That's his first name, all right. What a shame they don't give his last.

I wipe my forehead. Get up from the sofa and grab my cell phone: 11:20 p.m. With this heat, it wouldn't surprise me if my brother, Nicolas, was already asleep. I phone him.

"Sorry to call so late, but on France 5 there's a show about the Trapèze."

"You know I don't like to see what's become of that area . . ."

"Wait, this isn't really about the redevelopment. They're interviewing an old guy, a former Renault employee. His name's Roland. I have a strong feeling that he's the one who used to hang around Maman. Do you remember him?"

Clutching my phone, I continue to stare at the screen. Roland is speaking in close-up. At the other end of the line, Nicolas exclaims, "Damn! You're right, it *is* him."

I'm hearing Roland's voice in stereo. He's gushing about the reconstructed neighborhood, the tree-topped walls, the glass-clad buildings. The camera zooms over Île Seguin—still a construction site—the new gardens, and then the famous Building X, rechristened Pierre-Dreyfus, the only visible remnant of the Renault empire, now partially hidden by scaffolding. Roland is reminiscing about his difficult circumstances as a factory worker.

"What bullshit!" I say. "The guy had a white-collar job!"

I clench my teeth. He was a foreman, while Étienne, our father, was only a semiskilled worker, subject to Roland's orders. I hear my brother expel his cigarette smoke.

"It's a good thing Nastasia didn't marry him. Imagine him as our stepfather . . ." He lets out a loud, sardonic laugh, which I'm in no mood to emulate.

A tracking shot shows Roland moving away, his tall figure leaning on a cane. He advances along the quay. To the left, brand-new buildings; opposite them, beyond the Seine, I recognize the closest houses on Île Saint-Germain.

We hang up. That's the end of the segment. I scrutinize the credits: Roland M. is acknowledged, but his last name is still not revealed in full. I turn off the TV and slam the remote down on the sofa. To see that guy again, after almost half a century. Alive.

We detested him. But Nicolas was too young. He couldn't understand. I, on the other hand, had been ten. Things were clearer to me.

How many times have I cursed him? How many times have I wished him an early death? An accident that would grievously disable him? A long, excruciating illness?

Because I'm sure he's the one who cravenly put two bullets in my father's back on the first of March, 1972.

1

Noon, Gare d'Amiens. I clamber onto an intercity train with dirty windows, headed for the Gare du Nord.

I hardly closed my eyes all night. I tried desperately to uncover Roland's last name, but in vain. I looked through my files: I possess very few items coming from my parents, and nothing relating to Papa's years at Renault. When Nastasia died, her second husband told me he'd thrown everything away.

Even so, I thought, *I should be able to find the man*. At three in the morning, I booked a hotel room near the Porte de Saint-Cloud.

Once past the Gare de Longueau, I close my eyes. I'm exhausted but find it impossible to sleep. Ever since watching the program, I've been dwelling constantly on that long-ago trauma.

It was a Monday, and it was cold. I was hurrying home from school, taking, as usual, rue du Vieux-Pont-de-Sèvres. I arrived at 270, boulevard Jean-Jaurès. We lived in a minuscule two-bedroom apartment on the second floor. From the hallway, I heard raised voices.

When I went inside, Nastasia was in the dining room. Her hair in disarray, she was screaming, and my aunt Olga was trying to calm her. Standing in a corner were two unfamiliar men in overcoats. Terrified, I called for my little brother, but Olga explained that she had come to take him to the apartment of Zoubida, who worked with my mother at a dressmaking shop.

I clutched my aunt's arm; she told me that "something very serious" had happened to Étienne. My eyes dry, I kept repeating, "Papa, Papa." I didn't really get it. The younger of the two men then escorted me to my room. He was a policeman and had to ask me some questions. Did my parents get along well? Yes, I said. I asked him how Papa had died, but he didn't answer. Then he asked me about my father's work at Renault. Did he fight with the leftists who were loitering outside the factory doors or at the gateway to the Seguin footbridge? I replied negatively. Then I broke into sobs.

I open my eyes and gaze out the window. A metallic voice is announcing that we are stopped at the Gare de Creil and that the train will arrive late.

Renault-Billancourt was a gigantic factory complex that, between the Trapèze and Seguin plants, employed thirty-five thousand people. At the beginning of the seventies, it was one of the preferred haunts for Maoists, who gathered regularly at the entrances to industrial sites to hand workers the sacred text of the Great Helmsman. Their presence gave rise to incessant conflicts with both the company's security guards and the CGT union, which, though left-wing, was not Maoist. But all that veered sharply for the worse when a certain Pierrot, a Maoist who had gotten himself discharged from the factory, was murdered in cold blood by a guard in front of the Zola entry gate. My father, normally taciturn about his work, had even spoken to us about it.

I remember oversize posters stuck up everywhere in Boulogne, showing the face of this Pierrot: a bearded, bespectacled man with round cheeks and an Afro.

In fact, it was this "leftist" angle that the police had immediately chosen to pursue. Papa had no enemies; he was the very soul of kindness, and all his fellow workers appreciated him. As for those closest to him—our mother, Nastasia; his sister-in-law; and his friends—everyone had an alibi. And one detail had immediately caught the investigators' attention: as

Papa's colleagues on the assembly line used to say teasingly, he was always "dressed to the nines." At Nastasia's insistence: my mother, for whom elegance was an absolute priority, couldn't bear to see Étienne badly dressed, even when he was leaving the factory. From that, the cops had deduced that an over-wrought young Maoist, intent on avenging the revered Pierrot, had mistaken my father, with his three-quarter-length checkered coat, for a supervisor or even a manager. The murder had occurred around three p.m. (Papa worked the day shift) in one of the passageways leading from the Trapèze to boulevard Jean-Jaurès. During my restless night at home in Amiens, I verified on Street View that the passageway no longer exists. There were no witnesses. The police officers had assured my mother that the assailant and the murder weapon would quickly be found.

But they never laid a hand on either the murderer or the gun. Papa merited only a snippet in *Le Parisien*, because three days later a big-shot Renault executive was kidnapped by a gang of extreme leftists, and the media turned exclusively to that story. The inquest concerning Étienne was wound up in perfunctory fashion.

The succeeding months were difficult. Nastasia was in a daze. Up until one evening the following autumn: while I was doing my homework and Nicolas was playing in the kitchen, our mother waltzed in, all dolled up, and announced that she was going to a movie with some friends. As soon as the apartment door had closed, Nicolas and I raced to the window. At the foot of the building, leaning against a car and sporting a stylish suede jacket, was Roland M., Papa's foreman.

2

When I emerge from the metro station, the heat is over-whelming.

The hotel is located on rue Gudin, a stone's throw from the Porte de Saint-Cloud. The desk clerk says my room is ready. I undress, take a shower, and stretch out on the bed. In less than ten minutes, I'm asleep.

With some difficulty, I wake up at six p.m. Decide to head over to the Trapèze neighborhood, named for its trapezoidal shape. In his interview, Roland M. recounted that he often strolled in the new garden along the quai Georges-Gorse in the late afternoon.

Feeling quite emotional, I leave the metro at the Billancourt station. Follow rue de la Ferme to the place Bir-Hakeim. Several old buildings remain, but between them I note gaps like missing teeth. I take avenue Émile-Zola and plunge into the reconfigured Trapèze.

I expect to encounter changes, but not to such an extent. Everything has been demolished, both industrial and residential buildings. The new structures—apartment blocks and sharp-angled office buildings—are not hideous in themselves, and the urbanistic streetscape seems coherent: wide sidewalks, cycling paths, and greenery more or less everywhere. But the overall banality, which calls to mind every other redeveloped suburb, is quite dispiriting.

I wander for a good while in the famous Jardin de Billancourt. No one else there. After crisscrossing the garden from end to end, I exit and continue on my way. The sun is still beating down, and in a spanking-new, totally deserted Franprix, I buy a half bottle of Badoit. I drop the idea of going to Île Seguin. Take rue de Meudon back to place Jules-Guesde.

It's there that one of the main entrances to the factory was located. The white facade, with its strict art deco lines, is still standing, but its doors open into a void. Did someone forget to demolish it? The tall letters that once spelled out *RENAULT* have been removed from the rectangular pediment.

The intersection itself is almost unaltered. The cafés are still there. But their clientele has changed radically: the terraces are now occupied by a rather young crowd, reasonably well dressed, who no doubt stop by for happy hour after leaving the office.

I read somewhere that place Jules-Guesde was the regular gathering spot for former Renault employees. And yet, I notice not a single one, not on the cane chairs of the bistros or on the benches of the partially completed central pedestrian space.

I've seen enough. In front of a defunct café-tabac that announces the impending opening of a sushi bar, I suddenly visualize Mohand's brother's café on rue Carnot. Why haven't I thought of it sooner? I write him every January 1, and he always replies promptly. We exchange family news. Mohand was an assembler on the same line as my father, and his wife, Zoubida, worked with Nastasia in the dressmaking shop.

I cross avenue du Général-Leclerc, pass my old primary school, and return to rue Carnot. The Soleil de Kabylie hasn't changed, still occupying the ground floor of a three-story building whose yellow brick construction is typical of the old Parisian suburbs. Several tables are laid out on the sidewalk. The only customers are three old-timers with the characteristic look of retired Renault employees. They're chatting over iced tea in the shade of the blue-and-white-striped awning. The oldest is a bald guy with sparkling eyes, whom I recognize immediately even though he's gotten much heavier: Mohand.

I move closer. The trio raise their heads and size me up. Mohand, seated in the middle, knits his brows. It's been ages since we last saw each other.

"Irène?"

"Yes, it's me."

"But that's unbelievable! You haven't changed."

He speaks in Arabic to his companions, who greet me with respectful nods in consideration of Étienne. True to my intuition, the other two are indeed Renault retirees. Mohand invites me to sit and asks what I'd like to drink. Three minutes later, a dark-complexioned young man, whom Mohand introduces as his grandnephew Aziz, brings me an orange juice. Mohand's sidekicks discreetly disappear as my father's old comrade pats my forearm, his eyes misty.

"My little Irène. What pleasure this gives me!"

3

"But what are you doing here? Have you come to revisit the scenes of your youth?"

I tell him a little fib. "Yes. I'm in Paris for a few days. I'm taking advantage of a small chunk of free time to visit Billancourt . . ."

"So, you'll dine with me. Aziz will whip up something fresh for us."

I glance at my phone: 7:30 p.m. The August sun is beginning to decline. I nod. Aziz brings us a condensation-covered carafe and two glasses. Mohand serves us.

"Are you going to look at Île Seguin?"

"No. I've explored a large part of the Trapèze, from the park to the place Jules-Guesde. That was enough for me."

"Yes, what they've done is terrible. I know that the people who live in those new buildings must be faring well, with AC and all that. But for those of us who worked there for so long, to see all those demolitions . . ."

Aziz returns with two plates of mixed salad. I take the plunge: "I'd like to ask you something, Mohand."

"Yes?"

"Just before coming to Paris, I saw a program on France 5 about the renewal of the Trapèze. There was a guy who was talking about the Renault plant. I had a strong sense that I recognized him as someone who used to work with you and Papa."

Mohand frowns in thought. "Malquart?"

"On TV, they only mentioned his first name: Roland."

"Yes, Roland Malquart. I've seen him on occasion, when he comes to the association."

"What association?"

"When the site was permanently closed in 1992, the ex-employees decided to create an association. I had already retired, but the younger ones needed to relocate or even take up whole new occupations. At first, the group was a mutual-aid society, but it evolved into an organization of retirees working to preserve the heritage of Renault at Billancourt."

"And so, this Malquart, have you seen him lately?"

Mohand shook his head. "It's been a good six months since we've crossed paths. The program you saw was a re-broadcast. It was shown for the first time last spring. And you must've noticed that Malquart had all kinds of good things to say about the transformation of the island and the Trapèze redevelopment zone. I don't think our members particularly appreciated that."

"Do you have his address?"

"Why? You want to see him?"

"Yes. I'd like to pull together as much information as possible about Papa. The people who knew him, that sort of thing. To pass on to my kids."

Mohand scrunches his face just as he did before. "Listen, he's not a very nice person."

"This Roland, he used to chase after my mother, didn't he?"

"You know, Irène, lots of guys were courting Nastasia. She was so distinguished, so elegant . . . In any case, Roland wasn't the one she ended up marrying."

"I'd like to meet him anyway."

He smiles. "Still as stubborn as when you were a kid, eh?" He takes an old flip phone out of his pocket and puts on a pair of reading glasses. Scrolls slowly through his directory. "It's a landline number. Can you write it down?"

I leave the terrace of the Soleil de Kabylie around eleven p.m. I've listened to Mohand talk about his family and then about my parents. But when I mentioned Papa's murder, he was convinced it had been a leftist who gunned him down. I almost shared my own suspicions, but I held back.

I decide to walk to the hotel via avenue Édouard-Vaillant. It's still hot out, but the air is moving a little. Despite the late hour, I make several attempts to call Roland Malquart. The ringing resounds uselessly. Back in my hotel room, I consult the phone book. Malquart lives on rue Reinhardt, a little side street near the Hôtel de Ville of Boulogne-Billancourt.

4

The next morning, I force myself to get up early, since sweltering temperatures are again forecast for the entire country. At the Porte de Saint-Cloud, I catch a bus that drops me off near the Hôtel de Ville.

Malquart's place—15, rue Reinhardt—is a very modest two-story house. It's made of brick, topped with a flat roof, and partially concealed by a solid fence. Before ringing the bell, I have a moment's hesitation. What am I going to say to this man?

I only have to push the gate; it isn't fastened. The shutters on the two upstairs windows are also open. I step into the little forecourt, where cardboard boxes and six Henry II–style chairs are spread around.

What does all this mean?

Noises are coming from inside. I hear a drawn-out "goddamnit!" Then a guy about my age exits the house. Tall and lean, with a curly gray mane and vintage sunglasses on his forehead. He's wearing jeans and an attractive print shirt.

"Are you looking for something?"

"Um . . . yes. I'm looking for Roland Malquart. Does he live here?"

"He did."

"What do you mean?"

"He died last November."

Oh shit. Mohand said he hadn't seen him for six months. And with good reason. Now I'll never be able to make him confess to murdering Étienne.

The man comes closer. "Are you all right? You look very pale. I'm going to make a cup of coffee. Would you like one?"

A cramped kitchen, with minimal, outmoded furnishings. The only touch of modernity is a shiny new Nespresso sitting on the counter. The man removes from the sideboard two white Arcopal cups decorated with matching daisies. We had the same tableware pattern at Jean-Jaurès. A wedding present that Nastasia hated.

While the sleek machine is heating the coffee, he extends his hand. "I'm neglecting my obligations. I haven't introduced myself. I'm Éric, Roland's son."

"Irène."

"Pleased to meet you!"

"I'm failing at my obligations too. All my condolences for your father."

"Thank you. Why did you want to meet him anyway?"

"Because he worked with my father."

"Then you're a Renault baby too?"

"Yes."

He lifts his cup toward me, a flirtatious smile on his lips. "Well, that's something to drink to. Shall we speak as friends?"

"Agreed."

"And your own father, is he still living?"

"No, he died in 1972."

"You must have been very young. What did he die of?"

"He was murdered . . ."

Éric snaps his fingers. I notice in passing that his hands are quite lovely.

"I'm sorry. Who killed him?"

"That was never determined. He was killed several days after Pierre Overney, and just before a Maoist gang kidnapped a Renault manager."

"Nogrette?"

"Right. I doubt the investigation was properly handled. In fairness to the police, Billancourt, in that era, was like the Wild West."

"And . . . you're looking for whoever killed him?"

I shake my head. It's impossible to tell him the truth. "More than forty years later, that would be difficult. I just want to round up information about my father. Incidentally, if by chance you found in your father's papers anything relating to him . . . His name was Étienne Moreau."

"Roland wasn't exactly the type to put things in writing. But there's a stack of papers in his bedroom. I had intended to organize them later, but considering the heat . . . What would you say to you and I taking a look? Only if you have nothing better to do, of course."

We climb the stairs to the second floor. Step into a tiny room, even smaller than mine on boulevard Jaurès. It's barely possible to squeeze between the bed and the armoire. Three bulky cartons are sitting on the quilt.

Éric touches my shoulder. "We'll take them down to the kitchen. Within an hour, this room will be unbearably hot."

Three hours later, we've finished. Roland Malquart didn't burden himself with useless paperwork. We found no personal documents among the piles of administrative forms. Except, at the bottom of one carton, a manila envelope with the Renault letterhead, which contained a bunch of black-and-white snap-shots. Some unknown people, Éric as a baby with his parents . . .

"Are there any photos of you as an adolescent?"

"No. You know, I was five years old in 1960, when my parents separated. After that, I lived with my mother at Is-sy-Moulineaux. And I hardly ever saw my dad again. He was supposed to take me for part of my school vacation, but he never did. On the other hand, he always paid child support right on time."

In the final photo, I immediately recognize Nastasia. She's wearing a pleated dress, buttoned down the front with a small collar. The photo must date from before her marriage to my stepfather. Éric lets out a whistle.

"I don't recognize that beautiful woman."

"That's my mother."

5

"My father kept a photo of your mother . . . So, did our parents go out?" The idea seems to amuse him.

"When she was a widow, I believe they used to see each other. But that didn't last."

"That's insane!" He sets the photo on the sideboard. Examines it. "In any case, if my father kept this photo, he must have been very attached."

I don't tell him that, to my eyes, it's further proof of Roland's guilt.

"What was her name?"

"Nastasia."

"Were your grandparents Russian?"

"Yes, they were White Russians. You know, there were a lot of them in Billancourt between the world wars."

"Did you know them?"

"No, they died when my mother was a child. Her older sister Olga was responsible for most of her upbringing."

Éric wipes his brow and glances at his handsome watch.

"How about lunch? I can only offer you sandwiches from Monoprix, fruit, and Perrier. But we could also go somewhere . . ."

Traipsing through the white-hot streets does not excite me. "Let's go with the sandwiches."

We sit in the cozy kitchen. Éric plugs in an old fan made of green plastic. We eat our lunch. He asks about my life at Amiens, my daughters, my job as a French teacher. I quiz him in turn. He explains that he is a bass player, that he has toured for a long time with some of the big names of French rock, that he's divorced like me, that he has a grandson and lives in the fifteenth arrondissement.

After our picnic, I help Éric clear the serving cart from the dining room, which contains an impressive collection of Baccarat glassware. He's arranged to offer the whole lot to a bric-a-brac merchant, who shows up around five thirty. I disappear.

Returning to the hotel in the nearly empty 175 bus, I gaze at the photo of Nastasia that Éric gave me. Then I muse about Roland. If I had confronted him face-to-face, would he have admitted to killing my father?

My cell phone rings, startling me. The screen shows a number I don't recognize. I answer anyway.

"Hello?"

"Irène, it's Mohand . . ." His voice seems different.

"Yes?"

"I absolutely have to see you."

"Do you want me to come by tomorrow?"

"No. Tomorrow I'm flying from Orly to Algeria. Could you possibly come now?"

It's almost eight p.m. Returning to Billancourt now doesn't thrill me in the least.

"Is it really that urgent?"

I rummage through my suitcase for a T-shirt to change into. My supply of clean clothes is beginning to run out.

A half hour later, I arrive at the restaurant. To my astonishment, all the outdoor tables are occupied by a group of elderly people clad in sporting attire. The indispensable Aziz, assisted by a young man, bustles about, bearing a platter. As soon as he notices me, he approaches briskly.

"My uncle is waiting impatiently for you."

"Excuse me, but do you know what's going on?"

"He has something to tell you, that's all I know. He's in the courtyard. You can get there through the bar."

It's very hot inside, despite all the open windows. I slide behind the counter, cross a dark room cluttered with cases of bottles, and emerge into the building's center courtyard. A few potted plants are set here and there on the antique tiled surface. Near a pair of French doors, Mohand is sitting in an armchair, at a pitiful bistro table.

"It's good that you've come, Irène."

I look closely at him. His face is drawn; he's the antithesis of yesterday's jovial man.

"Will you have something to drink?"

"I'd very much like a coffee." I take a seat at the table.

Speaking Arabic in his powerful voice, Mohand hails the second server, who quickly returns with an espresso and a glass of water. As soon as he leaves, I pull my chair closer.

"What is it that you're so intent on telling me, Mohand?"

He fans himself with a large sheet of paper. "Did you go to see Roland Malquart?"

"I went to his house, and I happened to meet his son, Éric. Malquart is dead."

"Really?" Mohand seems truly surprised. Then he makes a resigned gesture. "Well, as I mentioned, he hardly ever saw any of the retirees. Especially after what he said on TV. Not being informed of his death is just more of the same . . . What did his son say to you?"

"Not much. He was five when his parents separated. He barely knew his father."

Silence. Mohand looks at his hands. "In point of fact, you wanted to see Malquart because you thought it was he who killed Étienne."

"I still think so. In Roland's papers, Éric found a photo of Nastasia. And yet he generally kept nothing of his past."

"You're wrong, my dear. Malquart had nothing to do with your father's death."

His words have a sharp edge. I furrow my brow.

"But what do you know about it? Do you honestly believe that some young Maoist shot Papa?"

A new silence. I will myself to be patient.

"No, it wasn't a Maoist who killed your father, Irène."

My heart starts racing. "Mohand, you aren't going to tell me that it was you . . ."

He lifts his head. Stares at me with his brown eyes. "No, my dear, I didn't kill Étienne. It was Nastasia who killed him."

6

"Maman?" What is this all about? "Hold on, Mohand. Why would Maman have killed Papa? That's absurd! In any case, on the afternoon of the shooting, Nastasia was at the dressmaking shop with Zoubida and one of your cousins. They were working on a wedding dress . . ."

I distinctly remember that dress. A bodice embroidered with pearls and a taffeta skirt with clean lines. A marvel: Nastasia had outdone herself.

"I know, Irène. But your mother stepped away. Étienne worked the morning shift; he left the factory at two thirty. On his way home, he always took avenue Hugo, where most of the houses had been condemned. Your mother knew that, obviously. She hid behind a gate and waited for him to come along—"

"This is nonsense!"

Mohand hushes me with a dismissive wave of his hand.

"Nastasia killed him and then returned to the shop. She was fairly calm. Zoubida phoned me. I was on leave from the factory that day, helping my brother here at the restaurant. I went to the shop. You mother told us everything. She told us she would not turn herself in to the police. She had the courage to return alone to her home on boulevard Jaurès. Two inspectors were there waiting for her. They told her that her husband had just been gunned down. She immediately became hysterical. Zoubida took charge of your little brother, and your aunt Olga arrived . . ."

"I remember, Mohand. I got home from school at that very moment."

"Zoubida and I spent all night discussing whether we should report Nastasia. By morning, we had made our decision. We'd say nothing. The next afternoon, the cops came to interrogate my wife. She told them that Nastasia had not left her presence. They also questioned our young cousin. But she was newly arrived from our native village, and knew almost no French . . ."

I have the sense of being submerged in a nightmare. I shake my head. "Wait a minute, Mohand. On top of everything else, you're telling me that you and Zoubida covered up the crime? That's delusional. I'll say it again: Maman had no reason to kill Papa. They got along fine. He adored his 'Russian princess,' and she was attached to him! Do you recall the years of hardship that we endured after he died? A number of times, we were almost evicted from the apartment . . ."

"Yes, Irène, but Nastasia had a very good reason."

"What?"

I must have raised my voice. Aziz pokes his head through the door to the bar. Mohand waves him away.

"Étienne wanted to leave. To desert your mother. He'd fallen madly in love with a woman at Renault. An assembler named Nicole."

"But that's not true!"

"It is. Your father had indeed loved his 'Russian princess,' as he used to say. She dazzled him. But very quickly she became harsh with him. You were too young to realize that. Every chance she got, she reminded Étienne that he, a humble workingman, had been extremely lucky to marry her. This was all the more unfair in that your grandfather Kanchine, when he fled Russia, had been delighted to land an unskilled job in Monsieur Renault's factory . . ."

I say nothing. I'm floored.

"Your father had enough of that. He made plans to leave and settle in Flins with that Nicole."

"In Flins?" I stare at Mohand in confusion. Then it comes back to me. Flins. Renault's other giant assembly plant. More modern than the Seguin factory. And at the same time, less grandiose.

"For beautiful, elegant Nastasia, to be jilted and left with two kids . . . It was worse than humiliating. It was quite simply impossible. And that was why she shot Étienne."

I run my hand over my face. Try one last objection: "Papa was killed by a gun. How could Maman have gotten her hands on one?"

Mohand sighs. "Before arriving in France, your grandfather had been a soldier in the famous army that fought the Communists. I forget what it was called."

"The White Army? Under General Wrangel?"

"That's it. He'd kept his revolver. And I know he taught both his daughters how to shoot."

"But what happened to the gun?"

Mohand wipes his forehead. He's drenched in sweat. It's stifling in that fucking courtyard.

"I threw it in the river. From the island. For me, it was easy."

Epilogue

Two in the afternoon. It's a nice, bright day, and after the previous night's turbulent storm, the temperature is more tolerable.

Éric and I are leaning our elbows on the railing of the Pont de Sèvres. In front of us, the northern tip of Île Seguin. The solar panels on the new Seine Musicale auditorium are gleaming in the sunlight.

"It's not such a bad thing that they built a concert hall on that site," I say.

Éric concurs. I squeeze his wrist. The other evening, after Mohand's revelations and my return to the hotel, I telephoned him and tearfully told him everything: that I had always believed his father to be guilty of murdering mine, but that in fact it was Nastasia. He couldn't get over it. Asked me which of my parents I resented more. I couldn't answer him. Then he announced his intention to interrupt his "morbid inventory" to go spend a few days in Brittany at a friend's house near Vannes. He asked if I wanted to come with him. I told him I'd think about it.

I have trouble averting my gaze from the island. There once stood the steamship-shaped factory on whose stern the word *RENAULT* was inscribed in black capital letters. I ponder the generations of workers succeeding one after another in that blue-collar fortress, among them my grandfather Kanchine, Étienne, Mohand, Roland, and that damn Nicole who seduced my father. To try to answer the question posed by Éric the other night, I wonder in my heart of hearts if it isn't Étienne who I blame the most.

My companion grips my shoulder. "Shall we go have a drink? In a café on avenue Vaillant that won't have changed since our distant youth?"

"That's going to be hard to find, but why not . . ."

A long stretch of the quai Georges-Gorse is taken up by

construction projects. We wait at a temporary traffic signal. Although we're in the August lull, the traffic on the bridge remains heavy. Éric wipes his sunglasses with the tail of his stylish shirt and favors me with one of his irresistible smiles.

"By the way, what have you decided about Brittany?"

STRANGE MARTYRS

BY ANNE-SYLVIE SALZMAN

Arcueil

Translated by Katie Shireen Assef

Nothing could've been easier, after dark, than sneaking a ladder out of the Roure community center and leaning it up against the stretch of wall where the aqueduct begins. It was enough to bypass the ring of steel spikes that deters trespassers—the most inexperienced ones, at least. This was how—most often with a few beers, a bottle of rum, and a baguette (a little pâté too, probably, the makings of a basic sandwich)—we'd manage to spend some time above the valley. Not necessarily the whole night, but enough time to take in the city where we lived, the network of orange-lit streets circumscribing shadowy areas. During the last of these expeditions, it had started raining around four a.m., and we'd all climbed back down with a certain urgency. As we walked along rue Paul-Bert, which runs parallel to the RER tracks, the sidewalk crunched under our feet; it was littered with snails that must have been brought out by the rain.

"They're there for the taking," you said.

"Yeah, except then, you have to purge them for two, three days," said Azlat. "And it's pretty disgusting."

But you knelt to scoop up a few handfuls anyway, and as we made our way down toward the old town hall, your stride was careful, punctuated by a rattling noise: the shells, in your pockets. The next morning before class, in the hallway, Pham asked you if you'd eaten them.

It was with this group of friends and a few others that, around the same time, we'd tried to push through the barbed wire surrounding the old Curie laboratory on rue de la Convention, the holy grail of loitering, if you will; the radioactive zone. But now that I think about it, I don't know if you were with us then. I remember you on the aqueduct and in the house that, for mysterious reasons (perhaps because of the rings of gilded mosaic tiles around the windows), we called Villa Byzantine. There, you prayed, after a beer or two, over the corpses of dead pigeons. Villa Byzantine had been marked for demolition after years of disuse. We rummaged the closets and lifted the floorboards in search of some imagined booty or, idiots that we were, a cadaver as mummified as those birds. I even seem to recall you bragging about having slept there alone one night. The Byzantine was on rue Templier, number 9 or 11, I can't say for sure; in those days, none of us thought to photograph the scenes of our petty little crimes. It was destroyed, along with the house next door, after being occupied by some Togolese students, evicted from their massive squat in Cachan—but I knew nothing of this story before my recent return. In Villa Byzantine's narrow front garden, ailanthuses grew, unfurling their foul-smelling flowers; in the spring, their powdery pollen covered everything. The trunk of one of those trees had pushed up the front steps. There are no more stinking ailanthuses at 9 or 11, but a cube-shaped house, all glass and wood. The immense bay window on the first floor reveals a dining room straight out of a magazine, a room where no one ever sets foot (but you, having haunted these streets until the day you died, would no doubt say otherwise).

To tell the truth, I'd forgotten you. Villa Byzantine, the

forbidden lab, the aqueduct, the Parc du Coteau, the Bièvre valley crossing, the cottage once rented by the Marquis de Sade: I remembered all that well, but without you. I can't say when exactly our paths diverged for good—not long after the last visit to the aqueduct, of that I'm certain, but when this expedition took place, I don't know anymore. And it wasn't as if we'd slowly drifted apart or simply fallen out of touch; on the contrary, the break had been clean. It happened on an afternoon we'd spent at your house, on rue Bougard—at your grandfather's house, where you lived. He was sick and could no longer get around without an oxygen tank attached to a little cart. While he listened to music in his office, we smoked a cigar you'd "stolen" from him (he wasn't allowed to touch them anymore). The walls trembled slightly and there, in your room, where no sunlight could penetrate, you showed me your collections: photos cut out from magazines that my parents would surely have forbidden me to look at—I often dreamed about them later, wandering in sleep through dozens of buildings and houses in search of that pale room wallpapered with dead flesh; I crossed yellow valleys that opened up in the middle of the city, fixated on the particular smell of your skin, which, in these dreams, was no longer yours, but simply the smell of the earth stretching out beneath the sidewalks, a pungent smell of engine grease and ancient filth—daggers that you claimed were German, books bound in black faux leather that indexed the horrors of the previous century. Then, moving toward me, head lowered, you breathed an apologetic sigh and pushed me up against your absurd bookshelves, a kitchen knife in hand. I remember that I'd been able to escape your lair only when the music stopped and a terrible ringing sounded: a dragon's cry, a wailing of martyrs that made you freeze. Was it the sound of a defective alarm, your ailing grandfather hollering in pain? I never found out. I fled. I ran all the way up rue Bougard, my head swimming with images of your headless children laid out, limbs flaccid, on lab benches; of your suicides in pools of blood, your women hacked to pieces, my eyeballs throbbing in your room of staged torture.

I never spoke to you again after that and, if my memory is correct, you never took part in another of our nocturnal adventures. Following my lead, the group turned away from you, even though I'd never brought up your room, your weapons, or your wall of the dead. These things were like easily forgotten small abysses that came back only intermittently, in dreams or in the strange moments of vertigo that precede sleep. Your disappearance from the group and, eventually, from school (which I can't quite place in time, either) made this erasure complete. A year later, after graduation, I left my parents' house at the end of rue Politzer. It was only recently—some twenty years later, on my return to France—that I bought that same house from my parents (my mother, who'd moved to Port-Bail, kept a room). I'd been living there again for three or four months when I saw you on the square in front of Laplace station. To this day, I remain vaguely suspicious about your identity; perhaps you were only a body without a consciousness that I had decided to animate, for some reason, with the wayward spirit of a childhood friend. And yet you looked like him, and your smell was the same, concentrated: a vile stench.

In the days that followed this reunion of sorts, I learned that you still lived in the cinder-block cottage on rue Bougard. I saw you again one night in front of the station, lying on a stone bench. You were scratching your stomach. Then you got up and walked right past me. A shell that had been hollowed out and filled with who knows what other soul, you didn't recognize me; you had no clue who I was or who I'd been to you. I watched you make your way to the café at the bottom of avenue Laplace, and fell into step behind you. On rue de Stalingrad, you started to shadowbox in circles, letting out cries that sounded more like a dog's barking than any kind of human voice. You shook your fist at the sky, you howled and laughed. A young woman passed in front of you, walking a big dog with shaggy gray fur. From the way you looked at her, I knew it really was you, even before I saw you open the cottage gate.

It was that cannibalistic look you must have wanted to give me in your horrible room—impossible, in those days, when all you could do with your dark thoughts was read, photocopy, and paste.

My mother didn't even remember your name. I'd probably never told her about you. Azlat, Pham, Aline Sallé, yes: they'd all come over to our house.

"And you mean to tell me that with this guy, you would all climb up onto the aqueduct in the middle of the night?"

"Only on Fridays and Saturdays, Mom. We weren't out of our minds."

Your frequent appearances were governed by two simple laws: your level of filthiness, and your beard. A kind soul must have given you a shave and a bath and a change of clothes every couple weeks. You slept on the benches of the station square or under the shelter of bus stops, and passersby—women, especially, whom you leered at, scowling—would move away with unnerved looks on their faces. You always had a beer in hand, and yet I never once saw you eating. When I spotted you, I'd often think of the snails. You pissed against walls without trying to hide, at all hours of the day, probably at night too. And one day, waiting for the bus, I noticed you crossing avenue Laplace, a sneer on your face, to take a shit in a bed of flowers. You wiped your ass with a fistful of iris leaves, then held them out toward the avenue, toward us, with furious glee.

Always, in your wanderings, you would curse the sky, invoking gods with names no one could understand; always, the acrid smell of grease and stale piss in your wake, your frantic dances before the statues in our few city squares, your shirt raised to reveal an enormous, hairy stomach. Those wanderings sometimes took you farther. I once caught you on the other side of the aqueduct, in the Parc de Cachan, emerging from the bamboo garden, stooped over, a hand on your lower abdomen. You'd just masturbated, I think. Your face was flushed with ecstasy, eyes rolled back. I doubted for a moment that, with so much joy under your belt, you could ever have been the sad teenager with a kitchen knife.

Two or three months after I returned—and this has nothing to do with you—I'd gotten into the habit of taking inventory, street by street, of the plants that grew along the base of the walls. Dandelions, carnations, pansies, and violets that had escaped from nearby gardens, mugwort, catchflies, daisies, poppies, gypsywort, nettles, fig trees whose roots pushed up through the walls and made cracks in them. It was March or April, maybe a little later, after a winter when we'd had more than a full week of snow (I don't know how you managed to stay alive during that time, and I didn't see you for months). I would walk along rue Paul-Bert, by the tracks of the RER, or rue de Stalingrad, which becomes a bridge over the A6 motorway—a bridge now on the edge of ruin and from which, when I was young, I sometimes thought of jumping to smash my skull on one of the rails below. It would be a hideous death, the kind you would have been thrilled to document at that age. I'd take rue Benoît-Malon, rue Victor-Basch, rue Albert-Legrand, rue Cauchy, occasionally streets on the other side of the valley. Once, I found myself on the Voie du Fossé where, by an extraordinary stroke of luck, the gate had been left open; there, a stone path stretches between two concrete walls, covering the Bièvre River that flows underground with a hollow sound. That was where I found the first bird: a pigeon, probably killed by a cat, its chest torn open, lungs gone—head missing too. Almost all that remained were its wings and feet, stiffened and slightly spread apart. The next day, wanting to listen to the river again (I don't think our group had ever bothered with this route, too easy for us), I found the gate closed. I walked instead through the grounds of the old Cité des Irlandais—so unfamiliar to me that they may as well be on foreign land—and almost all the way to Villejuif and the Maison Marin, an art supply store where Pham used to steal tubes of paint for her mother, a penniless artist. I had helped her only once or twice; my hands tremble when I steal, with shame and inexperience.

I even called Pham one day to tell her about you, because I needed these repugnant visions—your bald head and weary fat face, your inarticulate cries, whatever you exposed, your flabby stomach, your dirty ass, your flesh that I sensed was already rotting on your bones—to leave my head and wear out someone else's conscience for a while.

"Now that you mention it, yes," she said. "But it's an effort to remember. That whole time is a blur. We really were all over the place then."

And then—every two or three days, maybe?—more headless

birds began to appear along my route. There were pigeons, a magpie, crows, and, one day, even a baby seagull. It lay there, the poor thing, on rue Paul-Bert, beside the gate that blocks access to the rail embankment, in a clump of poppies. Everything in that place seems to be falling apart: near the grating, the sidewalk, already very narrow, is crumbling from years of use, crammed with poorly parked cars and battered trucks; cobblestones jut out of the pavement, the asphalt broken up by shrubs with gnarled branches that scratch at your legs and face.

I found the seagull in the middle of a heat wave. Feeling adventurous while returning from the lab, I decided to walk from Bagneux to my house on rue Politzer. I took rue de la Gare, which leads from the highway—swept clean that day by a strong, warm breeze—to the Arcueil-Cachan station. The street is lined with low houses. Above one of them sits the marquee of a cinema that no longer exists. As I walked past the ground-floor window, I heard a dull noise: a small child, pale and almost naked, beat his fists against the bars that separated him from the street. Then he slowly inserted his head between the bars and pulled it back quickly, doing this several times, until his temples turned red. Too late, I begged him in a low voice to stop. The boy looked at me unblinkingly, with a kind of surly satisfaction that was uncanny for his age.

He was just making a face, I told myself. And I thought of the other children I'd come across recently, who were playing with plastic swords in the otherwise vacant garden of the community center, and how it seemed as if they were the only ones left, along with me, in this radioactive city. And farther on, just past the aqueduct, a pile of beige feathers mottled with dried blood—the seagull. Its head was missing, as were some of its insides. It was on that day, I think, in the white heat, that I recalled our nights up on the aqueduct—I had found the exact spot where we'd placed the ladder—and the night we walked home in the rain: the crackling of snail shells, the avid smile that crossed your face as you knelt to scoop them up. The day of the seagull, whose rotting carcass I didn't want to touch—it was still there the next day but gone the third time I passed—I caught sight of you from a distance, resting your elbows on the railing of the bridge on rue Berthollet, above the tracks, watching the trains go by. You raised your arms in that wild way of yours, and you howled.

I took a much longer route home than usual. The idea came to me as I stood in front of the statues of dancers in the Cité Zola, a man and a woman, both naked, their outstretched palms raised (only the skies know if they're screaming): these birds along my route were your doing, an obscure message you were trying to send me, even if you didn't seem to recognize me. Not an offering, nor a threat. No. I saw in all of this an expression of the humanity that had stayed locked away in the squalid room of your youth. An invitation to join you there? Probably not. Nevertheless, I was careful to avoid you in the days that followed. I no longer went down to avenue Laplace, where the chances of spotting you skulking under the RER bridge or lying on a bench—eyeing groups of children, the corn vendor, the Korean students from the Catholic residence, never me—were too great. But soon enough I found three dead rats, one each day, in front of my house: the first one beside the neighbors' garbage can, the second in the gutter, the third at the intersection of avenue de la République. And I imagined you all at once as a comedian, a phony bum, and an actual monster; a crazed hunter filled with a growing rage that would drive you, fatally, closer and closer to your victims. My mother and the two friends to whom I spoke of you—too evasively, probably—responded separately with the same odd reproach. I'd been so happy since my return, they said, that I had to invent some misfortune or a reason to worry myself into a frenzy. One of these friends, who is also a neighbor, claimed that she had never seen you before. In short, you were my ghost, my shadow, my doppelgänger. Your sadness and failures might have been my own, extracted from my body like oil, refined and concentrated in this drifting soul who walked the streets that sweltering summer, methodically beheading little animals. I decided to photograph, in addition to the plants along the walls, the corpses you'd left, which seemed to be quickly growing in number. I noted the locations on maps I found online and looked for geographical connections. On the verge of sleep one night, I thought I understood that you were bringing the heads of these creatures to the Bièvre, a short walk from your place, via the Voie du Fossé; that you alone had the key to the gate and that you left these offerings in the gaps between the stones that covered the river, which you worshipped as a deity. But I recognize that this *you* was not you at all, that this servant of a river goddess who'd been quashed, defiled, poisoned, and finally buried was really nothing more than an invention of my mind.

But. All the same, *where were you trying to lead me?* After this vision of the Bièvre, I wanted to abandon these pursuits that were pointlessly distracting me from my work, from my ordinary routine; I vowed to stay away from the Vanne promenade, from the caved-in sidewalks of Paul-Bert, and even the bird shelter on rue Branly, where an old woman fed chickadees, sparrows, and, I believe, a goldfinch. It was in these places that most of your corpses could be found. The one you left me as an offering (yes, finally) in the Parc du Coteau put all the others to shame.

I should say, first, that I had wanted to go down to Gen-tilly and walk around awhile—the weather had cooled—so I made my way to the end of rue des Champs-Élysées. I saw you there, lying in the communal vegetable garden across the RER station, scratching your back. This time, you made an effort to look at me, perhaps even to recognize me. Your gaze was clear, I thought, and rather cold. I turned around and, with-out looking back, walked all the way to the Parc du Coteau. I wanted to stand there by the skate park, watch the kids, let the din of their boards wash over me. If need be, I would walk all the way up to the sloping prairie, I would close my eyes and let images rise up from the recesses of my mind: in the hollow of the valley, the sea-green goddess of the Bièvre, who had nothing more to do with you; atop the embankment, the hun-dreds of girls who, in the time of the Zone and the fortifications, had mysteriously honored the river with their dances. It was on the climb up that I found the animal. A dog, it must have been, though its body resembled no known breed, its fur gray blue, its paws lacerated—and, yes, its head was missing. Flies buzzed at its wounds. As I approached, they swarmed away in clouds.

I climbed the stairs that cut through the park to reach two large new buildings, two apartment complexes with undulat-ing balconies. I trembled, imagining myself headless, my own orifices swarming with crazed flies. More than fear, a terror so great that I felt I no longer had a body: each molecule buzzing separately and repelling the others.

It was impossible to sleep soundly in the prairie as I'd hoped to. Every passerby—man, woman, young, old—dressed in your cloak of sweat, came drifting toward me with a knife in hand. And yet, I was at least able to doze, first on my stomach, face against the ground—thinking, despite my supposed happiness, that it would be easy to die like this, and adjusting my shoulders in preparation—and then on my back, elbow bent over my face, listening to the noises from outside blend with those—my heartbeat, the dull-sounding movements of my intestines—from within. *Met Pierre Soulié's mother. Soulier. Leave your sister alone, will you? Come back, I said. You don't have a cig? I'll give one back to you tomorrow. Forgot my pack. A lighter. Come on, now, come back. All you ever do is smoke, you bum. Omar, d'you see? Vassouri. It's Vassouri, I'm sure. Sure. Time to go home. Vassouri!* Hours spent staring at the sky, my arm over my face like a shield. As I walked back down, I thought I saw, at a distance, three children leaning over the hole where the dog lay. I took care to move away before they could call an adult for help. Or maybe, in the excitement of finding their first corpse, they wouldn't need help burying it.

I walked without thinking about where I was going until I reached rue Bougard. My muscles felt strong again; my legs carried me along with remarkable ease. I made my way around the edge of the cemetery—it's where my father's buried, and I'll no doubt join him there one day, above the Bièvre, I thought, turning my gaze away. Another footbridge passes over the Voie du Fossé, just before the city hall. I understood, looking down from above, the meaning of the huge spray-paint mural that covers the wall (a little man in a red hat, his mouth wide open, swallowing rabbits). A woman wearing a turban was taking pictures of some rosebushes. A boy I often see at the skate park cruised down avenue Laplace on his board, with his long red hair, soft features, and curved lips. If only I could slip into his skin and skate far away from here.

Instead, I took rue de Stalingrad, toward Gentilly. I have

a particular fondness for three of the houses that stand side
by side—les Figuiers, les Églantiers, Villa Valentine—even if,
of these three, only Villa Valentine seems occupied; the two
others have had their shutters closed since my return, and not
long ago, I think I saw a foreclosure notice on the door of les
Figuiers, whose facade is decorated with ceramic tiles depict-
ing a number of demons sticking out their tongues. *I wish I
could save them*, I thought as I passed in front of the door, rein-
forced by a metal plate and two padlocks, for the day is near, I
fear, when les Figuiers will be torn down. And standing above
the highway, now, I remember a snowy night when everything
had come to a standstill: the train tracks lay covered in snow,
drivers in anoraks walked circles around cars that had stopped
running, flapping their arms and exhaling streams of fog. With
Pham? Yes, certainly. I remember that we'd gone to drink a hot
toddy at the Nelson, or maybe the Costa Brava, at the corner
of rue Bougard and avenue Pasteur. And smoked, probably;
what comes back to me is a mixture of the taste of cigarettes
and hot chocolate. And on a snowy night like that, we never
would have tried to walk down the steep slope of your street
(you're already gone, it's the winter before my departure).
The gate isn't closed; the small courtyard in front of the house
is overrun by gooseberry and butterfly bushes; baby fig trees
grow at the foot of the front steps. Through the half-opened
door, I hear an indistinct breathing sound, more mechanical
than human. I go in, my bare hands soon pulling the corner of
my shirt up to my face; the stench is so thick, so insinuating,
it darkens everything. And yet I remember the path to your
room that I followed only once, and even if I'd forgotten it,
the stench would lead me there. It grabs my wrists, it drags me
toward the staircase; with its long hair, it could strangle me or
make me trip and fall. It leads me to you.

* * *

In your room, lying among the heads, the beaks, the dead feathers, the shells; in your room, arms and legs already blackened; in your room, your stomach bloated with gas, ready to explode. In your room, a man without a head, eyes resting on the hollowed-out neck and pointing—I believe—toward the sky, toward the gods who let you down.

THE DAY JOHNNY DIED

BY PATRICK PÉCHEROT

Nanterre

Translated by Nicole Ball

T hat's when I made up my mind, I think. The guy kept repeating: "It happened the day Johnny died." He tried to explain. He didn't mean to kill. The kid falling, the noise of his skull crashing on cement. He didn't want any of that. But the day Johnny* died was special in the mighty chain of cause and effect. Solar eclipse, total blackness. Then, that guy, with his sarcastic look . . . "Jojo's gone? You're all alone now?" No, the kid had said nothing of the sort. He just idly leaned on the wall like he did every day, glancing at him scornfully, yes sir, scornfully, like every day. He let out a glob of spit like he did a hundred times a day, like every day. But that's just it—nothing would be like every day anymore.

That's what landed me back in Nanterre. Just a human-interest story. A short mention in the paper. A possible topic for a writer out of inspiration . . . Michel Darget was the name of the murderer. People who knew him were left speechless. They'd suspected nothing. I quickly realized that it had been a while since they'd seen him. Michel Darget had made himself scarce. He no longer signed up for boccie tournaments, deserted the Association of Retired Bus

---

* Johnny Halliday (6/15/1943–12/5/2017): the most famous French rocker. From the 1960s until his death, his songs accompanied several generations. His funeral attracted hundreds of thousands of fans of all ages.

and Metro Drivers; nobody ever ran into him at the union anymore . . .

The not-quite-old men I'd met wondered what could have possibly gone through his mind. They knew that solitude had grabbed one of them, and that their turn would soon come.

Over the course of our meetings, I had started to paint a portrait of Michel Darget.

He'd make a beautiful subject for a story.

In his youth, in the middle of the previous century, Michel screwed nuts and bolts at the Simca plant, located between the rond-point des Bergères and place de la Boule. He was sixteen, old enough to be a factory worker back then. As for the shepherdess of the rond-point, she had stopped taking her sheep to the meadow many, many years ago. The girls who came after her were now learning stenography at Pigier before ruining their fingernails on the keys of typewriters. They'd paste photos of their favorite rockers on their locker doors—Eddy Mitchell, Dick Rivers, Elvis, or Johnny Hallyday—and dream of *retenir la nuit* ("spending the night with them"). In the spirit of the time, Michel had picked an American name: Mick. It made perfect sense and sounded good.

With his first wages, Mick got a moped. Orange, with the gas tank on the side, motorcycle-style. In his free time, he'd make his bike backfire in front of Pigier. Eddy Mitchell and his Chaussettes Noires sang "Dactylo Rock." The girl he had his eye on was named Sylvie. *Cette fille-là, mon vieux, elle est terrible* ("That girl, man, she's terrific").

Before going home, he'd have a beer and play a few rounds of pinball at the Saïdani café behind route des Fusillés; twenty years earlier, during German occupation, resisters and hostages were driven down the same road on the way to the firing squads at Mont-Valérien.

Sporting a pompadour, a faux-leather jacket, and jeans introduced by the American GIs in Saint-Germain, he would act tough, surreptitiously admiring his reflection in the mirror of the café. On summer nights, Mama Saïdani hung Chinese lanterns in her yard. Stuck between a garage and a mattress shop, her sorry-looking yard turned into a festive little dance hall. The jukebox alternated between accordion trills, the syrupy love songs of Luis Mariano, and Dick Rivers's Chats Sauvages. Side by side but in separate groups, you had the café regulars, Nanterre's junkyard dealers, working families out for a good time, the neighborhood youths . . .

Mick had just started working an old pinball machine. A tough guy with a leather wristband admired his playing style. They grabbed some beers. Two drinks later and Mick was a pal of the junkyard crowd. Flattered to be accepted into the tribe. Wild, outlawed, out of society, out of everything—scrap pickers, small dealers in copper, lead, zinc, old pots and pans recoated a dozen times, bedsprings, washtubs, and car wrecks. Bums with empty pockets, pierced hearts, and crucifixes tattooed on their biceps, their faces roasted by brazier fires and cheap wine. Clocking in and out, breaking your back on the assembly line? No way; not for them. Scrap metal likes to grow on work sites, so gleaning it is tempting. Mick got pinched as he was hauling rebar on a tarp-covered truck. The moon can't help but shine. Lovers love the moon. So do cops.

All the reported thefts from the work sites—they would eventually be used to build the high-rises of la Défense—were pinned on them by a judge in a fancy robe. With no criminal record, Mick got six months. He spent them at the district penitentiary where small-time hoods, beggars, and old bums were sent to rot. And for good measure, they added a short stay at la Santé, the big jail in Paris.

Johnny, the youth idol, had not sung "Le pénitencier" yet. Mick was ahead of him. He was also ahead of him when he joined the army. He had enlisted before call-up, sick of being turned down for jobs.

Algeria is a beautiful country. You can even practice pigeon shooting in the sun out there. A young recruit, not too many ideas in your brain—forward march! Your pompadour shaved off, your bag too heavy, chores, long empty hours, stupid jokes in the barracks, fart and beer-can competitions, yomps, waking with a start, trudging with constant fear in your gut, being ambushed, decomposing corpses, flies, shit, curdled blood, dirty whorehouses when you're on furlough, cheap booze, bad headaches, and all the other stuff you will never tell. When the time comes, you'll either shut up or rewrite history to forget the real one, hideous and smelly like an eviscerated corpse. Mick chose to keep quiet. God knows what's gnawing at your guts when demons are prowling inside you.

The shabby premises of the ARAC, the Association Républicaine des Anciens Combattants, on rue des Anciennes Mairies, smelled musty. Its glory days were long past. The vets of the Great War, the war to end all wars, were gone. The troops of the following one were now joining them in the graveyard, as were those from the wars that didn't have names.

I wouldn't learn much from the Algeria vet who had arranged to meet with me. Mick didn't attend their events much. He'd joined because the association defended their right to a retirement pension.

"Your rights, if you don't fight to keep them . . . You get the picture . . ."

I did.

Mick never attended commemorations, but he rarely skipped the annual lamb barbecue. "A hearty appetite!" That changed after he got into a fight with another attendee. "I can't even recall what it was about. The Sidi Brahim we serve with the méchoui does go to your head. But he never came back. Too bad, there's not many of us left . . ."

The veteran poured me coffee in a plastic cup. He noticed the magazine I had put on the desk.

"*Mademoiselle Âge tendre*? I completely forgot about this one. When she was fifteen, my sister would wait for it to be out like you wait for spring to come . . . Where did you find it?"

At the market on rue des Trois Fontanot, named after the three heroic brothers who joined the MOI*, a secondhand bookseller had spread out his stock of dated magazines and rarities. I found what appeared to be a "girly" equivalent to *Salut les copains*, year 1967. The picture of Françoise Hardy on the cover had attracted me. The old guy couldn't believe it: this issue of *Mademoiselle Âge tendre*, a magazine for teenage girls, covered Johnny's concert at the Majestic Cinema in Algiers. The poster, plastered on the theater, announced that Johnny would be accompanied by a band called les Black Burds.

Majestic Cinema. Stucco. Plaster, and caryatids . . . The French *pieds-noirs* had enjoyed their horchata there in front of Italian peplums. That was before they were compelled to choose between packing up and getting shot.

* * *

* *Main-d'œuvre immigrée*, a Resistance network of the Communist Party. Mostly composed of immigrant workers, among them many Jews from Eastern Europe.

In 1967, while Johnny danced the twist in Algiers, Mick was working at the Seine paper mills. A low-paying job. Seventeen acres of factory, machines, and smokestacks.

The working-class suburbs, the Red Belt communes, were hard at work. They smelled of gas, oil, tobacco, lunch-box food—but mostly dust. Cadum soap, made in the factory whose perfume coated Courbevoie, could never get rid of that dust. The endearing face of the brand, Baby Cadum, was painted on the gables of buildings. Tired workers returning home after work didn't know that the baby, featured prominently in la Défense, was Maurice Obréjan. In 1925, he was voted France's most beautiful baby in a competition held by Cadum. Fifteen years later he was stripped of his civil rights, in accordance with anti-Jewish laws enacted by the Vichy regime. His father was Romanian, his mother Polish. He joined the Resistance at seventeen. Deported to the Buchenwald concentration camp, he was the only survivor of his family, which had gone up in smoke.

At the paper mill, Mick exchanged his black faux leather for canadienne—more proletarian. A coworker gave him *Nous les garçons et les filles*, the Communist Party monthly youth magazine, like *Salut les copains* but Komsomol-style. Johnny was making the headlines. He'd just donated the proceeds of one of his concerts to the striking miners. From buddy to comrade, the distance is short. Mick crosses over. Sitting in his wallet now is his union card, next to an autographed photo of Johnny. A few months before, Mick went to Vincennes to attend la Fête de *l'Humanité*, the annual festival held by the Communist daily *l'Humanité*. Johnny was on the program. He didn't show up. He was found unconscious in his room in Neuilly. Attempted suicide. *Noir c'est noir* ("Black is black").

Open-air markets: marché Lénine, marché des Bergères

. . . Between the vegetable stands and the street peddlers, Mick sells *l'Humanité Dimanche*, the Sunday paper. His voice mingles with the patter of the tableware vendors. He's happy to spread the good word, even if it means freezing his butt off. In the early morning, black coffee and cigarettes. His pompadour is now more subdued; he smiles, Gagarin-style. When he returned from Algeria, Sylvie was gone. War has collateral damage. To be a veteran at age twenty is hard. You've got your whole life to carry the burden.

The Communist Party teaches Mick that the working class knows no borders. Yet he can't help but think of the many Algerians in Nanterre. Emergency projects with decrepit concrete walls, shantytowns. Muddy terrain, tin roofs, crumbling bricks, humid hovels where cribs are suspended to protect babies from the rats. Wretched living conditions, poverty, shame, injustice. But listen: they wanted to have their own country, so why cram in here? Peace, progress, friendship among peoples, blah blah blah—he's all for it, Mick. He agrees 100 percent. That's not the problem. Have you ever had to walk around heaps of trash, clutter that not even garbage collectors can pick up? That's the problem. *And believe me, it stinks!*

In the party, France's largest at the time, the problem elicits an embarrassed silence. Georges Marchais, its future head, has not yet declared: "Our immigration policy poses serious problems. We must stop immigration, both official and clandestine." For the time being, the mayor does what he can; he visits the shantytown, sends a comrade doctor there. No other doctors dare to go. Thanks to the mayor, transit lodgings and housing projects are built.

As for Mick, he lives in his parents' house. His father built it with his friends. Small garden allotments, workers with a beaver's spirit, everybody pitches in. *Souvenirs, sou-ou-venirs, je vous retrouve dans mon cœur et vous faites refleuri-i-r tou-ous mes rêves de bonhe-eur* ("Memories, me-e-mo-ries, I find you again in my heart and you make a-a-all my dreams of happiness come back again"). A bouquet on top of the roof, champagne. The sign on the wall: *Villa Jeannette.* His mother's name. A little tear at the corner of their eyes on the day of their house-warming party.

The working class, too, has property rights. It's been engraved in the cement of solidarity. Home is here! *Nous n'avions au fond de nos poches qu'un peu d'espoir, mais nous partions comme Gavroche, le cœur assez bavard* ("All we had in our pockets was a little hope, but we went forth like Gavroche, our hearts did not mope").

Villa Jeannette didn't resist the pickax of the demolition workers, but some of the individual houses still standing have kept growing geraniums at the foot of the concrete plaza where city hall stands. At the beginning of the eighties, when I tried to explain to an elected official that having quotas for foreigners in need of housing wasn't the best idea, he asked me to leave. A dialogue of the deaf between a Communist official and the young union representative I was then. I was accompanying a worker who'd been denied housing in the name of the party's new policy: "When the concentration of immigrants becomes too important [. . .] the housing crisis worsens; apartments in housing projects are sorely lacking and many French families can't have access to them." I argued that Augustine was not a foreigner: she was from the Caribbean and thus 100 percent French. They just showed me the door.

A photo on the page of a newspaper. Extracted from a folder by a man who wears a cap and a wool scarf. He's at the age when the cold grabs you with no warning. He's in charge of the archives of the Communist cell Maurice Barbet. A film of dust is dancing in the light. The man points at the bottom of the photo: "There!"

A Parisian boulevard, a human tide, banners, signs . . . Mick is marching in the third row, his gaze on the lens. Who is he smiling at? Someone not in the picture? The photographer? The people who will look at the photo? Above his head, a banner: *Seine Paper Mills*. Far behind it: *Citroën*. And *Panzani*. And other names you can't decipher because they're too deep in the crowd.

The photo was taken in Paris on May 13, 1968. Nanterre had lit the fuse of the big fat firecracker that was shaking France. Red Nanterre, black Nanterre . . .

Mick has put on weight. Hard work has a way of withering you before your time. The young fools who dreamed of Mao the way others worship the Virgin Mary have not yet broken their baby teeth on the assembly lines. Soon some of them will show up at Mama Saïdani's door to bring the good word to the working class wetting their whistle between the three shifts. More than one will ruin their liver there; cheap red wine mixed with the red of the flag. But right now, everything is possible. That's what Mick came to shout with millions of others on May 13, 1968. End the infernal speed of the production lines, allow freedom of speech, guarantee a thousand-franc minimum wage . . . There's a smell of spring and freedom in the air.

The newspaper has turned yellow.

The order returns, the hunt for union activists is on. Mick is left out. "After the strikes, he couldn't find a job," says the archivist. "Bosses would call each other before hiring . . . The party got him a job. Working for the city. Driver. One thing led to another and the RATP hired him as a conductor. We lost touch . . ." But the old man wants me to know: "Mick was a good man." Before closing the folder, he adds: "Those were different times." Times reflected in his eyes, despite their cataracts . . .

Working for the city, Mick meets Gisèle. She's a secretary at the registry office, where today he's delivering a load of administrative forms. On her desk, *Antoinette*, the union monthly for women. A glance, a burst of laughter. It's enough to start a life of thirty years.

Happy, quiet life. They buy their furniture at the Galeries Barbès. A two-room apartment with a kitchen. Nanterre lilacs, Nanterre wisteria. An evening stroll in the sweet smell of the linden trees. Snowy Nanterre, frosty Nanterre. Cuddling under the comforter at night. Decorated with pastel clouds, the round towers of the Aillaud projects shoot into the sky. The lovebirds never tire of kissing. "They look like candy sticks." Émile Aillaud wanted his buildings to look that way: no angles, no sharp edges. Nothing but curves, roundness. Dreams all the way, up to the windows that look like drops of water.

Que je t'aime, que je t'aime, que je t'aime . . . ("How I love you, love you, love you . . .").

But life, so fragile . . . The beautiful towers are falling apart. When did the first crack appear? Slowly, the rest followed. The smell of the garbage chutes, the noise when they dump stuff in them. Then they are closed and you have to take your trash can down and empty it in dumpsters swarming with rats. The graffiti in the elevator—when it's not out of order: *Jordan's cock, Nadège loves to be fucked, your sister's a whore, fuck the police, fuck the neighbors, fuck everybody!* The music isn't the same either; it jumps at you like a punch in the face from one of those young thugs who think they're from the Bronx. When they're tired of doing push-ups on the street and chin-ups on bus shelters, they hang around aimlessly, speak backward, and don't budge an inch at the entrance of the hallway. They spend the whole fucking day there with their ghetto blasters the size of trucks, bawling away.

Mick knows that boys will be boys, and he doesn't forget that he too was young. *Ma mère me dit régulièrement, tu ne fais rien, tu perds ton temps, tu ferais mieux de travailler au lieu de t'en aller traîner, hein-hein-hein . . .* ("My mom keeps telling me, do something, you're wasting your time, go find a job instead of hanging out all day, blah blah blah . . ."). That's no reason to break everybody's balls. In 1967, after Johnny's concert on place de la Bastille, France-Soir could have headlined: *Salut les voyous* ("Hello, Hooligans")—a parody of *Salut les copains*. But back then, they didn't organize dogfights in basements, didn't sell drugs at the entrance to the projects, didn't turn electric meters into dope cabinets. Mick doesn't care if the situation is the same at other projects, like the Zilina or the Pâquerettes; he and Gisèle live at Aillaud. The whole place has climbed near the top of the chart for crime? To celebrate such a feat, those pain-in-the-ass kids set off fireworks in the dumpsters.

Johnny votes for the Right. Mick isn't too sure anymore.

When the first Islamist preachers arrived, one minister of the interior was delighted. They would calm things down and set the little savages on the right path to prayer. Twenty years later, little brats stuffed with sermons cut themselves off from the world, the gang leaders were hooked on speed and sura cocktails, and the old imams were sent back to their studies.

"They don't listen, they say we don't know the Book. What about them? What do they know about religion? Do they wear the Prophet's qamis? So what? Religion, it's some-thing you wear in your heart. And what about these other guys there, wearing the gangster's T-shirts . . ."

"Tony Montana."

"That's right. Was Tony Montana halal?"

The old part of Nanterre feels like a village. Little squares, paved streets, almond-green shutters, shops, outdoor cafés, and small restaurants. I can never resist the tea they have there; that Gunpowder tea mixed with fresh mint is condu-cive to bonding. Especially when Akim serves it. From our high school days he's kept old loves. On the walls of his café, he's pinned the sleeves of LPs we used to steal in the super-market: James Brown, Otis Redding, Sam and Dave . . . brass and Hammond organ . . . Akim winks as he listens to the old man's speech. It's good-natured Nanterre here. Kebab and mironton beef stew, méchoui and Camembert. A post-card almost. In high school, Akim was already practicing the art of blending in. The cafeteria was split in two—one half with pork, the other without. He didn't care where he ate. At lunchtime, I don't think I ever crossed the invisible line that separated the guzzlers.

Mick never went to Akim's place. Neither did his vic-tim: the Aillaud Towers people don't bother to come that far down. "The 'suburbs'—a stupid word if you ask me! A Nutella term the newspapers love to spread all over their columns. The unrest in the suburbs . . . The suburbs . . . As if they were just one big thing. What a joke! Take Nanterre, for instance. We have two, three, ten suburbs here. The offices in the busi-ness district of la Défense, the Aillaud Towers, the Folie, the old neighborhood . . ."

Mick had locked himself inside the Aillaud, a stone's throw from the office towers. Like the tough kids he tried to stay away from. Maybe, in the long run, you could lose your-self there.

I continued up to rue des Suisses, hoping to retrieve a few images from my past. I recognized nothing. The silhouette of the beautiful girl who used to share the seat of my bike, and the many times I was kept after school at Lycée Joliot-Curie, had vanished. The massive headquarters of the right-wing Front National, recently renamed Rassemblement National, stood erect where her building used to be. I remember climb-ing the stairs of her house with a racing heart.

Chez Tonton, the Portuguese restaurant where the FN staff eats regularly. The iron curtain was drawn. My cell dis-played the clients' ratings. "Pleasant atmosphere. Delicious food. A place worth checking out . . ." Some joker had writ-ten, "The president's future chef." Google Images showed Tonton behind his counter proudly displaying his FN mem-bership card.

Looking back, I see us, Christiane and me huddled to-gether, listening to Bob Dylan on a stereo. I wondered if times had changed for the worse, against all hope.

I walked back toward the Fontenelles. On rue Chevreul, the fountain where kids used to splash each other stopped running forty years ago, but I could still hear it gurgling. Jürg Kreienbühl had no idea how much his paintings were worth on the art market when he painted Ahmed the street sweeper drawing water from the fountain. And he couldn't care less about it. The Swiss painter of the shantytown would have en-joyed some of the graffiti that decorated the area, for sure.

I was taking a photo of a Saint-Exupéry tagged on the wall of an abandoned plumbing workshop when a tough guy stepped out. Surprised, he pulled back. Then, as my cell was focusing, he said sharply, "No photos here, sir." His tone had the sweetness of a warning. He obviously was someone who didn't need to yell to be obeyed.

"No problem, I'm just taking a picture of Saint-Ex, nothing else." I tried to win him over.

"If you're an artist, take a picture of him in your head, please . . ." Without raising his voice.

I thought it wise to put my Samsung away. The big guy thanked me with a nod and watched me walk away. I didn't bother to look for a good spot from where I could catch some bigwig boss with a fat gold chain leaving that building and hustling into an SUV with tinted windows. Under the watchful eye of his bodyguard.

What would I do with all that?

Centuries ago, when I was teaching high school, a girl asked me defiantly: "Noir novels? Why do you make life so dark? You're bringing us down. There are lots of good things happening in our suburbs . . ." I didn't know how to answer. I'd always been just passing through, and once again I was about to put definitive words on something I knew nothing about.

On the allée des Demoiselles d'Avignon, right where the tragedy took place, a poster invited the locals to a discussion on the future of the towers: *Renovation or demolition?*

The question summed me up. I was interested in Michel Darget because he provided me with a character. I started to sketch him as I wandered around. I didn't have a clear picture of his victim yet, but his turn would come. I had some idea about him that I needed to refine.

He was young and his name was Jordan. I'll put the inescapable baseball cap on his head and dress him in a matching sweatshirt and pants. Nikes too. He'd draw his cell phone the way gunfighters draw their six-shooters, and greet his buddies with "checks." I could never figure out what those checks meant. The big boss with the SUV entrusts him with his car keys when he comes to collect. "Here, kid. Keep an eye on it." Or something like that, to boost his ego, make him proud that Pablo Escobar trusts him. Soon, he's promoted to watcher in the big free market of the business. But he won't get a chance to work his way up. A mean headbutt stops his career short. The career of a poor kid dragged into the machine that turned him into a petty criminal.

He, his buddies, and their big brothers have ruined the lives of the residents, to the point where some retired old guy, usually quiet, goes nuts because some kid happened to look at him a bit too insistently.

The fine youth of the towers may be less accessible to me than Mick, but why bother inquiring when I already knew how they'd react to my questions? "It's for a book? Can you talk about me?" Or: "Jordan wasn't doing anything. The old guy just arrived, we didn't get it, he gave him a headbutt, right there. For nothing, I swear. I was shocked!" Or this: "You're a reporter? Yes, you are a reporter . . . We don't need no reporters here. Fake news, that's all they write!"

All of a sudden, I felt drained. This up-and-down, roller-coaster kind of mood was familiar. Feeling your heart sink in front of a ripped photo, the smile of a child, a stray dog, or an old poster yellowing on a wall . . . Renovation or demolition?

On a tous quelque chose en nous de Tennessee . . . ("There's a bit of Tennessee in all of us . . .").

I didn't return to Nanterre to follow in Mick's footsteps, but in the hope that I would retrace mine. I was clinging to my past the way Mick was hanging on to Johnny. With the illusion that I could retain a life. Mama Saïdani, Algeria, *l'Humanité Dimanche*, la Défense—all that brought me back to myself. As always. I was going to shape it all my way on paper, and through them, I would talk about myself. About me and my compassion. How generous that would make me.

Jordan had died for that. Mick had killed for that. For me. For my name on the cover of a book worth two bucks.

Before his funeral and the silent march to demand justice, Jordan was resting in the funeral home. Mick was waiting for his trial in the psychiatric ward of some hospital. According to the policeman I talked to, he was devastated when he learned that the young man he'd hit did not survive. To explain what he'd done, he kept repeating, over and over, in a litany, something about the death of Johnny Hallyday. In telling me that Mick had asked to see his wife, the cop made this gesture of screwing his index finger into his temple, to signify the guy was nuts: "His wife died ten years ago . . ."

The esplanade was swarming with men in three-piece suits, women in fashionable jackets and pastel jeans. Young executives on scooters were skating with this grotesque movement that would propel them faster from their offices to their homes where they would work remotely and feel indispensable. Later, the invisible army of nocturnal, tired immigrants would arrive and storm the towers of la Défense with their vacuum cleaners. I hurried up to cross the large square linking Nanterre to Puteaux. Gisèle was asleep in her family vault in the old cemetery. Wilted flowers on the grave. Since Mick's arrest, nobody came to replace them. In a beige marble plate, a photo of Gisèle in midlife, smiling confidently. And another picture. With Mick. Under their happy faces, a heart and two concert tickets: Johnny Hallyday, Las Vegas, November 24, 1996 . . .

An inscription on the stone: *Gisèle Darget, May 3, 1948– December 5, 2007.*

December 5 . . .

"The day Johnny died . . ."

Ten years to the day Mick had buried his love, he was burying what was left of their lives.

I didn't have the courage to go any further.

The interchange of la Défense led me to the highway. I avoided looking at the towers in the rearview mirror. Driving along the concrete ship of the new Paris la Défense Arena, capable of offering forty thousand spectators to the kings of rock and soccer, I was imagining the grandiose stage entrance The Boss could have treated himself to.

A tunnel engulfed me, interfering with the summer series devoted to Johnny. When I emerged into open air again, the rocker's voice burst out. I didn't know it could be so wrenching:

Regarder tomber la pluie
Écouter le souffle du vent
Accepter de ne pas comprendre le pourquoi des choses (. . .)
Et s'endormir seul . . .

Watch the rain fall
Listen to the wind blowing
Accept that you can't understand why things are the way they are (. . .)
And go to sleep all alone . . .

ABOUT THE CONTRIBUTORS

KATIE SHIREEN ASSEF (translator) is a writer, translator, and some-time bookseller living between Los Angeles and Marseille, France. A fan of international noir fiction, she has translated stories from Akashic Books's *Brussels Noir*, *Montreal Noir*, and *Marrakech Noir* anthologies. Her translation of Valérie Mréjen's novel *Black Forest* was published by Deep Vellum in 2019.

DAVID BALL (translator) has won two major prizes for his translations: from MLA (1995) for *Darkness Moves: An Henri Michaux Anthology*, and from the French-American Foundation (2014) for Jean Guéhenno's *Diary of the Dark Years*. His most recent work includes translating, introducing, and annotating Roger Gilbert-Lecomte's *Coma Crossing*, and translating Abdourahman Waberi's *The Divine Song* with frequent collaborator Nicole Ball. He is Professor Emeritus of French and Comparative Literature at Smith College.

NICOLE BALL (translator) has translated, from French into English, novels by Maryse Condé, Lola Lafon, Laurent Mauvignier, and Abdourahman Waberi, often in collaboration with David Ball. From English into French, she's translated thrillers by Jonathan Kellerman and William Casey Moreton, and most recently a graphic biography of Thelonius Monk, which won a 2018 French Jazz Academy prize. Retired from teaching, she spends her time between her native Paris and her adoptive town of Northampton, Massachusetts.

GUILLAUME BALSAMO was born in 1980, far from Île-de-France. Raised on a diet of pop culture, he is the coauthor of *Papier culture geek* and *Votez Cthulhu*, both published by Marabout. An enthusiast of crossing the boundaries between Paris and its suburbs alone and on foot, he divides his time between Ivry-sur-Seine and Paris's thirteenth arrondissement.

PAUL CURTIS DAW (translator) is a lawyer turned translator. His translation of Évelyne Trouillot's *Memory at Bay* was published in 2015 by the University of Virginia Press, and his translation of Olivier Targowla's *Narcisse on a Tightrope* is forthcoming from Deep Vellum's Dalkey Archive imprint. Daw's renditions of stories and other texts from France, Haiti, Belgium, Quebec, Réunion, and Romandy have appeared in numerous literary journals and several annual editions of the *Best European Fiction* anthology.

TIMOTHÉE DEMEILLERS was born in Angers, France, in 1984. He lived in the Czech Republic, Australia, and London before setting down his suitcases in Pantin. Passionate about the history of Central and Eastern Europe, he published his first novel, *Prague, faubourgs est*, in 2014. His 2017 book, *Jusqu'à la bête*, was awarded the Prix du Jeune Romancier Le-Touquet-Paris-Plage, the Prix Calibre 47 du festival Polar'Encontre, and the Prix du Deuxième Roman de Grignan.

HERVÉ DELOUCHE is a noir literature specialist, columnist, conference moderator, and noir festival coordinator. He was in charge of the full reissue of Jean Amila-Meckert's writing for Éditions Joëlle Losfeld, and he works as a copy editor for Gallmeister, Rivages, and Seuil. From 2007 to 2016, he was the president of 813, the first French association of noir literature lovers.

MARC FERNANDEZ, cofounder of the crime-fiction review *Alibi*, has been a journalist for twenty years, covering Spain and Latin America for the *Courrier international*. He is currently an editor and novelist; his works include *Mala vida* (published as *Mala Vida* by Skyhourse Publishing in the US), *Guérilla social club*, and *Bandidos*. With Jean-Christophe Rampal, he has cowritten several investigative works, including *La ville qui tue les femmes* and a novel, *Narco Football Club*.

KARIM MADANI grew up in Paris's Chinatown in the thirteenth arrondissement. At an early age, he immersed himself in American culture: crime novels, comic books, noir films, jazz, soul, funk, and hip-hop. A contributor to numerous periodicals specializing in urban culture, he is the author of the novels *Le jour du fléau*, *Casher nostra*, and *Blood Sample*, and of nonfiction on Spike Lee and Kanye West. His latest book, *Jewish Gangsta*, was published in 2017.

CLOÉ MEHDI was born in 1992 in a suburb of Lyon and developed a passion for writing during her adolescence. She won several writing competitions and then published her first novel, *Monstres en cavale*, in 2014. Her second, *Rien ne se perd*, was awarded the Trophée 813 and the Prix Mystère de la Critique. Her third, *Cinquante-trois présages*, was published in 2021.

PATRICK PÉCHEROT was born in Courbevoie in 1953. He has worked in the social sector, the trade-union sphere, and the news media. In 1996, he published his first novel, *Tiuraï*. He won the Grand Prix de Littérature Policière for *Les brouillards de la butte*, and the Trophée 813 for *Tranchecaille*. His latest novel, *Hével*, was awarded the Prix Marcel-Aymé in 2018 and the Prix Mystère de la critique in 2019.

CHRISTIAN ROUX, born in 1963 in the Yvelines, is a pianist, vocalist, composer, screenwriter, and actor. He has published several noir novels, typified by characters in revolt: *Braquages* (winner of the Prix SNCF du Polar in 2002), *Kadogos*, *L'homme à la bombe*, *Placards*, *Adieu Lili Marleen* (winner of the Trophée 813 in 2016), and *Que la guerre est jolie*. He lives in Mantes-la-Jolie.

JEAN-PIERRE RUMEAU, born in 1952, lives in Fontainebleau. For more than thirty years, he has been a stuntman, stunt trainer, and consultant—for movies, commercials, and TV. He has directed around twenty theater plays and written several feature films, including *Siméon*, directed by the well-known French and American director Euzhan Palcy. His first novel, *Le vieux pays*, published in 2018, was awarded the Prix du Goéland Masqué in 2019.

ANNE-SYLVIE SALZMAN is the author of three novels (*Au bord d'un lent fleuve noir*, *Sommeil*, and *Dernières nouvelles d'Œsthrénie*) and two story collections (*Lamont* and *Vivre sauvage dans les villes*). She has also published a book of poetry, *Dits des xhuxha'i*, and translates literature from English under the name Anne-Sylvie Homassel. She has always (or almost always) lived along the Bièvre.

INSA SANÉ was born in Dakar, Senegal, and was raised in Sarcelles. He is a writer, actor, comedian, and performer. In 1996, he created the Guérilla Collective with other artists and organized a theater group. His debut novel, *Sarcelles-Dakar*, was published in 2005. Four novels have followed, including *Du plomb dans le crâne* and *Tu seras partout chez toi*. Sané tours with the Soul Slam Band and is currently working on an album, *Un gars trop compliqué*.

RACHID SANTAKI was born in Saint-Ouen in 1973. Called the "Victor Hugo of the ghetto" by his friends, Santaki has published more than ten novels, including *Les anges s'habillent en caillera*, *La légende du 9-3*, and *Les princes du bitume*. Very active in the public housing projects, he has successfully organized spelling bees and gone on tours to popularize French literature. To the same end, he participates in programs with prisons and correctional facilities.

ANNE SECRET is a media librarian for an employee representatives' council. She does not write thrillers or detective stories, but rather noir novels in which the places—their history and sociology—play a major role. In that spirit, she has published *La mort à Lubeck*, *L'escorte*, and *Les villas rouges*, as well as two novellas, *Moskowa* and *La chanceuse*.

MARC VILLARD lives in Paris. He has been a rock columnist for *Le Monde de la musique*, and has written articles for *Jazzman*. Since 1979, he has written noir short stories (*Démons ordinaires*, *La Fille des abattoirs*), scripts for graphic novels (*La guitare de Bo Diddley*), and autobiographical narratives (*J'aurais voulu être un type bien*, *Avoir les boules à Istanbul*), among others. He directs In8's Polaroïd collection, which publishes short fiction.

Also available from the Akashic Noir Series

PARIS NOIR
edited by Aurélien Masson
252 pages, trade paperback original, $15.95

BRAND-NEW STORIES BY: Didier Daeninckx, Jean-Bernard Pouy, Marc Villard, Chantal Pelletier, Patrick Pécherot, DOA, Hervé Prudon, Dominique Mainard, Salim Bachi, Jérôme Leroy, Laurent Martin, and Christophe Mercier.

"The dank and sweaty crime scenes in *Paris Noir* testify to the fact that the French invented 'noir.'" —*New York Times*

"Rarely has the City of Light seemed grittier than in this hard-boiled short story anthology." —*Publishers Weekly*

MARSEILLE NOIR
edited by Cédric Fabre
240 pages, trade paperback original, $15.95

BRAND-NEW STORIES BY: François Beaune, Philippe Carrese, Patrick Coulomb, Cédric Fabre, René Frégni, Christian Garcin, Salim Hatubou, Rebecca Lighieri, Emmanuel Loi, Marie Neuser, Pia Petersen, Serge Scotto, Minna Sif, and François Thomazeau.

"Gritty from east to west, Marseille is the perfect venue for the latest in Akashic's venerable Noir series. While earlier entries in this 70-volume series have sometimes been bleak and atmospheric, this one is all red meat. . . . Just as Marseille is tailor-made for noir, this dark banquet is tailor-made for noir fans." —*Kirkus Reviews*

BRUSSELS NOIR
edited by Michel Dufranne
288 pages, trade paperback original, $15.95

BRAND-NEW STORIES BY: Barbara Abel, Ayerdhal, Paul Colize, Jean-Luc Cornette, Patrick Delperdange, Sara Doke, Kenan Görgün, Edgar Kosma, Katia Lanero Zamora, Nadine Monfils, Alfredo Noriega, Bob Van Laerhoven, and Émilie de Béco.

"Brussels, Belgium's cosmopolitan, multilingual capital, has it criminal underside, as shown in the 13 dark—and sometimes darkly humorous—stories in this strong Akashic noir volume."
—*Publishers Weekly*

"Akashic Books deserves kudos for their fine service to noir . . . If these volumes are designed to give crime writers a nifty forum and also capture the local flair and flavor, *Brussels Noir* is a fine come-hither." —*New York Journal of Books*

HAITI NOIR
edited by Edwidge Danticat
316 pages, trade paperback original, $15.95

BRAND-NEW STORIES BY: Edwidge Danticat, Rodney Saint-Éloi, Madison Smartt Bell, Gary Victor, M.J. Fievre, Mark Kurlansky, Marvin Victor, Josaphat-Robert Large, Marie Lily Cerat, Yanick Lahens, Louis-Philippe Dalembert, Kettly Mars, Marie Ketsia Theodore-Pharel, Evelyne Trouillot, Katia D. Ulysse, Ibi Aanu Zoboi, Nadine Pinede, and Patrick Sylvain.

"A wide-ranging collection from the beloved but besieged Caribbean island . . . The 36th entry in Akashic's Noir series (which ranges from Bronx to Delhi to Twin Cities) is beautifully edited, with a spectrum of voices." —*Kirkus Reviews*

HAITI NOIR 2: THE CLASSICS
edited by Edwidge Danticat
264 pages, trade paperback, $15.95

CLASSIC REPRINTS FROM: Danielle Legros Georges, Jacques Roumain, Ida Faubert, Jacques-Stephen Alexis, Jan J. Dominique, Paulette Poujol Oriol, Lyonel Trouillot, Emmelie Prophète, Ben Fountain, Dany Laferrière, Georges Anglade, Edwidge Danticat, Michèle Voltaire Marcelin, Èzili Dantò, Marie-Hélène Laforest, Nick Stone, Marilène Phipps-Kettlewell, Myriam J.A. Chancy, and Roxane Gay.

"A worthy sequel that skillfully uses a popular genre to help us better understand an often frustratingly complex and indecipherable society." —*Miami Herald*

MONTREAL NOIR
edited by John McFetridge and Jacques Filippi
320 pages, trade paperback original, $15.95

BRAND-NEW STORIES BY: Patrick Senécal, Tess Fragoulis, Howard Shrier, Michel Basilières, Robert Pobi, Samuel Archibald, Geneviève Lefebvre, Ian Truman, Johanne Seymour, Arjun Basu, Martin Michaud, Melissa Yi, Catherine McKenzie, Peter Kirby, and Brad Smith.

"Akashic Books has produced more than 80 city-noir collections, from Atlanta to Zagreb. Toronto has had a turn and Vancouver is in the works. The Montreal edition brings together a bicultural roster of talent by some of the city's best crime-fiction specialists, with tales from the city's many neighbourhoods." —*Toronto Star*